# THE SWEET BOUNTY

## EW FINKE

Copyright © 2014. All rights are retained by the author.

This novel is a work of fiction. Resemblance of any characters to persons living or dead is purely coincidental. Characters, events, organizations, businesses, places, and incidents are either the product of the author's imagination or are used fictitiously.

To Bethany, Heidi, and Dan,
who have always given me great joy.

And to Nadine,
who brings me a new kind of joy.

## CONTENTS

| | |
|---|---|
| Acknowledgements | i |
| Chapter 1 | 1 |
| Chapter 2 | 11 |
| Chapter 3 | 19 |
| Chapter 4 | 33 |
| Chapter 5 | 37 |
| Chapter 6 | 50 |
| Chapter 7 | 56 |
| Chapter 8 | 69 |
| Chapter 9 | 82 |
| Chapter 10 | 88 |
| Chapter 11 | 98 |
| Chapter 12 | 109 |
| Chapter 13 | 122 |
| Chapter 14 | 133 |
| Chapter 15 | 139 |
| Chapter 16 | 145 |
| Chapter 17 | 159 |
| Chapter 18 | 167 |
| Chapter 19 | 179 |
| Chapter 20 | 186 |
| Chapter 21 | 190 |
| Chapter 22 | 202 |
| Chapter 23 | 215 |
| Chapter 24 | 225 |
| Chapter 25 | 234 |
| Chapter 26 | 242 |
| Chapter 27 | 256 |
| About the Author | 266 |

# Chapter 1

One of the paramedics sighed with palpable frustration and I lifted my eyes to meet hers. I understood why she sighed – three harried paramedics were unable to check the declining condition of this once vigorous man, now rapidly fading on the gurney beside me. Over the muffled whine of the turbines I heard the pilot of our helicopter announce to the controller that Med-Evac One was 13 kilometers out and we would be landing at St. John's General Hospital in five minutes.

I said condition because the paramedics don't seem to know what ails this man. His hands and body shake, and he jabbers incoherently with an exaggerated form of the same illness at least fifteen others of my Tribe suffer. The long, richly black hair he used to tie in a ponytail is brittle, matted, and unkempt. The eyes once full of spirit stare vacantly at the space above him. The medicine pouch around his neck, once his protection, is now an unsettling reminder of the hideous evil extinguishing his life.

# EW Finke

I had known him as a strong and capable man – wise, alert, and compelling. Today, soiled and wrinkled clothes, worn and slept in for weeks, disguise the frail carcass of a man I barely recognize. I haven't seen him since my French mother moved me away from the Reserve 19 years ago. Had he not had the lucidity to locate me during his last days of consciousness, I might still be in Montreal knowing nothing of his fate. 'It's something you must know!' he had said, and it was urgent that I come right away. I had no idea this was why.

Our Puoin had already exhausted every healing ceremony on this man. To me, 34-year-old Peter Joe, he is Nkekkunit Abram, my godfather Abraham, who raised me to the age of 15 after the Mi'kmaw father I never knew abandoned my mother and me on the Reserve. And now he, too, is abandoning me – for the second time.

"Blood pressure and pulse erratic, tremors and incoherence increasing, condition unstable." It was the paramedic speaking into the headset of her helmet. I hoped the person on the other end of that transmission would know what to do when we land. As a boy on the Reserve, I had fantasized about riding in a helicopter one day, but I never imagined it would be under circumstances like this.

The whine of the turbines declined a little and the pilot suddenly became very busy. I looked out through my tiny window to see us approaching St. John's from the Atlantic side. My stomach rose and fell back again as we bumped in the turbulent air over the coastline. The paramedics didn't seem to mind the ride, but I felt queasy and tried to steady myself by gripping the handholds beside me. We slowed and descended until, only a few feet below us, the trees gave way to the sprawling campus of St. John's General.

Nearly still in mid-air, we rotated in a half circle and settled onto a flat roof. The turbines wound down, leaving a rhythmic *foof foof foof* as the only sound inside the fuselage. The paramedics took their positions around the gurney and sat poised and motionless, as if something prophetic were about to happen.

Moments later, the latch turned from the outside and the fuselage door jerked outward and rolled away on its track. Two orderlies and a nurse, their hair blowing wildly askew, appeared in the doorway.

"Let's do it!" snapped the nurse, shouting over the gusts of rotor wash. The paramedics sprang to action, rotating the foot of the gurney to the open door and sliding it partially out. One of the paramedics steadied the attached stand with the IV bag. The other two paramedics jumped out and intercepted the head of the gurney as it continued its slide. Three paramedics and an orderly toting the gurney bearing godfather Abraham quickly disappeared through double sliding-glass doors into the hospital, with the nurse and second orderly in tow.

With the rush of emergency well on its way, I picked up my bag and jumped out of the helicopter onto the landing pad, ready to follow. As I did, a third orderly, this one carrying a clipboard, ambled toward me. A short, stocky build gave him a rocking gait, and his arms angled away from his body like an over-inflated doll animated for this occasion.

"You Peter Joe?" he asked.

"Yes."

"Come with me," he ordered.

We passed through the same double sliding-glass doors and turned down a short hallway into a small white room containing only a desk and two chairs. With an open hand, he wordlessly showed me the chair in front of the desk as he continued past it. Taking the hint, I sat while he rounded the desk to the other side.

"Paperwork," he said to no one. Shunning the pleasantries and with pen in hand, he leaned over the desk, glued his eyes to a printed form on the clipboard, and began asking me questions about godfather Abraham.

"Name Abraham J-e-d-d-o-r-e?"

"Zhed-ore," I pronounced for him.

"Age?"

"65."

"Address?"

"Conifer, Newfoundland. Mi'kmaw First Nations Reserve."

"Surviving next of kin?"

*He's not dead yet, you thoughtless ...* "Me," I said more calmly, knowing his wife died years ago from the relentless, plodding ravages of intestinal cancer. The three years of her suffering had wrenched far more than that from his face.

"Relationship?"

"Godson."

He looked up at me. "Godson's a relative?"

*My godfather is dying, would it hurt to do this later?* "Yes," I said with a sigh. Then I remembered the white world is different. Mi'kmaq godparents are vital members of every family. They help raise the children and vow to be there for them if there is trouble, a promise they make in the Kekkunit Ceremony. They are second parents. "In Mi'kmaw society," I added.

"I'll put that down for now," he said with a

begrudging grunt, and then returned to his form. "How can we reach you if we need more information?"

I wondered about that, too. I had only $100 and a ruddy gym bag with two day's clothes in it. "I don't know. I'll have to stay somewhere until I can get back to the Reserve. I'll leave a number when I find out where."

Then he sat back from the desk, tossed his pen onto the clipboard, folded his arms, and looked at me like a general about to issue a command. "Don't forget," he scowled.

I stood, and with the Mi'kmaw patience I learned from my godfather, I thanked this inconsiderate man. "Now, where can I see him?" I asked.

He pointed down the hallway. "ER. One floor down."

I followed his finger to the elevator and descended one story to the main floor. Large, blue overhead signs directed me to the Emergency Room. I immediately encountered nurses and aides rushing about, too busy with a crisis to notice me standing in an empty corner of the room. From the bits of frantic conversation and rapid orders I could make out, I learned they were in the midst of a triage, uncertain how to treat the patient on their hands. I watched and listened, trying to follow the events unfolding before me.

The focus of their uncertainty was my godfather, strapped to a bed in a small room off to the side. The privacy curtain had been pulled completely open. He lay on his back, convulsing erratically against the restraints. A heart monitor on a rolling stand beside the bed chirped unsteadily, and the clear tubing from the IV bag still dripped its life-giving solution into the back of his right hand. The three paramedics, appearing to await further orders, stood together out of the way.

Into this confusion came a barrel-chested doctor in a pale blue scrub shirt. He wore butched-off hair and appeared to be in his mid-forties. A reddish face and a military demeanor told me he was in charge. "Do we have those lab results yet?" he demanded, almost shouting, from the head nurse. There was a hint of Scottish in his voice.

"No, Doctor, nothing yet," she responded.

"Mother of Jesus," he muttered. He pulled a cell phone from its belt holster, flipped it open, pressed a single key, and held it to his ear.

"This is Dr. McGovern. Get me the lab director immediately," he demanded. Ten seconds passed before he spoke again.

"Bob. This is Drew," he began impatiently. "Look, I have a serious situation here. An elderly man in tremors and convulsions. Highly irregular pulse and BP, elevated body temp. I ordered a full panel – blood, urine, stool, hair, fingernail scrapings. I need any piece of information you can give me, and I need it now."

Another ten second pause, then he spoke again.

"Thanks, Bob. I owe you." He flipped the cell phone closed and clicked it back into its holster.

He turned to the head nurse still there beside him. "Far from ideal, but we could have something from the lab within a quarter hour," he said.

He moved to address the rest of the staff. "People!" he shouted. The ER staff and the paramedics turned his way. "Everyone, over here. Let's look again at what we're dealing with." They all moved toward him. "Medics, review the symptoms when you made the pick-up."

One of the paramedics, a tall, fair-skinned

woman in glasses and a dark blue jumpsuit, stepped forward. Her blonde hair was pulled back into a tight ponytail. She lowered her eyes and read from a clipboard.

"Pulse irregular, blood pressure variable, temperature 105," she began efficiently. "Labored breathing. Lethargic but easily excitable. Slurred speech. Long-term memory loss – couldn't remember his name or the name of his town. Narrowed visual field. Poor hand-eye coordination." She paused and looked up. "And highly progressive tremor."

"Theories?" asked the doctor.

"Senile dementia, Alzheimer's," she responded. "Parkinson's, cerebral palsy, sleep deprivation, malnutrition. Could be any one of those ... or all of them for that matter."

"No help," he muttered and turned again to the head nurse. "Present conditions?"

She, too, read from a clipboard. "BP still highly variable. Pulse irregular and waning in strength. Temperature 105. Breathing irregular. Tremors, convulsions, uncontrolled perspiration and blushing. Unresponsive to touch, voice, and light."

"Theories?" he asked again.

"None you haven't already heard," she responded.

"Where in hell are those lab results?" he demanded of no one in particular, shifting his feet as if he were beginning to pace. Just as he spoke, a young, male technician in a white lab coat entered the emergency room and approached him.

"About time," he said turning toward the technician. "What do you have?"

"The lab director said you needed this right

away. The hair was the easiest to get a fast result on, but it's only a screen ..."

"Meaning?" the doctor interrupted.

"Meaning I ran a quick test to look for anything unusual. It's only pass/fail, tells you present or absent, but it doesn't quantify anything. We're processing the rest of the samples as fast as we can, but it'll take a full day to get complete results. A preliminary read off X-ray fluorescence gave me this." The technician handed a printed analysis to the doctor.

The doctor stared at the report for what seemed like half a minute before shooting the technician a look of disbelief. "Are you sure?" he asked.

"As sure as I can be right now. Give me the rest of the day to confirm."

"Confirm it. And bring me the rest of those results as damn fast as you can!" ordered the doctor.

"On it," the technician said. He turned and left the room.

The doctor turned to face the rest of the staff. "OK, people," he said. "Explain this one. The lab gives us ..." His words were abruptly overpowered by the continuous, piercing *deeeeeet* of the heart monitor.

The ER team rushed immediately to my godfather's bedside. The first nurse to arrive took a pulse on his carotid artery. "No pulse!" she yelled. A second nurse pressed a manual bag resuscitator over his mouth and nose and began squeezing air into his lungs.

The head nurse shouted for electrode jelly and a defibrillator. She ripped open my godfather's shirt and squirted jelly on the paddles. "One-fifty! Clear!" she called out and pushed the paddles onto his chest. With a sudden jolt, his chest rose and thumped back down onto the table.

Irreplaceable seconds passed before the next report. "No pulse!" First Nurse called out again.

"Two-fifty!" shouted Head Nurse. "Clear!" Another jolt, and another rise and fall of his chest. More seconds passed. "Still no pulse!" First Nurse reported again.

A stocky male nurse with muscular arms stepped up to the table. "Beginning compressions!" he shouted, and he placed the heels of his hands on my godfather's sternum. "One ... two ... three ... four ..." he began. Every 30 compressions, the second nurse squeezed in another two breaths of air.

My heart pounded, but I could only watch with helpless apprehension as this crisis played out in front of me. *No, this cannot be!*

Sixty seconds later, the male nurse stopped compressions momentarily while First Nurse felt for a natural pulse. "Still no pulse!" she called out. The male nurse began again.

Forty minutes passed while the ER team administered CPR, but it seemed like hours to me. I had begun to wonder if they would ever revive him when, abruptly, the doctor called out, "OK, people, that's it, it's over. 4:09 p.m. Mark it."

My heart pounded and my knees went weak. *Is this really it? Is this how a wise and courageous man dies?*

The ER team ceased its frantic activity almost as quickly as it had begun. Head Nurse wrote something on her clipboard. First Nurse turned off the heart monitor, and a deep and sullen quiet filled the room. Even my own heart seemed to have stopped. Long sighs came from the staff – of relief, of sadness, of frustration, or maybe all three.

The doctor broke the silence once again. "Remember, people, you did your best. We'll have other lives to save. I'll see to the autopsy and the rest of the lab results. We need to know what the hell just happened here."

With heads hung low, the ER team gathered their equipment and walked slowly away from his bed. One by one, they drifted out of the emergency room.

I moved slowly to my godfather's bed and looked into his face. Abruptly, the undeniable realization of what had just happened struck me hard, as if a man of twice my strength had just boxed me squarely in the face. Distant memories burst unrestrained into my mind then left as fast as they came, each one followed by another. I turned away and tried to deny what I knew. Tears welled in my eyes. I reeled, grasping at the bed rail to keep my balance. I felt my heart beating within my own chest, and an unwelcome heat flushed my body. I strained to force my mind to confront the truth, but it struggled just as hard not to accept it. A score of emotions played havoc within me – grief, confusion, anger, frustration, fear, sadness, guilt. Too strong, they overpowered me and I sobbed.

Long minutes passed before I calmed. I regained my courage and turned to face him again, pressing the wetness from my eyes with my sleeve. I searched my godfather's eyes, wanting to see the strength and vibrancy I remembered from so many years ago, but they no longer looked back at me. The spirit of Saqamaw Abram Jeddore – Chief of the Mi'kmaw Band at Conifer, Newfoundland – was gone.

I breathed out a long, resigned sigh.

# Chapter 2

A uniformed figure moved to the emergency room desk. It was First Nurse, and I made my way toward her.

"Ma'am, can you tell me what just happened over there?" I pointed in the direction of my now-deceased godfather.

The pale woman in a white uniform looked up at me. Her milky-brown hair was tied into a bun behind her head. Pudgy upper arms and round body made the uniform appear too small, and she wore a scowl on her face. "Are you a member of the family? I can only speak to members of the family," she said with authority.

"In my society, yes," I responded. "He's my ... was ... my godfather. I rode the helicopter with him. I'm the only family he has left."

At that, she abruptly lowered her eyes and began rifling haphazardly through a clutter of papers, as if she were searching for something important. "Ah," she said finally with a look of relief on her face, "then you must be Peter Joe."

I nodded.

"Good," she said. "Sign this." She presented a printed form, pointing to the signature line with a short, chubby index finger.

"What is it?" I asked.

"Gives us permission to remove a few organs for testing, an autopsy. That was unlike anything we've ever seen here before. Dr. McGovern wants to consult a toxicologist in Ottawa."

I hesitated. Moments before we lifted off, our Kinap had warned me this might happen, and he had counseled me against it. This was a spiritual matter of great consequence. My godfather might be doomed to be forever in limbo between the earth and spirit worlds, or his spirit might be sent back to look for the missing parts.

Yet, I knew that at least fifteen others of my Tribe suffered the same illness that just claimed my godfather's life. Could not they die just as my godfather did? Are they not my People, too? Would not my godfather himself have acted to protect them? *Yes*, I heard myself say, to all of those questions. I could no longer save my godfather's life, but maybe I – or rather he – could still save theirs.

I prayed Kji Niskam would know this sacrilege was meant to preserve the lives of many of his People and was, in the end, no sacrilege at all. I stiffened at the thought of what I was about to do, but I signed and pushed the form back to her.

She must have seen the indecision on my face. "You can claim the body in a day or two," she said with a brief look of sympathy.

I lowered my eyes as I thought about where I might be in a couple days. I didn't even know where I'd be tonight. I thanked her and asked if she knew where I might stay.

"Well, there's the Captain's Inn, near downtown. Quite nice, but reasonable and not too far from here. The taxi out front could take you there."

I thanked her again, picked up my bag, and left the building.

Once outside, I stopped at the edge of the sidewalk. The sole taxi stand in front of me was empty. I was about to turn around and re-enter the hospital when I noticed an older car about 30 feet to my right begin to creep in my direction. In what seemed to be an eternity, the car eased its way into position on the other side of the street directly in front of me. It was outfitted with springy curb feelers, and they squeaked against the concrete as it came to a halt.

For a moment, I stood motionless, taking in what had just driven up. I was looking at a faded-brown Pontiac Catalina with a crack in the driver-side rear window and a taillight that had been taped over in red. It gently rocked in time with the low rumble of its exhaust. The wheels bore star spinners, and a white magnetic sign on the side of the car read *Speedy Taxi* in italicized red lettering. Even with all that had just happened, I could not prevent the wide grin that crept onto my face.

Still grinning, I moved closer and stooped to address the driver through the open front window. "Downtown inns?" I asked.

A pale, round head, bald except for a few stray hairs, turned to face me. It belonged to a wiry, elderly man of about 75 years of age wearing large, rectangular, wrap-around sunglasses. The head rose barely above the steering wheel, which he gripped firmly at the top with both hands. I wondered how those sunglasses stayed on such a frail face.

"Anyplace y' wants," the driver said in a heavy Newfoundland dialect.

I opened the rear door, tossed my bag inside, and hopped in beside it. The hinge creaked and the window rattled as I closed the door. I had just fastened my seat belt when I glanced up and noticed the driver staring at me through the rear view mirror. I stared back.

"Where to, b'y?" he asked.

"Captain's Inn," I said.

"Da'd be King's Bridge Road. Have ye dere dareckly." The driver returned his gaze to the front, and rotated the column shifter into *D*. The curb feelers squeaked again as he crept forward.

Without warning, the driver suddenly spun the wheel to the left and jerked the Catalina to an abrupt halt. I thrust my hands against the back of the driver's seat to arrest my unexpected movement, and craned my neck, wondering what pedestrian or animal the driver had swerved to avoid. Then he spun the wheel to the right, shifted into reverse, accelerated, and again jerked the car to a halt. To my surprise, he performed this maneuver yet again, this time completing a U-turn and reversing our direction.

His driving became much more predictable as we headed east on Clinch Crescent Drive, and I settled in for what I hoped would be a long, uneventful ride – a few empty minutes would help settle the events of the past two hours. He unknowingly granted my wish, and I mindlessly read the street names along the way.

After waiting for an oncoming car, the driver turned left into the parking lot of the Captain's Inn and brought the Catalina to a stop. 'Lev'n dol'rs' was the fare, so I handed him a ten and a five and told him to keep the change. I grabbed my bag, said, "Thanks for the ride," and quickly exited the car.

Inside the Inn, I found the check-in desk on my left vacant, but a small placard on the counter said the staff and management of the Captain's Inn were pleased to have me as a guest. Beside it, a brochure said the Inn had a long and varied history in St. John's. Built between 1843 and 1849, it had once been a house, formerly owned by prominent merchants, businessmen, a superior court judge, a president of the Reid Newfoundland Railway Company, a prime minister, and several other people with Sir or Honorable in their titles.

The floors were narrow planks of polished, amber-white wood, aged by years of use and mottled with worn-in scuffs. The walls were papered in an embossed motif of dusty-red roses. The Inn appeared to have been restored, but it still recalled an era over 150 years gone.

Voices from the pub across the narrow hallway caught my attention, suggesting I look there for the clerk. The gaze of a tanned, trim woman of about 50 met my entry. Her long black hair, tinged in gray, was pulled to the side of her head with silver combs. She had perky, hazel eyes and an inviting smile.

"Good evening," she said. She had an easy-listening voice, one I would have liked to hear more of had the circumstances of the day been different. Three locals on bar stools interrupted their conversation to shoot me glances that asked if this Indian-boy had come from away.

"Room or drink," said Easy-Listening Voice, not quite making a question.

"Room, please."

She moved smoothly from behind the bar and crossed the hall while I followed. She let herself into the room that was the lobby office and stood before the counter facing me. "One person one night?" she asked politely. I noticed how easily her eyes fixed my gaze.

"Please," I said.

She checked me in and handed me a key. '9' it said. "Upstairs," she chirped, adding "we serve a complimentary breakfast in the reception room from 6:30 to 9:30 am," and she pointed to a large room behind me. I thanked her, picked up my bag, and turned away from the counter.

Room 9 was a short way down the hall at the top of the stairs. Once inside, I dropped my bag, removed my jacket, and threw myself onto the bed. I was drained and exhausted in ways I never thought I could be. What I wanted most was to drown in a long, deep sleep. What I got instead was a long gust of memories I had stifled for nearly 20 years.

Nkekkunit Abraham had been more a father to me than a godfather – he was the source of everything I learned before the age of 15. Firm, yet kind and attentive, in the Mi'kmaw custom of teaching he never directed me. But I learned well from him. To live with honor and integrity, in harmony with my physical and spiritual world. To live the way of patience, non-interference, sharing, teaching, independence, and respect for all. These were the examples he set for me. *Why did he let her take me away?*

From him I learned to hunt and fish, and to honor the animal giving itself so that I may eat. He taught me the message of the Medicine Wheel and the Power of Four, the healing magic of the sweat lodge,

## The Sweet Bounty

and respect for the words and ideas of others in the Talking Circle. He showed me the strength of conviction, the power of belief to change the course of men's lives, and the wisdom of the old ways.

From him I learned of Kji-Niskam, the Great Spirit Creator, and of Elder Brother Kluskap who taught the Mi'kmaq about the World. He told me how our People came to be, and how the sacred pipe, sweet grass, and tobacco came to us. I had listened on his lap to the teaching stories of Mikcheech, Muini'skw the Bear Woman, Ki'kwa'ju the Wolverine, Beaver, and Rabbit and Otter. We had hunted eels at night by canoe, spearing them in the torchlight like the old Mi'kmaq had done, and the Beothuks before them. I smiled as I remembered the times he let me win at the coin and stick game of Waltes.

Together we had built a canoe of birch wood and rowed it from Pjila'si Bay onto the Atlantic and back. And he reminded me that our People had traveled that way from Cape Breton Island and back even while the Beothuks still inhabited this place.

But something had bothered my mother deeply in those years. We had to leave, she said finally, she could take it no longer. I asked why, but she had buried it and would not say. I begged her to let me stay here on the Reserve with my godfather and the People and the life I loved so much. But she refused to listen. She took me from the Reserve when I was 15. *He knew I didn't want to go! Why didn't he stop her! He abandoned me, just like my father did!*

She said French relatives in Montreal would take us in until she could make a better life for both of us. One thing led to another as years added upon years. I had accepted a scholarship at Concordia University and was just a term short of a doctorate in cultural anthropology when my godfather called. Now, against all that knowledge of human behavior, I found myself wondering how I could be so conflicted about the man who had once meant so much to me. *Where did it come from, this anger I haven't felt for years?*

At 15, things seemed all so very clear. Now, 19 years later, lying right here on this bed, nothing seemed clear. How would ... how could ... I ever find the harmony in this? *He should still be here for me!*

I drifted into tormented sleep with a pain searing in my heart.

## Chapter 3

Something jarred me awake ... the telephone, I thought in a sleepy fog. I rolled to one side and searched for the clock. Squinting, I read 8:55. I groped for the handset. "Hello?"

"Peter Joe?" It was a woman's voice.

"Yes?" I said. I rubbed my eyes with the fingers of my free hand.

"Front desk, Mr. Joe. A post. The delivery said it was for you."

I was still too groggy to think clearly. "OK, I'll be down in a little while." I returned the handset to its cradle, wondering why I needed to know about this post right now. Then it suddenly hit me. *Who even knew I was here?*

I rose, showered, dressed in jeans and a black cotton pullover, and pulled my straight, black hair into a ponytail behind my neck. I had to stoop to bring myself into the mirror. The meager bulb over it cast a yellow pall over my light brown face and blue eyes, imparting a jaundiced color to my prominent round cheekbones. A few pockmarks, a genetic carryover from my father, peppered my nose and cheeks. I splashed cold water on my face and dabbed it dry with a towel from the rack beside the sink.

I flipped off the lights, left my room and headed for the main floor. As I stepped off the last stair and made the left turn toward the reception room for breakfast, a voice from behind caught my attention.

"Mr. Joe?"

I turned. It was Easy-Listening Voice.

"You are Mr. Joe, aren't you?"

"Yes," I answered.

"Your post," she said and smiled. She handed me a cylindrical package wrapped in white paper, like a gift-wrapped wine bottle but lighter. She had an expectant look on her face and wasn't turning to leave. I returned her smile, and to satisfy her curiosity I thanked her and joked that maybe it was a bottle of Screech from last night's barstool boys.

The room that now served as the breakfast room appeared to have been the focal point of this house in the 1800s. A mantle of sculpted and polished white stone framed a fireplace in the corner. The sitting area looked out through glass-paned French doors onto the garden, its once flourishing growth now waning with the season. On the far side of the room, an elderly couple stood with their backs toward me gazing at the collection of photographs, perhaps of former occupants or owners, that adorned the walls and mantle shelf.

I chose a Danish roll, poured myself a tall glass of orange juice, and sat at a vacant table near the French doors. I drank a swig of juice, bit off a mouthful of Danish, and unwrapped my package.

It was a rolled and rubber-banded newspaper, the early edition of today's St. John's Telegraph. I spread the front page on the table before me, wondering what could be so urgent about it. An article in the bottom right corner soon answered my question.

TOXIN CLAIMS INDIAN CHIEF?

St. John's –

Anonymous sources at St. John's General Hospital report Saqamaw Abraham Jeddore, Conifer Mi'kmaw Indian Chief, died late yesterday. He was 65. Cause of death was not yet determined.

Jeddore became widely known in 1983 when he led 31 Mi'kmaq Indians to occupy the Provincial Rural Development Office, protesting Newfoundland's treatment of its First Nations people. While in a St. John's jail, he began a hunger strike lasting eight days before being released.

Recently, he charged the Provincial government's approval of the Sweet Bounty mine was yet another violation of First Nations rights, alleging the government intentionally ignored probable effects on the Mi'kmaw homeland on the false pretense of jobs and economic development. He claimed waste from the mine would release mercury into the Conifer River, contaminating the salmon aqua farm in Pjila'si Bay, a major source of income for the Tribe, and poisoning his people.

The Provincial Poison Control Centre warns methyl mercury is toxic to the central nervous system.

      I rubbed my face to forge clear-headedness, new questions searing my mind like hot iron. Other than a few hospital employees and me, who knew he died? How did that news make the very next morning's edition? And there's a mine?

Someone could answer those questions, and I intended to find out who. I finished breakfast, went back to my room, and dialed the offices of the St. John's Telegraph.

A computer answered in the overly pleasant voice of a young woman. "Good Day!" it said. "You've reached the offices of the St. John's Telegraph during regular business hours. If you know the extension of the person you wish to reach, you may dial it at any time, or simply stay on the line for the next available operator."

I decided to stay on the line. Subscription music was playing a 60's rock-and-roll tune when a real person came on.

"St. John's Telegraph," said Real Person. "How may I help you?"

"News editor, please," I requested.

"I'll connect you. One moment, please."

After a series of electronic clicks, I heard, "Kahn."

"Mr. Kahn. Peter Joe. What can you tell me about a front-page story? 'Toxin Claims Indian Chief,' it says."

He said I'd have to talk to the journalist himself on that, and Jimmy Nolan was his name. He transferred me. After a few more clicks, a voice said, "This is Jimmy."

He sounded young, and his voice carried a light but discernible brogue. "Jimmy Nolan?" I asked.

"That's me. Who's this?"

"Peter Joe," I answered.

Silence followed.

"Mr. Joe," he stammered at last. "I didn't expect to hear from you quite so soon."

*So, you are the source of my mystery package.* "You have a disturbing way of making acquaintances," I said.

"Yeah, that. My apologies, Mr. Joe. I wanted your attention."

"You have it," I said, and I waited for him to say why.

"There's something you should know. About your Chief Jeddore, I mean."

"I'm listening."

"I can't talk here. Meet me at the sidewalk benches across from Murray Premises on Harbour Drive, 10:15."

*A reporter who can't talk about his story on the telephone?* "Why should I trust you?"

The question caused him to pause. "Your Chief Jeddore just died, Mr. Joe, and I know why. Unless you want to see more of your people suffer the same demise, you should hear what I have to say."

Now it was my turn to pause, weighing what I had just heard. "How will I know you?"

"Auburn hair, black mackintosh. Take King's Bridge and Hill O' Chips to Water. Right on Water, left on Prescott to Harbour. Right on Harbour about a block." Then he hung up.

I checked the clock. It was now 9:50. In 25 minutes, I could learn something about my godfather's death from a Jimmy Nolan – maybe. Or I could ignore this whole conversation and take my godfather's body back to the Reserve now. What's passed has passed – no revelation can change that. I sighed.

I unfolded a tourist map of St. John's from the bedside table. It told me that in 15 minutes at the outside I could walk to Murray Premises, leaving me 10 minutes to check the area before meeting Jimmy Nolan. I made my decision – I grabbed my charcoal-gray safari jacket and left the Inn.

Outside I felt the start of a drizzle and donned my jacket. It was an easy walk along King's Bridge, but a steep downhill on Hill O' Chips. As I made my right turn onto Water Street, the familiar, fishy smell of a saltwater harbour caught my attention.

Water Street was an avenue of shops, offices, second-story homes and apartments, and a number of tourist havens – restaurants, down homer gift shops, pubs, and espresso shops – all housed in the reclaimed buildings of an earlier St. John's prime. This corner of Canada is indeed old, laden with little remembered but important events in history. St. John's claims to be the oldest city, and Water Street the oldest street, in all of North America.

Prescott Street. I made my left turn and arrived a block later at Harbour Drive. I turned right, walked past a Russian trawler, and watched a trio of stationary cranes unload a container ship up ahead as I walked. Just half a block ahead was the Murray Premises Hotel, and across the street from it were the benches where I was to meet Jimmy Nolan.

I still had a few minutes, so I entered the Hotel. I was awed. Its decor held the aura of a much older time, yet still felt elegant and new. Refurbished red brick and heavy, polished wood posts and beams, reinforced at strategic places with bolted steel plates, dominated the room. A stout wood pillar bearing a bronze plaque burst from the marbled white floor to support a labyrinth of polished joists and rafters overhead.

## The Sweet Bounty

The plaque told me the Hotel was part of a larger Murray Premises, the oldest collection of cod-shipping warehouses in the Province, a once-prominent place of business among the merchants, fishermen, and noblemen who built St. John's, and one of the few structures to survive the Great Fire of 1892. It was now a collection of boutique shops, executive suites, and meeting rooms.

I entered a gift shop, nodding to the clerk as I made my way to a window facing Harbour Drive. Looking out, I saw a figure dressed in a mackintosh standing at the benches, leaning against the railing at the quay. It was him, I surmised, but his hair was more red than auburn. I left the gift shop and crossed the street, preparing to meet reporter Jimmy Nolan and wondering if other aspects of him might not be what he wanted me to believe.

He must have heard my footsteps, because he turned to greet me as I approached him from behind. "Mr. Joe?"

I nodded. "Jimmy Nolan?" I asked. I was looking into the fair-skinned face of a young man with a scant red beard who could be no older than 25. He was lean and a good ten inches shorter than me. Black dress slacks projected from under his mac and ended at a pair of brown hiking shoes, small even for a man of his diminutive size. The left pocket of his mac was torn at the corner, and a triangle of cloth dangled there from a bundle of loose threads.

He nodded in return, and extended his hand. "Pleasure, Mr. Joe."

We shook hands and more or less simultaneously turned to look out over the Harbour, he on my right. He leaned his forearms onto the railing and settled into them with folded hands. His right thumb fidgeted with its mated knuckle. I stood with my hands in my coat pockets.

Aboard a red and white Coast Guard cutter berthed on the other side of the Harbour, six blue-uniformed men busied themselves at unseen tasks. A tug puttered from right to left across our view.

"You wanted to tell me something about my godfather," I said.

He didn't answer right away, as if he hadn't already organized his thoughts, still deciding what I would want to hear first. Then he began.

"I've been writing your Chief Jeddore's story for quite some time, Mr. Joe. I was there three years ago when he first brought press to the Conifer River and the mine site. His face was bruised and bloody then, did you know? Some of his people were protesting at the mine entrance before construction of the mine workings had even begun. On the morning they were to begin pushing up topsoil, he and five others chained themselves to the main gate. They were forcibly removed and beaten by some of the Sweet Bounty's hulking goons. He was one of the lucky ones that day – three others got their hands broken.

"But they couldn't slow him down, you know? He showed us where the Conifer River began, how it went right through where the diggings and leach pads were to be, and where it flowed into Pjila'si Bay. He brought us back when the mine was operating and showed us how the River had been forced around the mine by a series of dikes, where the dikes leaked and allowed the River in anyway, and where that water later sank back into the ground. He showed us the seeps on the banks below the mine, discolored red by iron and acid. That was clear evidence, he said, the mine had already contaminated ground water, the Conifer River and Pjila'si Bay. It wouldn't be long before the mercury would follow.

"Then he took us to his home at the town of Conifer. He said it was the sacred tradition of the Mi'kmaq to live in harmony with their surroundings, fishing the Bay as the Old Ones had done for centuries. We saw the aqua farm, too. He said studies by the States had found deadly methyl mercury in seafood, and he reminded us of the warnings our own government has been giving us about it in the seafood we eat. He told us the Mi'kmaq were proud that each one of their salmon was clean, free of mercury. He said that's what kept Mi'kmaq salmon in the restaurants and supermarkets all over the eastern seaboard.

"He described how the mine would use cyanide to dissolve gold from huge piles of crushed ore called leach heaps. But the cyanide would dissolve other minerals too, and it was mercury that worried him the most. Gradually, he said, the mercury would escape from the used-up heaps into the groundwater below them. It would find its way to the Conifer River and flow with the River to Pjila'si Bay, where it would contaminate the salmon and poison his people.

"He told us about Minimata, Japan, where every-day, hard-working people believed their government would protect them. But the government was naive and corrupted and it played down the danger while thousands of Japanese convulsed uncontrollably from the methyl mercury poison. In the 1950s, hundreds of them died without ever knowing why.

"Then he brought it all home, Mr. Joe. Standing with us on the shore of Pjila'si Bay, he asked us to find out for ourselves what would prevent the same thing from happening right there on that very spot in Newfoundland.

"He knew what was coming, Mr. Joe, but he couldn't prevent it. Not in time to save his life. Mercury from the Sweet Bounty – that's what killed him, just like in Minimata. It was in the water he drank, in the fish he ate, and it's sure to be poisoning even more of your people right now."

Unexpectedly, I flushed warm and my world closed within me, shutting out his words. I did not want to believe him, did not want to believe my godfather had really died, and I felt indignant and wrathful at Jimmy Nolan, as if he himself had killed him. I looked away, rattled by the unruly feeling and ashamed he might see my emotion.

"There's bribery here, too," he went on, oblivious to my change of mood. "I feel it sure as I'm standing next to you, but I can't prove it. Maybe you can help me prove both of those things. If you do, I'll make damn sure the rest of the world knows the story. That's where we can work together, Mr. Joe – you prove it, I print it. This may be the biggest environmental crime since Love Canal in the States, and I want to tell it. All I want is the exclusive rights to print whatever you find out."

At that, he became silent, which I took to be a wordless invitation for my agreement. It was clear he knew a lot. But there was something in his manner that troubled me. Or maybe it was just the wariness I learned a long time ago – a wariness around making agreements with white men.

"Tell me about the bribery," I said, looking over at him.

## The Sweet Bounty

He rose up off his forearms, grabbed the railing, leaned into locked elbows, and cocked a face with a matter-of-fact look in my direction. "At high levels of Provincial government, Mr. Joe – the Ministry level at least, maybe higher. Think about it. Newfoundland's had 14% unemployment, the highest of any Province, ever since Canada first shut down the Grand Banks cod fishery in '92. Thirty-thousand Newfoundlanders out of work as fast as you could snap your fingers." He demonstrated. "And it's never recovered.

"Four years ago, Ceborro Minerals Company out of New York proposed the Sweet Bounty gold mine. We're accustomed to mining in this Province, Mr. Joe – the Hammerdown at Baie Verte, the Wabush and Voisey's Bay mines in Labrador, the Duck Pond at Buchans. Mining is nothing new to us.

"But this ...." He was momentarily drowned out by the tug's horn, blaring as it began a new maneuver. It ceased and he began again. "... this one got special treatment. It flew past government reviews and got very little publicity. If your godfather hadn't raised a fuss, I doubt people would even know it existed. And when he finally exposed it, the government fell all over itself telling people the mine promised high-paying jobs, wages unheard of around here for 20 years. In an economy like this, you'd think if the government planned to approve any enterprise with jobs like that, they would want everyone to know right from the start.

"Well, I dug into that claim, and I found out the Company planned to bring in its own workers from the States. I stumbled onto a tip that the equipment was so high-tech they needed people already skilled with it. It was cruel, Mr. Joe, the government playing on the desperate hopes of the people that way." He lowered and wagged his head, as if to show me his disgust.

"I think the government was trying to cover its tracks," he began again, "which means either the government's inept or someone's on the take. Now, I don't have much faith in the government to do anything sensible, but I'd wager a tickle full of new ships somebody got paid to grease that mine through channels."

"What makes you so sure?" I asked.

"I can't prove that, not yet, anyway. There's a mine plan, every mine has to have one – gold, copper, gravel, whatever. The plan tells how the mine will be operated, how it'll extract its mineral, and how it'll reclaim the mined area when it's done. The government has to do an environmental review and approve that plan before the mine can move a single bucket of dirt. I don't believe even an ignorant bureaucrat would approve a mine plan if there was any half-clear indication it could poison either people or a bay full of salmon. There's plenty of prejudice against Indians in the government here, your Chief Jeddore knew that well enough, but it isn't suicidal. My hunch is the mine plan is pretty good but the Company never planned to operate by it, and the payoff assures no one will find out the Sweet Bounty mine isn't what the plan says it will be."

I looked away and contemplated that. Some distance to our left, the tug began to nudge the trawler back against its mooring.

"It may be your Chief Jeddore had a hunch about that, too," he continued. "He went to see the Minister of Environment at the time the mine was approved three years ago. Albert Winslow's his name. Maybe your godfather figured out something the government didn't want anybody to know."

He paused for a moment. I was trying to make sense of it all when he added, "One more thing. There's a professor who's made a career out of studying mines like the Sweet Bounty. She's at Sir Wilfred Grenfell College in Corner Brook, but you can see her here in St. John's. Maybe she can help you." At that, he handed me a newspaper clipping, and I pushed it into my left pocket without reading it.

Throughout this conversation, the drizzle had gradually become a rain, and I pulled my collar up to fend it off. Soon, I would need to get out of it altogether. "One last question," I said. "How'd you find me, or even know who I was?"

A grin came to his face, like I had just uncovered a proudly kept secret. "Scanners, Mr. Joe – police, aircraft, hospital. A man in my line of work has to make it his business to know what happens before it happens, if you know what I mean. I heard the Med-Evac pilot call the tower, I heard the paramedic call the hospital. Once I learned Chief Jeddore was on that chopper, I knew it had to be serious. After that, it was a simple matter to call the ER desk and ask who else was on board. I got lucky when I got the nurse who knew where you were staying."

The rain suddenly became a downpour, like it so often does this time of year. I pulled my jacket up over my head, said a hasty I'll-get-back-to-you, and ducked into the Hotel to wait it out. While shaking the rainwater from my coat, I remembered the clipping in the left pocket. I pulled it out and began to read:

Memorial University Continuing Lecture Series

Dr. A. Chartier of Sir Wilfred Grenfell College

Professor of Geologic and Environmental Chemistry

"Bio-Alteration and Bio-Magnification of the Heavy Elements"

Music Auditorium, Memorial University of Newfoundland

Tuesday, September 4, 7:00 p.m.

    That was tonight. I decided I'd take Jimmy Nolan's suggestion and meet this Dr. Chartier. But first I would try to find out what my godfather learned from Minister Albert Winslow.

# Chapter 4

It was about noon when Paul Ceborro walked the south boundary of the Sweet Bounty, the gold mine his father had gambled on to drag the Company back from the verge of bankruptcy. As he walked, he ran the fingers of his right hand through tight, curly, black hair and grinned with the early morning news.

Paul liked that name, The Sweet Bounty of Newfoundland. It had been his creation. He thought it conveyed just the right image – bringing to the people of Newfoundland the sweet, bountiful rewards of their own natural resources. He laughed to himself at the thought of how he had been able to divert most of those bountiful rewards to Ceborro Minerals Company.

Unexpectedly, the Company's assays had generously under predicted the wealth within the ore body. In its first year of operation, the mine produced enough gold to accelerate repayment to its private investors and produce an unprecedented twenty percent profit for the Company in each of the last three quarters of the year.

But if Paul had prevailed he would not be here at all. He would have preferred to stay in his Puerto Rican neighborhood of the Bronx where he had lived quite well as Vice-President of Ceborro Minerals Company for the past ten years. He wondered if he might still be there had he not answered that interoffice phone call from his father three and a half years ago, but it would have been difficult to not respond to Company President Ricardo Ceborro. His father was both demanding and intimidating, and Paul had learned early in his childhood not to ignore him. 'I'm teetering on bankruptcy, Paul,' his father had said, 'and you'd better come through!' Paul knew the only acceptable answer was 'Yes, Sir.' He hated calling his father 'Sir.'

Then, as if that wasn't already enough, along came Saqamaw Abraham Jeddore, 'that sack-a-maw Jedder', as Paul referred to him.

With his father and the Company lawyers behind him, Paul had always prevailed, and he'd trumped many. Militant, hermit landowners who threatened personal violence because their wells went dry when the Company de-watered an aquifer. More sophisticated landowners who brought class action lawsuits when their property values plummeted near the Company's mines. Government bureaucrats who always managed to find one detail or another that was 'contrary to the policies of this administration.' And environmentalist lawyers who invented all manner of procedural flaws under endangered species laws and regulations.

But this man was a different kind of opponent. In all his years in the mineral business, Paul encountered very few men with such single-mindedness of purpose and devout attachment to cause as Chief

Jeddore, willing to endure personal sacrifice to achieve what they believed to be right. He had offered a significant sum of money to Jeddore, too, but he had refused it, and with some ferocity, Paul remembered. He was not used to dealing with men in positions of influence whose most basic motivations were not some form of personal gain, men to whom greater wealth and more power meant little. Everyone, his father had taught him, could be swayed by either power or money, and for those who could not be so easily swayed, it was only a matter of time before he would find their Achilles heel. 'Then,' Paul recalled his father saying, 'I have them by the short hairs!'

Jeddore claimed the Company had deceived the public and that the government had intentionally overlooked the insidious danger the seeping mercury would pose to the Mi'kmaq of Conifer. A reporter with the St. John's Telegraph had taken Chief Jeddore's cause back to his editor, and the public was now seeing the Mi'kmaq people as a neglected minority trampled by a corrupted government courting a selfish international business. Two dozen sympathetic non-Indians had joined the protest line at the mine site, and a human rights law firm had offered Jeddore free legal services to take his fight all the way to the Supreme Court of Canada if necessary.

Worse, 70-year-old Ricardo Ceborro was not pleased to hear about any of this. 'My instructions were simple,' he had rasped to Paul on the phone. 'Keep the Chief quiet and make it look good in the papers up there. No room for mistakes!' he had shouted. There was no misunderstanding the insinuation of failure, and the ulcer in Paul's stomach had throbbed at his father's rising tone.

But today things looked a lot brighter and Paul's grin broadened. The Telegraph's early edition told him Jeddore would no longer be a problem. That was excellent news. But although the Telegraph said cause of death was unknown, there was still the troublesome implication that mercury from the Sweet Bounty had killed him. There was no mercury coming from the Sweet Bounty, Paul was sure of it. He knew the real reason Jeddore had died. Paul decided that meddling reporter was just trying to make something out of nothing, trying to make a story for himself at the Sweet Bounty's expense. And now that Jeddore was out of the picture, he doubted the reporter would get very far with it.

After all, it didn't really matter how Jeddore died, it only mattered that he did.

## Chapter 5

    I didn't like how I found myself just now, sardined in an elevator with townies I didn't know. Crowding put me ill at ease. From the back of the elevator, I surveyed my temporary companions – seven people in tailored business suits separated from each other only by the thickness of the fabric at their shoulders. At the front, two women alternately tilted their heads toward each other, whispering and laughing with hushed voices as people might do when sharing a remembered moment among strangers. An elderly man with thinning white hair groped for the handrail to steady himself against the impending motion. A pretty, young woman with long black hair and fair skin, clutching a notebook to her bodice with folded arms, momentarily turned her head and gave me a brief smile. I returned it, hoping my uneasiness didn't show.

    The doors closed and the elevator jerked, carrying us abruptly upward. I stiffened at the jolt and my stomach rose in my throat. The mix of aftershave, perfume and antiperspirant suddenly created a foreign air, and I felt my airway constrict in a futile attempt to bar the invading scent.

It seemed like an eon had passed before the elevator stopped, opened its doors, and wheezed out my seven compressed companions. As each rushed to their separate missions, I felt the relief of now being able to take my first comfortable breath, alone, since boarding the elevator.

I stepped out and looked both left and right down long, empty hallways before I noticed a small, green sign with black lettering on the wall directly in front of me. The words 'Department of Environment' and an arrow directed me down the hall to my right.

The walls of the plushly carpeted hallway were adorned at shoulder height with photos of previous Canadian Prime Ministers and Newfoundland Premiers. Above them all, at a level reserved for royalty, hung a much larger photo of the Queen. I made my way down the hallway as the sign instructed, eventually reaching the office of the Department of Environment.

Approaching a large, mahogany desk, I introduced myself to the prim-looking, female receptionist wearing horn-rimmed glasses and a wireless telephone headset. "I have an appointment," I added.

"I'll notify the Minister you're here," said Prim, barely making eye contact. "Please be seated." She spoke something quietly into the mouthpiece of her headset and returned to her work.

I glanced at my watch. It was 12:57 p.m. I turned and seated myself in a white leather armchair a few steps away. In the few minutes remaining, I scanned the room.

To my right, Prim now typed away at a keyboard hidden from my view and stared at an oversized computer monitor centered on her desktop. She sat perfectly upright, her forearms resting on their properly adjusted armrests. Tidy stacks of important-looking documents fenced the perimeter of her desk.

On the wall directly opposite me hung a large, opulently framed photo of the Minister receiving a plaque of some sort from the Premier, both men smiling for the camera. In real life, the Premier was of unimpressive height, but from my present angle both gentlemen in the photo appeared to be imposing figures and I wondered if that was intentional.

The wall supporting the photo was papered in burgundy felt. A thick burgundy carpet covered the floor and carried the distinct odor of having been freshly shampooed, and a wainscot of elegant and unfamiliar marbled wood circled the room.

There was a large window to my left. I rose from my chair, brushed my jeans down my thighs, tugged the cuffs of my jacket down to my wrists, and moved toward it for a better view. From my high perch within the Scotia Bank building, I looked down on the city.

Directly below me were long rows of bright, crayon-colored shops and houses on Duckworth, Gower, and Water Streets, together known as Jelly Bean Row. The steeply rising cross streets carried traffic away from the St. John's Harbour, through the bustling downtown business district, and on to the historic residential areas to the west. Overhead, the remains of an Atlantic hurricane, wrung haggard by the unrelenting journey northward from its Caribbean birthplace, darkened the sky and threatened rain again.

My attention was abruptly interrupted by Prim's voice, and I turned. "The Minister will see you now," she said, pointing to her right. "Through that door, please." Three dark-suited men with scowls on their faces filed out of the appointed door and closed it behind them. I lightly cleared my throat and moved toward it. Words etched in black on a silver plate beside the door read "Albert Winslow, Minister of Environment."

I turned the knob and entered. Passing four white leather chairs arranged around a circular marble conference table, I proceeded toward the second mahogany desk of my day. Two flags stood at its sides – on my left, the red maple leaf of Canada, and on my right, the blue, red and gold of Newfoundland.

"Mr. Joe!" came the greeting a little too loudly. The voice came from a short, balding, portly man of about 50, wearing a black, tailored, three-piece suit and a garish red tie. Pale features crowded his chin, as if they had been pushed down to make room for a tall forehead. Mousy-brown hair, grown long on the right side of his head, was combed over the top to the other side, and a double chin bulged over the too-tight collar of a red and grey pin-stripe dress shirt. He pushed himself up from his high-back leather executive chair, leaned over his desk, and extended an open right hand in my direction. "My door is always open, but you cannot know how lucky a man you are, Sir! If that blasted lunch meeting had gone even a moment longer, I would have missed you," he said with a smile.

For a moment, I stared at the hand hovering over the empty plane of mahogany. When I realized the hand and its owner would not be coming around to my side, I leaned over the desk and accepted the handshake. The hand pumped a little too hard for my liking and the grasp ended only after I had begun to

The Sweet Bounty

wonder if it would.

"Do have a seat, Sir!" The Minister broke the handshake and indicated with the same open hand a simple wooden chair neatly centered on my side of the desk. The Minister sat and so did I.

"Now, Mr. Joe, what brings you here today?"

My lips parted to speak, but before I could begin I was interrupted by the chime of a cell phone. "Sorry, do you mind, Mr. Joe? I have to take this. I won't be but a minute." The Minister unholstered his cell phone, flipped it open, and swiveled away, leaving me to stare at the back of his chair. I chose instead to look elsewhere.

Through the nearly floor-to-ceiling glass window directly ahead, I took in a full view of St. John's Harbour only partially blocked by the Minister's chair. A forest of trawler masts bobbed out of rhythm against their moorings. White caps grew and died in the Narrows at the harbor entrance. Two container ships anchored beyond the Fort Amherst lighthouse waited for calmer water and tugboat escorts. The stationary cranes I had seen earlier in the day were still unloading the third container ship already in the safety of the harbor. Not far beyond them rose Signal Hill with its 105-year old sentinel Cabot Tower providing watch over the city from the highest cliff on the ocean shore. Beyond the Tower lay the endless blue-gray of the North Atlantic.

On the left side of the Harbour stood the weathered houses of Battery Road, built by fisherman more than a century ago so close to the water they seemed in constant danger of drowning. Yet, on my side of this body of water stood a bustling downtown of multi-story office buildings, hotels, parking garages, and the 20-story, glass-sided high-rise in which I sat at this very moment. *A clash of cultures,* my godfather would have remarked had he been seated here in my place.

I shortened my gaze to objects more immediately in front of me. Except for a sleek, black desk phone, a leather blotter, and matching silver pen and pencil in a silver stand engraved with the letters 'AW,' the Minister's desktop was vacant. An open laptop computer on an extension of the desk beside the Minister's chair flashed a screen-saver image of Newfoundland scenery every ten seconds. On the wall to my left hung photographs of the Minister with the four previous Premiers. The wainscot and burgundy decor from the waiting room extended into the Minister's office, and the carpet was immaculately clean.

The Minister finished his call, spun back around, and set the cell phone beside his laptop. Leaning forward, he crossed his arms and propped them on the blotter. "Now then, Mr. Joe, what can I do for you?"

"Minister Winslow," I began, "I'm a member of the Band of Mi'kmaq First Nations at Conifer. I'm inquiring about the Sweet Bounty mine."

"Ah, yes. It seems I had the pleasure of meeting your Chief Jeddore. Off and on over the last few years, I believe. Wonderful man. Have you spoken with him about this?"

"I have, yes," I hesitated. "He was unable to come himself, he's ... occupied with other matters at the moment. I'm here on his behalf, you might say."

"A pity, I would have enjoyed visiting with him again. Do give him my best."

"Thank you, Minister Winslow, I will. I'm here because the people of my Reserve are falling ill. Many of them believe it has something to do with the Sweet Bounty mine."

"Really. What illness would that be?"

"Hand tremors, slurred speech, the sort of thing that might be associated with mercury poisoning. They wonder if mercury from the mine is contaminating the Conifer River and Pjila'si Bay."

"Well," the Minister began sympathetically, "please tell them I'm deeply saddened to hear of their illness. But I can assure you the mine couldn't possibly have anything to do with it. My Department thoroughly reviewed the potential environmental impacts from the Sweet Bounty three years ago. We looked at a host of hypothetical contaminant releases and concluded the Sweet Bounty would have no significant impact on ground water or the Conifer River whatsoever. I have complete confidence in our results. Why, I wouldn't be afraid to dip a little downstream water and drink it myself!" He gave an unnatural chuckle, then became serious again. "I'd be happy to provide you a copy of the report."

"Thank you, that won't be necessary, but I would like a copy of the mine plan."

"Can't help you there, Sir. You'd have to get that from the Department of Mines. Try the Confederation Building, Prince Phillip Drive."

"I'll do that, thank you," I said, wondering how his Department could have done its job without the mine plan. "I've heard the Sweet Bounty isn't following that plan. What can you tell me about that?"

"Again, you'd have to ask the Department of Mines." He paused. "Mr. Joe, may I ask where you're going with these questions? The mine has been in operation for several years now, and I'm certain your

Chief Jeddore was quite well aware of it."

"Just following up on rumors, Sir. I'm sure you've heard them – the mine not operating in accordance with its plan, a bribe to move it through governmental review with a minimum of scrutiny..." I paused.

He began to flush pink, and an unmistakable sternness crept into his voice. "Mr. Joe, these issues were put to rest quite some time ago, I see no reason to resurrect them now. There's not a shred of evidence to indicate the Sweet Bounty is operating in any way other than in complete accordance with its plan and in compliance with every environmental standard. Your time to raise objections was during the public comment period three years ago."

He was skilled at avoiding the question, but I pressed him. "The Mi'kmaq raised objections, Sir, but I believe your Department ignored them."

At that, he stiffened his back, unfolded his arms, and rested his fists on the table. He began to scowl. "Poppycock, Mr. Joe! You're welcome to review the administrative record. My Department's files are open, we have nothing to hide. I'm sure you'd arrive at the same conclusion I have."

"Minister Winslow, what is your Department doing to assure the mine operates as planned and continues to meet those standards?"

"Mr. Joe, you plainly bother yourself with matters beyond your understanding. It's my job to protect the people of Newfoundland and Labrador. You need only trust me to do that."

The man had a cocky and offensive way, and he was stonewalling again. I wondered if he addressed all his visitors in this manner. "I understand the Sweet

Bounty received approval faster than other mines in the Province. Can you tell me why?"

Minister Winslow rocked back into his chair. His eyes glared squarely into mine for what seemed like minutes, and his nose began to run. He pinched it between thumb and forefinger and wiped them on his sleeve. He leaned abruptly forward and crossed his forearms, landing them once again on the blotter. "I challenge that assertion, Mr. Joe, but even if it did, it was well justified by the economy of this Province," he said. "Jobs, Mr. Joe. Jobs which are at this very moment rescuing Newfoundland from a double-digit unemployment rate higher by far than any other province in Mother Canada. And foreign investment, too – hundreds of millions of US dollars.

"We have some of the richest untapped gold reserves in North America, and it would be a shame not to take advantage of them. This mine taps into the largest of them, an ore body underlying more than 300 square kilometers of Newfoundland real estate. If you haven't read the papers lately, the price of gold is sky high. The Sweet Bounty is putting Newfoundland on the world's gold map, and this is just the beginning!" His face became red and his hands animated the excitement in his voice. "Think what that means, Mr. Joe!"

I was already thinking what that meant – the history of the Mi'kmaw struggle in Newfoundland is repeating itself yet again. I strained to keep my composure.

"Where people used to think of Australia, South Africa and Nevada as gold capitals," he exclaimed, "they now think of Newfoundland! This Province once led the New World economy with codfish, and now we're doing it with gold!"

I wasn't prepared for such a blatantly ignorant analogy, and my surprise must have shown because he stopped in mid-thought. I knew the truth of how Newfoundland once led the cod industry, having read the studies and the accounts from many years ago.

The development of highly efficient trawlers made the cod harvests of the 1900s enormous. At any given time, 40 to 60 vessels could be seen mining the Grand Banks of cod, each year gathering more and more into their nets until, in 1968, they harvested a previously unthinkable 893,000 tons.

During the next 20 years, harvests plummeted mysteriously. By the early 1990s, the commercial catch dropped below that which had been caught by hand lining from shore a hundred years earlier.

In 1992, the Canadian government outlawed cod fishing for two years, promising the fishermen of Newfoundland the cod population would restore itself in that time. The ban was extended and extended again. Eleven years later, they still showed no sign of recovery. The once-teeming cod of the Grand Banks fishery had been decimated.

Finally admitting the full scope of the disaster, the Canadian government reinstated the ban again in 2003, and to this day harvests are so closely controlled no cod fisherman can make a living. Within the span of two decades, 30,000 people were put out of work. Newfoundlanders permanently lost a livelihood that had thrived against uncountable natural odds for almost five centuries.

I had wondered how a seemingly limitless food supply could just disappear. Many Newfoundlanders had asked those same questions, and from many came self-serving blame and ill-pointed fingers. Some high Provincial officials even blamed harp seal predation and advocated killing off every last one of them, too. The real answer lay somewhere among the synergistic insults of unrestrained fishing, absentee management, shortsighted politics, greed, and bad science. Mostly, no one accepted responsibility for preserving an abundance like the world had never seen, nor will see ever again.

The Minster suddenly leaned even farther forward, his excitement now blooming, and I startled out of my thoughts.

"And think of what this can do for your people, Mr. Joe! Executives and mining engineers could be crawling all over your place if you people played your cards right! Take them hunting, fishing, show 'em the best spots. Charge double for lodging and guide services!" His face glowed with excitement for this idea, and I could see the arteries bulge from his temples. "They'll never miss the money, and they'll love you people for it!"

The Minister suddenly relaxed back into his chair, folded his hands on his lap, and exhaled aloud. "Besides," he continued more calmly, "regulations require double-lined leach pads and holding ponds, with run-on and run-off control. No water leaves the site. It's impossible for anything to get to the Conifer River or Pjila'si Bay. It's as secure a design as I've ever seen.

"Sorry, Mr. Joe, there were just too many unknowns to impede something as important to Newfoundland as this mine."

"And the rumors about bribery?" I asked. "Who's being paid to look the other way?"

Crimson anger bled from the unnatural constriction of his collar to the top of his head. He sat suddenly upright, his hands gripping the armrests of his chair. "Mr. Joe, I am a loyal servant of the Queen and a steward of the people of Newfoundland and Labrador! All of my Department's dealings with the Sweet Bounty have been completely above board! You are impertinent, Mr. Joe, and now I must ask you to leave!"

"Very well, Minister Winslow." I said as I rose from my chair, offering a handshake. "Thank you, I think I've learned all I came for today." The tinge of sarcasm surprised me, as if it had come from someone else. He glared in return and chose not to rise. I withdrew my hand and turned to the door.

"My receptionist will show you to the elevator," he said finally, his words thick and acrid.

I slowed as I came to the receptionist's desk, anticipating some sign of recognition, but Prim did not look up from a calendar entry she was making. Taking the hint, I showed myself to the elevator. I pressed Down and watched the number above the elevator door change from G to 2. As I waited, I considered what I had just heard and what I knew of the history of my People. *This will not be the first time we have faced a challenge from the government of Newfoundland*, I thought, and the litany of those events now quickly returned to memory:

1949 – Newfoundland joined Canada. All mention of native people was removed from the Terms of Union.

1981 – Newfoundland refused to sign a Canada-Newfoundland-Native Peoples Agreement if the "Indians are allowed to sign as equals."

## The Sweet Bounty

1982 – The Conifer Band of Mi'kmaq Natives filed charges of human rights violations against the governments of Newfoundland and Canada. Its Chief and an Elder were mysteriously killed in an automobile accident, though no connection was ever proven.

March 1983 – The Conifer Band protested the untenable conditions placed on a native-peoples grant of $820,000. Newfoundland canceled the check.

April 1983 – With my godfather, a young Saqamaw Abraham Jeddore, as their leader, 100 Mi'kmaq men and women marched on St. John's. Thirty-one of them occupied the Provincial Rural Development Office to protest Newfoundland's treatment of its First Nations people. Twenty-three, including my godfather, were arrested. He and eight others began in a St. John's jail a hunger strike lasting eight days before they were released.

April 1996 – Newfoundland filed six claims to traditional Mi'kmaw territory. Again under Saqamaw Jeddore's leadership, the Mi'kmaq protested. Eventually, Newfoundland backed off its claims.

My thoughts were interrupted by an unfamiliar ding and I looked up. The elevator light now read 15 and the doors opened. I boarded the elevator, pushed G, and clasped my hands at my waist.

Minister Winslow had cemented my resolve. Somehow, the Sweet Bounty, corruption, and mercury were related to my godfather's death and the poisoning of my People, and I was now determined to find out how.

*A clash of cultures,* I reflected. The elevator doors closed.

## Chapter 6

"Holy Mother of Christ!"

It was just about 2:15 p.m. when Albert Winslow, Minister of Environment for the Province of Newfoundland and Labrador, sat alone at his desk and swore at no one in particular. With his hands on the desk, he abruptly pushed himself up from his wheeled executive chair. The force of his sudden movement drove the chair into the floor-to-ceiling window behind him. It thumped hard against the glass and bounced back, rolling into the Canadian flagpole beside his desk. He stormed to his office door and shouted at his secretary that he was not to be disturbed and to hold all calls for the rest of the day. He slammed the door so hard that a microburst of air riffled the pages of a budget report still open on the conference table eight feet away. He went to the phone and punched Speaker followed by 11 numbers. The phone shook with the force of each digit.

Albert Winslow was having a very harried day – three unexpected phone calls from members of the House of Assembly complaining about how the Ministry had handled one matter or another, a budget meeting which overran its three-hour limit, and a visit from an irate woman complaining the city killed her horse when it pumped a sewer line empty onto her pasture. Then, just when he thought he'd get a break after a working lunch, his secretary informed him of a last-minute appointment with Peter Joe, a man asking snooping questions, a man as meddlesome as Chief Jeddore had been three years ago. He loathed having to follow the Premier's open-door policy.

He was a man of temper easily lost, especially when the ordered events of his life were upset. He only just now found time to read today's early edition, and what he saw upset his order more than if the entire House of Assembly, the irate woman, and Peter Joe had all descended upon him at once.

Had he not worked hard to get where he was now, covered all the bases? Was he not a high government official, a commander of public laws? Certainly, he was not a man to be trifled with. It wouldn't do to be connected with the death of even a single one of the Queen's subjects. He had plans, aspirations. Surely a Premiership lay in his future, and he deserved it, didn't he? Nothing less. There was a lot at stake here. This couldn't be happening. Not to him, not now.

Still standing, he listened impatiently as the phone rang a third, fourth, fifth time. His face was red, arteries bulged at his temples, and his nose began to run. He sniffed it back. "Answer, damn it!" he seethed. Finally, a click told him someone picked up.

"Ceborro," said the voice on the other end of the line.

The Minister anchored his hands wide on the

desk and hunched his shoulders into the phone. "Ceborro!" he shouted. Drops of spittle flew onto the phone – he wanted to breathe his anger directly into the other man's face. "What in God's name are you doing down there? Have you seen today's paper?" He began to pace the floor between the desk and the window.

At first, the man on the other end of the line didn't recognize the bellowing voice. Then it struck him, and Paul Ceborro acknowledged his caller quite calmly. "Well. Minister Winslow. How nice to hear from you. And yes, I have seen today's paper. But I have a feeling you're going to tell me about it anyway."

"You're damn right, Ceborro! Jeddore's dead, and that damn Nolan is making it look like your operation killed him. He claims it's just like Jeddore said it would be – your mine leaks mercury into the river and contaminates the salmon, people get sick and die. Jeddore was in here three years ago spewing that crap and it was all I could do to get him to leave me alone. I told him he had nothing to worry about, just like you said. 'Safest design I've ever seen,' I told him. You'd better have a damn good explanation why Nolan's wrong, Ceborro! If he tries to pin any of this on my Department, I'll make damn sure you go down with me!"

Paul Ceborro remained unperturbed. "Don't get your panties in a wad, Winslow. No one's gonna pin anything on anybody. And of course Jeddore's dead, but I can assure you it has nothing to do with the mine. Besides, you should be thankful he's out of your hair."

"Of course I'm happy he's gone, Ceborro! The man was a thorn in my keister. But that's not the point, is it? The point is I'll have investigators swarming all over my Department as soon as somebody tries to make a connection between his death and your mine. Then we all go up in smoke – you, me, everybody!

"And get this," he continued. "Jeddore signed up someone to do his bidding before he died, and the bastard just paid me a pleasant little visit. Somebody named Peter Joe, asking a bunch of nosy questions, trying to take over where Jeddore left off, and the sonofabich didn't even mention Jeddore was dead!" The Minister broke into a sing-song whine. "'Let's just say I'm here on his behalf', he said." Now he growled. "A damn sneaky pest, just like Jeddore himself."

Paul Ceborro paused, taking in this new piece of information. "Hmm. Peter Joe, you say. Don't know of him. What did you tell him?"

"Not a damn thing more than I told Jeddore or anyone else who's ever asked about your operation."

Paul Ceborro took a moment to size the Minister's answer. Was Winslow covering his tracks again? He waived that question for the moment. He could always find out later.

"Good," he said finally. "Well, then, I would remind you, Winslow," he continued with easy disdain, "I won't go up in anybody's smoke. I'm the one paying the lovely extraction tax your government is putting to such good use, remember? So relax. I'm not paying you to fluster, I'm paying you to keep your mouth shut and think. I suggest you keep that in mind. As far as you know, Chief Jeddore died of unknown causes, just like the article says. And it'll stay that way if you pipe down and pay attention."

The Minister fumed at those words and paced again. *How dare he address me with impudence!* he thought.

"I suggest you take the high road on this one," Ceborro continued. "Put your Department out in front of it. Send your own people out here, run extensive tests on the Conifer River, the overburden, the tailings, the leach heaps, everything. Show the press your Department's doing its job of overseeing this operation, and you're making sure no one's harmed by anything as long as you're standing watch. You'll show them the Sweet Bounty meets every standard, just as you said it would when you approved that environmental review three years ago. And now that Jeddore's gone, there's no one to say differently. Confidence in the Premier's administration will jump five points, and your Jimmy Nolan will have to go elsewhere for the story of his career."

"And what about Peter Joe?" the Minister shot back.

"Don't worry your pretty little head, Winslow. Dead Jeddores don't talk, and if you didn't tell Joe anything I doubt he knows enough to make trouble."

Minister Winslow paused, taking that in. A solution was beginning to gel and his blood pressure waned. *Of course! Get the crisis under control before it became one!* "I'll consider that," he huffed, bitter he hadn't thought of it first.

"I'm certain you will, Winslow, and I'm confident you'll do it quickly. Now, I have a mine and you have a department. I suggest we both get back to running them." Then Paul Ceborro hung up.

"You damn, cocky, Puerto Rican son of a ...," the Minister started to say, stopping when he realized Ceborro wouldn't hear him. He punched the Speaker button again, terminating the empty dial tone.

## The Sweet Bounty

Still miffed, he rolled his chair from the flagpole over to the window, sat down, leaned back with his hands clasped behind his head, and crossed his feet on the floor. Looking out on the expanse of the Atlantic always helped him clear his head, and right now he needed a clear head more than anything else.

Then it hit him. He decided to send a team of his best investigators out to the Sweet Bounty tomorrow, get them on their way at daybreak. Using Jeddore's death, he could justify this as a priority – the investigators would have to drop everything else. He'd issue a press release announcing his action just before they reached the Sweet Bounty.

Their forthcoming reports would, of course, clear the mine of any wrongdoing, he'd see to that. But if the investigators found something, if the tests proved Nolan was right, he'd hold that information for later, for just the right time, as insurance just in case Ceborro tried to screw him over. *Bases covered,* he thought. He grinned, awed by his own ingenuity.

With that grin still on his face, he swiveled toward his desk and rolled himself forward with his heels. He pushed Speaker for the third time today and dialed his Director of Investigations.

\* \* \* \*

As he hung up the phone, Paul Ceborro wondered about this new character, Peter Joe. Where had he come from, what did he want, and why now? He hadn't heard the Mi'kmaq protesters mention that name. He decided to do a little inquiring, have one of his men hang out around the Conifer Reserve to see what he could find out.

## Chapter 7

It was 8:40 p.m. as I approached the gray, three-story, stone edifice housing the Music Auditorium. I would miss most of Dr. Chartier's lecture, but I decided that was for the best. Bio-whatever-she-called-it was way out of my field. My intention was to find out what she could tell me about the Sweet Bounty.

Earlier, after the rain let up, I went to back the Inn to extend my stay, arrange for my godfather's body to be flown back to the reserve, and to phone the Tribe to be sure they knew what had happened. They knew, of course, having already seen Jimmy Nolan's story in the St. John's Telegraph. But more disturbing news came my way during that call – five more tribal members were showing signs of my godfather's condition, bringing the total to 20. I ended that call thinking there may be some truth to Jimmy Nolan's hunch, and it strengthened my resolve after my visit with Minister Winslow. I was now convinced foul play was involved in my godfather's death, but exactly who and how were still big questions, and I had no idea where to find the answers. I dozed at the Inn with the troubling thoughts of the day's encounters on my mind, waking only in time to make it here before Dr. Chartier ended her lecture. I hoped she could offer me some useful information.

The Auditorium was dimly lit when I entered. A carpeted center aisle flanked by tiered rows of upholstered reclining seats led down to the stage. Her lecture must have appealed to many because only a few of those seats were vacant. The lower walls of the auditorium were paneled in a light-colored wood, and vertical sections of red-brown curtains, hung like overlapping flags, concealed the upper walls. A stylized motif of silver and blue organ pipes graced the wall behind the podium where a Baby Grand piano had been pushed to make way. A series of overhead spotlights were trained on center stage, illuminating Dr. Chartier. Echoes and background noise were noticeably muted, and her voice reached me as clearly as if I were standing next to her.

I could have walked the center aisle to the front row but I decided to remain where I was. She had just finished her lecture and announced she would stay a few minutes longer for questions. To standing applause, she thanked her audience for coming, and several of the evening's patrons began making their way to her.

I held back until I was certain the last of them, a woman discussing a particular detail of the lecture, had finished. Then I walked to the front of the auditorium and introduced myself.

"Dr. Chartier, Peter Joe. Jimmy Nolan suggested I contact you," I said, extending my hand.

"Monsieur Joe. Annamarie Chartier, a pleasure to meet you." She responded to the offer of my hand with a grip surprisingly strong for such a petite woman. "Oui, Monsieur Nolan and I, we have spoken in the past."

Her deep brown hair was cropped short in boyish style, and she wore large, bright red button earrings. She looked to be about 40, with golden brown skin and a slight, turned-up nose. Her green eyes sparkled in the overhead glow of the spotlights. Above her blue jeans she wore a white cotton turtleneck and a vest hand woven of black wool. At five-feet-four, she was slender but strong and outdoors-looking. She sounded very French. *Not the dowdy college professor type*, I thought as I returned her greeting.

"It seems he wants to be certain I learn everything I need to know about my godfather's death. He thought you could help me."

"Oh, I am very sorry, Monsieur Joe. Please accept my condolences," she said. "As to whether I can help you, perhaps. But that may depend on what you are expecting to hear."

"I'm trying to find out how he died. Many of my people have the same condition. Jimmy Nolan seems to think mercury from the Sweet Bounty mine is poisoning them."

"Oui, that is Monsieur Nolan's theory. But I have my doubts, it is unlikely in my view."

"What can you tell me about Minimata?" I asked. "Could that happen here?"

She raised her eyebrows, and her eyes smiled. "I see you did not hear my lecture tonight."

"Yes, ma'am," I apologized. "I arrived just as you were finishing."

"Then we must discuss this at a deeper level than I first thought. The University will close these doors in a few moments. If you have the time, I suggest we move to a more convenient place."

"That would be fine," I said. "But I'm on foot."

"Very well, I have my car. If you will allow me to gather my things here, you may follow me out."

Once outside, we walked a short way to a parking lot illuminated only by a few yellowed street lamps. We approached a red MGB, about 1980 vintage, its black ragtop up to shed the frequent rains of fall. I moved around to the passenger's side and let myself in.

The MGB was a close fit – my legs squeezed up against the dash and my knees stood at almost the same height as my shoulders. The black leather squeaked as I twisted to find a comfortable position. I thought I heard her stifle a giggle at my look of discomfort, though she assured me "It is a short ride, Monsieur." I slid the seat back as far as it would go and was at last able to stretch my legs under the dash. *Much better.*

She pulled the MG's leather-booted stick into reverse, turned the wheel to the left stop, and eased out the clutch. With a little gas, the motor responded with a confident, well-tuned rumble, and she spun us into a tight, 180-degree turn in the lot. A shift into first and a little more rumble put us onto Elizabeth Avenue and on our way.

I soon found myself on Water Street once again. She slowed and pulled the MG over to the curb. "Here we are," she said, and the motor died smartly when she turned the key. I let myself out and stood on the sidewalk facing an overhead sign that read 'The Guv'nor's Pub.' Dr. Chartier passed in front of me and I followed her in.

The Pub seemed a favorite place tonight – most tables were taken and the conversation buzzed. A small, waist-high sign on its own post told us to seat ourselves, the lights were dimmed, and by the time I spotted a table Dr. Chartier was already on her way to it. She chose a two-top in the corner by a window and we sat down on opposite sides. The light of a street lamp brightened the window-side half of the table. A wine-bottle candle stood between us, which she quickly moved to the window sill.

She waved a waiter to our table and ordered a locally-brewed Killick. I asked for the same. As the waiter went on his way, I turned back to see her lean forward, plant her elbows on the table, and fold her hands under her chin. She looked me squarely in the eye.

"I will start with Minimata," she began without hesitation, lowering her still-folded hands to the table. "From 1932 to 1968, the Chisso Corporation of Japan disposed of nearly 27 tons of mercury waste into Minimata Bay as the by-product of manufacturing a chemical called acetaldehyde. It was a key ingredient in the making of drugs, perfumes, and plastics." Her face and hands now became animated while she spoke, emphasizing a point here and a point there.

"In the mid-1950s, the people of the fishing towns of Minimata and Hachimon on the Bay's edge became mysteriously ill. They developed numbness in their lips and limbs, their speech became slurred, and their vision constricted. Many convulsed and shouted uncontrollably, as if possessed by a demon. For those most affected, the illness progressed to high fever and coma. Many died. Birds quite literally fell from the sky in mid-flight." She fluttered her open hands downward over the table. "Domestic cats launched themselves into a mad frenzy, spinning and whirling about. That is how it first became known as the cat dancing disease.

"In 1959, medical researchers at Kumamoto University discovered the Chisso Corporation's mercury waste was somehow converted to methyl mercury in the Bay. Over the many years, it accumulated in the fish of Minimata Bay that were later consumed by the townspeople, their cats and fish-eating birds. They learned Minimata Disease, as it finally became known, was caused by methyl mercury attacking the brain and nervous system."

The waiter returning with our Killicks interrupted her train of thought. I thanked him, and we both took the opportunity of that interruption to drink. Before I finished my first draw, she began again.

"The government of Kumamoto Prefecture responded by warning the townspeople to limit the number of fish eaten from the Bay, much like the Canadian government warns us about certain fish today. But that was not enough. Similar symptoms later occurred in Niigata and Ariaketcho, two other towns on the edge of another bay also with an acetaldehyde plant. No one knows precisely how many people contracted Minimata Disease, but estimates have ranged up to several thousand. What we do know is that 158 Japanese people died of this disease.

"Since then we've learned naturally-occurring, sulfate-reducing bacteria convert inorganic mercury, the form of mercury most commonly found in the environment, to an organic form. It is an extremely complex biological process we call methylation, and it results in methyl mercury, the kind of mercury responsible for Minimata Disease. Because it is organic, methyl mercury is particularly good at finding its way through digestive and circulatory systems into living tissue. It first shows up in tiny amounts in plankton, the tiniest of sea creatures, and it gradually accumulates up the food chain from prey to predator, increasing in concentration in each higher order species.

"We call that bio-alteration and bio-magnification, and you would know that if you had attended my lecture tonight," she said, another smile appearing in the corners of her engaging green eyes. "It just happens we humans eat those higher order species, which explains how the Japanese acquired the disease – they fished the Bay and ate their catch. In humans, it concentrates in brain and nerve cells where it disassembles the protein sheath around the nerve fibers. The fibers curl and tangle, nerve paths become confused, and random impulses are routed to unintended destinations."

Our attention was drawn to a burst of laughter from across the room. After a few seconds, I asked if the fish get it, and although the look on her face when her attention returned told me it was a naive question, she answered cordially. "Each species has its own level of susceptibility to any toxin, Monsieur Joe. But most fish don't accumulate enough mercury to reach that level before they die naturally, or are eaten by something else."

"You said you doubted Jimmy's theory. Why?" I asked.

"You mean is it possible your godfather died from Minimata Disease? As a scientist, I would have to say it is possible. But it is not probable. The odds oppose it for several very good reasons. Think about how long it took for symptoms to show up in the Japanese – about 20 years. During that time, I would estimate Chisso dumped 10 to 15 tons of waste into that Bay. The ores of the Sweet Bounty contain mercury, and, though much higher than typical ores, it is still less than one-tenth of one percent. If it were released from the mine, it would be released in an entirely different manner than the mercury at Minimata. It would seep very slowly from the leach heaps or tailings piles into groundwater, which itself moves very slowly. I doubt it could reach the Conifer River even many, many years from now."

I contemplated that.

"The methylation process is driven by many factors," she continued, "but the presence of freely-available inorganic mercury is absolutely critical. Even if every bit of that mercury was released into the Conifer River, and not all of it would be, the concentrations could not be high enough to produce enough methyl mercury to result in any symptoms, especially in such a short time."

"But I watched my godfather die," I protested. "I saw his body convulse, his hands tremor, heard him slur his words and babble. He fell into a coma before he died. It was just like you described at Minimata."

"I would not begin to tell you what you saw did not happen, Monsieur Joe, but many other illnesses produce the same symptoms. Alzheimer's, Parkinson's, senile dementia are just a few, which explains very well why poisoning by mercury is so hard to diagnose – it mimics at least half a dozen far more common illnesses.

"Since Minimata, there have occurred only three other confirmed mercury poisonings," she continued. One occurred in Iraq in the 1970's. The starving Iraqi people ate seed grains from Mexico that had been fumigated with methyl mercury as a fungicide. At least 6,500 died and many more became brain-damaged. The news of that catastrophe was suppressed by Saddam Hussein's regime for many years.

"The second occurred in Peru in 2000 when a truck carrying a load of mercury, a secondary product from the Yanacocha gold mine, spilled some of its load near the village of Choropampa. The villagers gathered up the droplets of the shiny, liquid metal and took it home, as if it were a precious gem. Children tasted it. Adults, remembering how mercury had once been used to recover gold, heated it over kitchen fires, hoping to find gold in it. What they found instead was highly poisonous mercury vapor. The Peruvian government estimated over 900 people fell ill.

"And the third much closer to home – northwestern and southern Ontario to be more precise. Between 1962 and 1970, the Dryden Chemical Company dumped 20,000 pounds of mercury waste into the Wabigon-English River system, and later disposed of it in a waste dump near Sarnia. Though we know of no one who died, by the late 1960s many members of the Sarnia, Grassy Narrows, and Whitedog First Nations became ill with mercury poisoning, and 500 kilometers of river are expected to remain contaminated for another 50 years or more.

"In all of those instances, and at Minimata, mercury or its derivative was clearly present. In your godfather's case, Monsieur, without a battery of corroborating medical and field tests, a confirmed diagnosis would be next to impossible."

"So then what killed my godfather?"

She relaxed back into her chair and dropped her hands to her lap. "That, Monsieur Joe, is a very good question."

I mulled that thought for a few moments. Then I remembered the tests the hospital would conduct on my godfather's body. "What kind of medical evidence would be necessary – an autopsy and a panel of lab tests?" I asked.

She sat forward again. "Oui, perhaps, but that would depend on what they were looking for and how they tested for it." Her eyebrows furrowed, as if a renewed interest overtook her. "What do you suggest, Monsieur?"

I told her about the autopsy and lab tests, and that the doctor had intended to consult a toxicologist in Ottawa. "The hair test was the only one completed before my godfather died. In a couple days, the rest of the tests and the autopsy should be done."

She seemed to contemplate the opportunity presented by this new information. "Did he mention the name of the toxicologist?" she asked finally.

I shook my head. "No, but I did get the doctor's name. Drew McGovern."

"Hmm. Well, if this Dr. McGovern knows the field, he quite probably meant Pierre Martin at the Centre for Chronic Disease Prevention and Control. He was a mentor in the early days of my career and he remains a personal friend. If you don't mind, I could call him and see what he would tell me. I will just tell him I have been assigned to follow up on those tests. If it turns out to be nothing, there will be no harm done." She dropped her head, paused again, and looked up at me from below raised eyebrows. Her eyes danced, like a child planning mischief, and she smiled again. "I am assigned, am I not, Monsieur?"

I gave back a quiet but frustrated sigh. "If it helps me find out what happened to my godfather, yes," I said.

At that, a silence arose between us and we gazed over the crowd, me not really looking, not quite knowing what to say next. I reflected that Dr. Chartier's information didn't help me. I was now questioning my former resolve and wondering who really knew the story behind my godfather's death. Jimmy Nolan swore corruption and deception surrounding the mine are responsible. He believed in my godfather and went to great lengths to tell his story. On the other hand, Dr. Chartier made her career studying mines like the Sweet Bounty. She was a woman of science, trained to distill facts from what otherwise might be no more than deceptive appearance. I even found myself wondering if the Minister actually had told me the truth. Who could I believe? The only thing I could conclude with certainty was that my godfather's death is still a mystery.

I was feeling overwhelmed when Dr. Chartier broke our silence. "Well then, what is next, Monsieur Joe?" she asked, drawing back my attention.

I clung to the only thing I knew with certainty. "I must return to the Reserve and bury my godfather," I answered. "A Mi'kmaw's body and spirit are one – it would be a dishonor to keep the body after the spirit has joined mntu. He guided his people to the old spiritual ways again, and they will honor that during the funeral. They will bury him with his most important possessions and the icons of his life, artifacts worthy of his role as Chief of his people. Then there will be a Salite, a celebration to honor his life, what some would call a wake."

"Well, then, I have an offer for you, Monsieur. I must begin my return to Corner Brook tomorrow. I will divert a short distance to the Sweet Bounty and take a few measurements on the Conifer River below the mine. It is time someone tested Monsieur Nolan's suspicions before he writes himself into trouble. A bit out of my way, but if nothing else, it will verify the mine is operating within its permitted limits. I could drop you off at the Reserve. It is not far from the mine, and I would appreciate the company."

That was a welcome offer. The government would fly my godfather's body home, but I was beginning to worry how I would get myself back. I'd have very little money after I paid the Inn – the scant stipend of a teaching assistantship hardly provided enough to holiday on. And it was an opportunity to see the Sweet Bounty itself, the mine that was rapidly becoming the center of my world. "That's very kind of you, Dr. Chartier. Tomorrow, then."

"Tres bien, Monsieur." She looked at her watch as I took another draw from my ale. "Ah! It is 9:45! I had better return to my room. I will have a very long day tomorrow." She looked up at me. "As will you. Can you be ready early, by 6 o'clock a.m.?"

She was right, it would be a very long day. The Reserve was more than 300 kilometers and a three-hour ferry ride from here, and I was familiar enough with the rest of Newfoundland to know she would be trying to do in one day what more tolerably would be done in two. But that was her matter, and I was too grateful for the opportunity to quibble about the time. "Yes, of course," I answered.

At that, we spilt the tab, left the pub, and she drove me back to the Captain's Inn. As I let myself out of the MG, I turned and stooped to thank her. She was smiling at me. "Tomorrow morning, Monsieur Joe?"

"6:00 a.m. it is," I said, returning her smile. I closed the door and backed away as the MG rumbled its good night with red taillights fading into the darkness.

## Chapter 8

The sleepy darkness of 6:00 a.m. brought little more conversation than 'hello', 'ready?' 'yes,' and 'OK.' We said nothing for nearly an hour as we rode, allowing the emptiness of the roadway and the steady, reassuring hum of the MG to lull us into a contented silence.

At Brigus Junction, the sun rose in a clear sky, lighting our way from behind with the yellow-white intensity of a lighthouse beacon. The bright morning sky was the perfect contrast to a sunless yesterday, and its clarity stimulated a pleasant wakefulness. We began with small talk, but I quickly felt the need to know more about the circumstances of my godfather's death. Many pieces of that puzzle were still missing for me. "Dr. Chartier, what can you tell me about the Sweet Bounty?" I asked.

"Monsieur Joe, if we are to continue our journey in this tiny car with a semblance of comfort between us, I insist you call me Anna as my friends do." She smiled, attractive even at 7:00 am.

"Very well, Anna," I consented.

"Much better, Peter.

"So," she began in earnest, "the Sweet Bounty is a deep mine with above-ground processing, which means it removes the ore underground and brings it above ground to extract the gold. I was hired as a consulting expert by the Ministry of Environment to review the mine plan three years ago, and I remember it quite well. Environmentally, it appeared to me a very sound proposal.

"Above ground are the waste piles, leach heaps, and facilities for crushing, grinding, and recovering gold from the pregnant solution ..."

She was moving too fast already. "Anna," I interrupted, "you're losing me. Leach heaps? Pregnant solution?"

"Oui, of course, Peter. I have assumed too much. Please let me start again, from the very beginning.

"Many years ago, in the gold rushes of California and Alaska, miners cleaned gold from the gravels of stream beds and valley floors using a process called mercury amalgamation. With high-pressure water cannons, they washed the gravels into elevated, manmade streams called sluices and made it flow along riffles where liquid mercury metal was added. The mercury bonded to the gold creating a mercury-gold amalgam that settled to the bottom of the riffle. The water was caused to flow a different path, separating it from the amalgam and allowing the gold and mercury to be collected. The mercury was then distilled off, leaving the gold behind, and the mercury vapor was condensed and reused again in the riffle.

"But there were two troubles with this process. One, mercury is very toxic, especially as a vapor, and two, mercury is a very heavy liquid. One-third of it, sometimes more, was just simply lost. Some of it leaked out the bottom of the riffle, but much of it flowed past the riffle into large ponds called after-bays. The contents of the after-bays, being of no concern to the miner, were simply left to chance. As a consequence, those valleys and streambeds to this day contain much mercury and are of great concern to ecologists and human health specialists. It has been reported more than eight million pounds of mercury were lost to the environment just in California alone during that time.

"However, with the use of cyanide beginning in the 1970's, mercury amalgamation was discontinued. I believe your godfather would have known this, so I am quite certain amalgamation is not the source of mercury that concerned him."

I acknowledged her assertion with a nod. Despite a life on the Reserve, my godfather was quite learned.

"Most modern day gold mining uses cyanide to recover gold in a process known as cyanide heap leaching. It is not very efficient, but it is very inexpensive and it allows profitable recovery of gold from even very low grade ores. It was pioneered in the 1970s at the Cortez mine in Nevada, proven on a larger commercial scale at the Zortman Landusky mine in Montana during the 1980s, and it is now in use worldwide.

"The ore is first crushed and ground to approximately grape size and placed into large piles called heaps. These heaps are indeed very large, often 200 feet high and covering 300 to 500 acres. Across their tops will be laid a network of hoses and nozzles to irrigate them with a weak mixture of sodium cyanide and water. As the cyanide solution percolates downward, it bonds with the gold and removes it from the ore."

We had just passed Blaketown, the site of Russell's Point where archaeologists had unearthed an ancient Indian camp occupied by the Beothuk long before my ancestors arrived. It has sometimes been alleged my People were responsible for the extinction of the Beothuk, that French colonists brought the Mi'kmaq from Cape Breton to Newfoundland and offered them bounties for Beothuk heads. But the stories of the Old Ones tell us the Beothuk were proudly independent and reclusive, and they avoided contact with new peoples. Competition for their coastal foods of seals, fish, birds, and shellfish drove them permanently inland along the Exploits River to Red Indian Lake. There, in the very heart of Newfoundland, they suffered disease and starvation, and there they perished.

"The pregnant solution," she went on, "the mixture of water and cyanide which now also contains gold, is collected at the bottom of the heaps on impermeable liners and conducted by channels or pipes to a similarly-lined holding pond."

I interrupted her again. "I thought cyanide was deadly, the gas of execution chambers."

"True, Peter. It is no longer used as such, but it once was the deadly gas of legal executions as you say, and of the death chambers of Auschwitz, too. But it is a poison gas only under certain conditions. If the acidity of the cyanide and water solution is controlled, it may be handled quite safely.

The acidity of plain water is enough to let the cyanide quickly escape as the deadly gas you refer to.

So before adding the cyanide, the miner will add quicklime to the water to make sure it is not acidic, and as long as he keeps the mixture that way the cyanide remains in solution. Accidents may happen, but the mine operator will take great care to prevent the poisoning of his employees.

"So, to continue, a lined holding pond now contains the solution of gold, cyanide, and water. This solution is then filtered to remove solids and pumped to a tank where the miner adds powdered zinc. The cyanide bonds to the zinc and releases the gold, which settles out as fine particles to be collected by another set of filters, then dried, melted, and cast into ingots. The remaining cyanide solution, now devoid of gold, is called the barren solution, and it is stored in another holding pond to be reused or neutralized or evaporated.

"It is all much more complicated than I have described, but now you should have a simple understanding."

"All well and good, Anna," I interjected. "But so far you haven't mentioned mercury. According to Jimmy Nolan, and my godfather, mercury is supposed to be coming from this mine."

"I was about to get to that, Peter. Historically, leach heaps and barren solution ponds have not been well controlled or well cared for after the mine closes. Perhaps this is what your godfather was concerned about."

"What do you mean?" I asked.

"Well, these ponds can become quite large, often covering 200 to 400 acres, and there are many examples of the dams bursting or overflowing. The dam at the Zortman Landusky mine in Montana overflowed several times in the 1980s, a dam burst at the

Homestake mine in South Dakota and at the Los Frailes mine in Spain both in 1998, as did one in Guyana in 1995. Or the dams may leak, as at the Summitville Mine in Colorado in the 1980s and 90s.

In all of those examples, long stretches of healthy and productive rivers were severely poisoned, many fish were killed, and drinking water sources were shut down or rendered unusable. The most severe event of this kind occurred in Romania in 2000. Within 14 days of the dam's bursting, over 400 kilometers of the Tiasza River were contaminated enough to kill more than 100 tons of fish. It even threatened to contaminate the beloved Danube River."

She adjusted her position and switched driving hands to gesture with her right. "In each of the instances I have cited, the cyanide itself was the poison. A very small amount of cyanide, a mere teaspoon of two percent solution in plain water, is enough to kill a human being, and less than that will kill many fish. It is very dangerous if left out of control."

"But surely that's not happening at the Sweet Bounty, right?" I inserted.

"I believe not, Peter. If it were, we would find the shores of the Conifer River and Pjila'si Bay lined with thousands of dead and dying fish and shore birds, and Jimmy Nolan's stories would be headlines in most countries of the world. But so far I have told you only half of what you should know."

"There's more? What could be worse?"

"Not worse, but perhaps more sinister. Not all of the cyanide solution percolates through the leach heap with the gold to the liner to be collected. Some of it remains trapped in the pore spaces of the ore, held there by capillary force, the same force that allows blood to creep upward against gravity through the tiny capillaries of your blood stream."

We were passing through the narrow isthmus connecting the Avalon Peninsula to the main island. At Come-by-Chance, in exactly the right place, one can see the North Atlantic on both sides of the highway. I was distracted by the keen smell of saltwater for the second time in as many days, and it brought me both a familiar comfort and an unfamiliar anguish. It reminded me joyfully of my boyhood years on the Reserve, and it reminded me sorrowfully I would bury my godfather in one day's time.

A rising emphasis in Anna's voice brought me back to the present. "Many ores contain sulfides, minerals comprised of metals and sulfur. As a result of the gold recovery process, most of the sulfides reside as waste in the abandoned tailings ponds and heaps.

"In the presence of air and water, the sulfur breaks away from the metal, and this chemical reaction releases acidic hydrogen ions. You may think of it as nature creating sulfuric acid, and she is aided in this change by naturally occurring bacteria. Sulfuric acid is very potent, capable of dissolving every other metal from the remains of the ore.

"So, now we have both cyanide and sulfuric acid within the abandoned leach heaps and the tailings pond, making a – what is the phrase? – double whammy? What is important about that is neither cyanide nor sulfuric acid are selective – they will both dissolve many metals from the heaps, including the toxic ones like mercury. When it rains, they are washed downward, percolating to tiny cracks in the liner, which by then is very old. They eventually seep through those cracks to the groundwater below and find their way naturally to surface water, or perhaps to someone's drinking water well."

We approached our turn off the Trans-Canada Highway at Goobies and headed west onto the two-lane Route 210. "Now," she continued, talking through the turns, "these metals are worrisome at best and a health hazard at worst. Their concentrations are frequently very small, often only tens of parts in a million, but even at such slight levels the living body does not tolerate them. They become a poison."

Something still was not clear in what she described. "But you said this would be a problem *after* the mine closed and the heaps were abandoned," I said. "My godfather has already died, and my People are ill *now*. That shouldn't be happening for years!" My frustration must have shown, and she held up her hand as if to stop me mid-sentence.

"Oui, the normal expectation is this would not happen for many, many years, and only if the heaps and tailings ponds were not properly cared for. However, something very similar could happen during the active life of the mine. If the liners are missing, cracked, or poorly constructed, those metals could escape to groundwater with the cyanide much sooner, even while the mine is still operating."

She acquired a look of conclusion. "That, I believe, is the scenario your godfather worried about."

I pondered that for a moment. "So, if I understand this, Anna, mercury and the other toxic metals could come from the heaps and tailings after the mine is abandoned, but they could be seeping from the heaps with the cyanide even now if the liners are cracked or missing. How would you know if that's happening?"

## The Sweet Bounty

"It would be difficult to determine that, Peter, unless the liners are leaking so badly one could already measure them in ground water or the Conifer River itself. I will test the Conifer for them while I am there, but I must caution you, it is highly unlikely I will find anything – it has only been three years since the mine began."

"But if you do find them, that proves Jimmy Nolan's theory, right?" I looked at her intently, anticipating her confirmation.

Suddenly, five dark gray vans, horns blaring, sped past us from behind at close range, barely squeezing between us and the oncoming semi desperately trying to widen the road between us. Their darkly tinted windows made it impossible to identify the occupants, and they bore no markings except the Newfoundland and Labrador Coat of Arms.

Anna swerved sharply to the right, still at highway speed. The diminutive MG shuddered in the wake of their passing. We careened onto the shoulder, the MG's brakes trying to find traction where loose gravel offered none. We bounced roughshod, dodging holes and rocks, narrowly missing an electric power pole and skidding toward the trees. Anna finally brought the MG to a stop with the help of a convenient stand of dense brush, and the motor stalled. I had braced myself with both hands on the dash, but my head still collided with the ragtop. Then she slammed the heels of her hands onto the steering wheel and cursed her anger in a long string of French phrases I had heard my mother say only a few times in my life. I was merely thankful we were unscathed.

We had been gathering our composure in silence for no more than a minute when, without saying a word, she restarted the motor, backed out of the brush, and rocketed toward the roadway, spewing gravel behind us. By the time she had third gear we were at highway speed. Fourth gear took the speedometer to 150 kph, needle still climbing. I was quickly learning what that subtle MG rumble could do when called to service.

I clung to the dash once more. "Anna, what are you doing?" I asked in surprise.

"They nearly killed us, Peter!" she exclaimed, finally returning to English. "That was the most rude and inconsiderate maneuver I have ever encountered! What could they have been thinking? We are going to catch them and report them to the authorities!"

"I don't think they were thinking, Anna. And those were government vans – they probably *were* the authorities."

"So much the worse, Peter!"

The motor screamed its delight, easily absorbing the distance she ordered it to consume. To my astonishment, she seemed to be enjoying the chase, and I looked over at her, bewildered. "V6 and a blower," was all she said, and with a wry smile she engaged the overdrive. Over the next 70 kilometers, Swift Current, Piper's Hole River, Long Pond, Toby Lookout, and Paradise River careened by in rapid succession.

At a passing road sign that announced our approach to Route 211, she geared down. The motor obliged with a high whine, cylinder compression slowing us to a docile 55 in jake brake fashion. She stopped at the fork and the motor rumbled lightly, as if patiently awaiting another sprint.

She studied Route 211, the way to Grand La

## The Sweet Bounty

Pierre and Terrenceville, then the road straight ahead. Our planned route would take us to the Bay L'Argent ferry, but it could also take us the full length of the Burin Peninsula to Marystown, Grand Bank, and the ferry to the islands of St. Pierre and Miquelon if we cared to experience a taste of France. She contemplated her options. There was no sign of the vans on either route.

"I am afraid I have lost them, Peter." The excitement in her manner was gone, her voice sounded almost despondent, and she sighed.

"We had best stay on our course," she said finally. "If we divert, we will miss our ferry and you will be delayed two days." Reluctantly, but to my relief, she engaged first gear and accelerated to a reasonable speed in our intended direction.

We arrived at the Bay L'Argent ferry terminal with only a few minutes to spare. After paying the toll, we were directed to the ramp and into the last position on the car deck. Anna turned off the motor and set the brake. No sooner did we stop than the ramp was closed behind us. We and what I guessed to be 50 other vehicles were now within the belly of the ferry, encapsulated by an echoing structure of yellow-green steel posts, dimpled wall plate, the now nearly vertical ramp, and a web of rust-red, steel I-beams supporting the deck above us. We seemed to be the only people still on the car deck.

I rubbed my eyes with the heels of my hands, weary from the drive and thankful for the stop. We gathered our jackets, climbed out of the MG, and closed the doors. We stretched, then wound our way through the narrow aisles between parked cars toward the side of the ferry where the stairway would take us to the upper deck.

Halfway up, something familiar caught my eye and I halted abruptly. I turned. "Anna, over there," I said with a directed nod of my head. She looked, then turned back, her eyes wide. At the very front of the car deck sat five, dark gray vans.

"Move 'long dere, be castin' off dareckly" called a Newfoundland dialect from below. I looked down to see a stout, dark-haired man in a yellow mac climbing the stairs toward us, urging us upward. "All riders on top deck, right?"

We climbed as he ordered and pushed open a steel bulkhead that led us along a short gangway to the passenger lounge. Anna announced she would leave in search of the van drivers, 'to give them a piece of her mind,' she said. I decided to ride on the foredeck – I would enjoy the salt spray and the sun on my face.

"I will see you in Rencontre," she called back, and she left in search of her quarry. Rencontre East would be the half-way stop before our terminus at Pool's Cove.

I stood on the foredeck, leaning alone against the rail as the captain gave a long blast of the horn. The motors wound up to a throaty roar and the screws churned hard to move the ferry away from the dock. Above the distant western horizon rose the shores of Corbin Bay and Pool's Cove, so much like the coast I remembered so well – serene, rugged, uniquely indescribable.

From the tundra plateaus of central Newfoundland, wooded canyons plunge steeply southward toward the Atlantic. At the sea's edge, towering cliffs are divided by inlets, bays, and coves, as if from walls of grey stone extending hundreds of kilometers an enormous, rooting bear had clawed out great fragments and hurled them into the ocean behind it.

On days when he had not been pressed with matters of tribal business, my godfather and I had walked many parts of the 100 kilometers from the headwaters of the Conifer River to Pjila'si Bay and the ocean shore. Through the steep and flowing tucamore-wooded canyon to the marble-green estuary of the Reserve we had trudged, and along the many arms of Pjila'si Bay to Hermitage Bay, where the fresh water of the Conifer River became the salt water of the North Atlantic.

A reminiscent smile stole quietly onto my face at that thought. It had never been a simple walk, as I recalled it. We had followed game trails where we could and bushwhacked where we couldn't. It was always a supreme effort for me – I was tall for my age, but lanky and awkward then. Barrens brush grabbed at my ankles and shins, and hidden depressions seemed to lay in wait just where I was about to place my feet. I stumbled repeatedly, tripping forward as if I would fall to my face, arms flailing to grab at some tree which all too often was not there. But to Saqamaw Abram Jeddore, my godfather, it was a very special place. Against the great struggle for common respect the white man's world would grant at only the slowest of paces, it cleared his mind, fortified his resolve, and brought a peace to his soul as could no other place.

The horn blared again and I came back to the present. The wind rose in my face and the crest of the first wave struggled to heave the bow upward out of its way. I was almost home.

## Chapter 9

"Fax for you, Jimmy!" she called out. It was Beverly, the older secretary whose desk was just across the hallway. She always called out whenever there was a fax, or a letter, or something for him. She never delivered it, she just called out, like she owned the place. He couldn't remember when Beverly appointed herself Matron General of the office, but she had, and she frequently took advantage of the lack of a challenger for that title.

Jimmy Nolan, reporter for the St. John's Telegraph, sat at the handed-down, three-drawer desk in the small office he inherited from its former occupant. His windowless room offered just enough space for that desk and the few accoutrements provided by his employer – the wooden swivel-chair in which he sat at this very moment, a metal, folding side chair for guests who never came, two four-drawer filing cabinets, and a coat rack which he seldom used. Two simply framed pictures of the harbour in his Ireland hometown hung on the wall beside the file cabinets.

Jimmy looked at the clock above his door. It was

## The Sweet Bounty

10:35 a.m. He rose from the chair, scratched the back of his right calf with the vamp of his left shoe, and walked the seven steps from his desk to Beverly's. She held up the fax and he took it, glancing at it only momentarily. "Thanks," he murmured, not meeting her eyes. He didn't like Beverly very much, and it showed.

Half a page was all it was. Probably a press release, he thought, dull just like all the other three, or five, or eight press releases he received nearly every week. He rolled it up and pushed it into his right hip pocket. Whatever the fax was, it could wait. What he wanted right now was a decent cup of coffee. Beverly had already made a pot in the lunchroom, but he had never liked her coffee. Besides, espresso shop conversation was sometimes a good source of newsworthy leads and he didn't have any right now. He walked back to his desk, donned his mac, and left the building.

Once outside, he turned right. The sun was shining through a pale blue sky. That, he observed, was a far cry from yesterday and a pleasant change for this time of year. It was only two blocks on Duckworth Street and one through the alley to the Common Ground on Water Street, his preferred morning coffee stop. But today he wished it was farther – he was enjoying how the sun warmed his face.

Now inside, he found himself to be fifth in line. Behind the elevated coffee bar, three staff waited on patrons and the line moved fast. Though the Common Ground was a small place, its red-brown brick interior and large street-side windows gave the feeling of being larger and almost open to the outdoors.

He ordered his usual tall skinny mocha with a double shot, made his way to the empty table at the back and sat, sipping and listening with newspaperman's ears for shreds of conversation that might give him a lead. The hiss of a steamer carved the buzz of conversation into seemingly unrelated fragments. He pieced together the usual banter about Progressive Conservatives this and Liberals that, but so far nothing to make good press.

    Remembering the fax in his back pocket, he unrolled it and pulled it back and forth over the table's edge to flatten it. He laid it out before him and sipped his mocha before getting down to business. His eyes widened at what he read.

Government of Newfoundland and Labrador

Department of Environment, Albert Winslow, Minister

For immediate release

Investigators Dispatched, High Priority Mission.

The Department of Environment today dispatched a team of highly-specialized investigators to the Sweet Bounty Mine in south central Newfoundland. Allegations of illegal operation and releases of toxic waste to the Conifer River triggered the investigation.

"I assure the citizens of Conifer the Sweet Bounty mine is a safe operation in compliance with every environmental requirement, and the allegations of the St. John's Telegraph are most certainly unfounded. Nonetheless, it is my duty as Minister of Environment to thoroughly investigate every allegation without regard to source, and I intend to do exactly that. Not a single citizen will be harmed by any operation under the jurisdiction of this Department while I'm on watch."

A perfunctory line at the end said to contact the Department for further information.

*Holy feck!* Jimmy thought. Elation swept over him as he began to realize the impact he, Jimmy Nolan, was now having on the course of events in Newfoundland. The future drama he would write had begun to unfold on the paper in his very hands. Surely, newspapers across Canada would carry his byline, even the CBC would pick up his stories. How many years had he worked for a break like this? Way too many to count.

He quickly folded the fax and drove it back into his hip pocket. He took a long sip from his mocha, stood, and hastily left the Common Ground, mocha in hand. In high spirits, he wove his way through the sidewalk crowds with quick strides. His mind was already composing his next story when he re-entered the Telegraph.

The Telegraph Block was the long building at 218 Duckworth. A very long time ago, it provided warehouse space for the largest supplier of nets, buoys, and fishing paraphernalia in a then independent Newfoundland. The Telegraph began elsewhere as the Island's only daily paper, a hand-pressed, single-sheet four-sider with a staff of six and a readership of 500. In the 78 years since, it grew handsomely, and its sale to the current owner became a small part of the largest financial transaction in the annals of the Canadian media industry. Somewhere in the midst of that history, the Telegraph had relocated to the reconstructed, three-story, white stone building Jimmy just entered.

He climbed the stairs to the second floor. Back in his office, he put down the mocha, threw his mac over the side chair, and sat at his desk. He wanted first to call Peter Joe, tell him the news. Now more than ever he needed Peter to find the cause of Chief Jeddore's death, expose the bribery, prove the mine was responsible, and bring him incriminating evidence. He dialed the front desk of the Captain's Inn and was greeted by the voice of a woman sounding Cockney and elderly.

"Sorry, dearie, Mr. Joe's no longer 'ere," she said. "Checked out this morning, 'andsome young Indian man, 'e was ... No, didn't leave behind no number for callers ... Didn't say where, must have been far, though, 'e and his young lady drove off in a sporty car before daylight."

"Thanks so much," he said with disappointment. He hung up.

A mild panic set in. He guessed Peter Joe was on his way to the Reserve, but it was 240 as-the-crow-flies kilometers from here to there. Roads in Newfoundland seldom go as the crow flies, which meant he could be anywhere on 300 to 600 kilometers of Trans-Canada Highway, or provincial route, or secondary blacktop, or coastal ferry, or who knows what. And who was his young lady?

*Of course!* Just then, he remembered giving a newspaper clipping to Peter as they talked by the pier, a clipping about Dr. Chartier's lecture. He must have contacted her that night, and he must be with her right now.

He remembered having her cell number ... somewhere. He rummaged hurriedly through the mess of paper scraps he had jotted phone numbers on in the top right drawer of his desk. There it was, under the Mexican takeout menu for Casa Grande, nearly on the bottom. He lifted the handset of his desk phone and dialed the number.

He was given without a ring directly to her recorded greeting, telling him she was out of range or her cell phone was turned off. He decided he would leave an urgent-sounding message and hope she would call him back quickly.

"Bonjour," said the greeting. "You have reached the Department of Environmental Chemistry, Sir Wilfred Grenfell College, in Corner Brook, Newfoundland. This is Dr. Annamarie Chartier. I am not available at this moment. If you please give your name and telephone number with your message, I will return your call as soon as possible. Au revoir!"

Jimmy did as requested. "Dr. Chartier, this is Jimmy Nolan, St. John's Telegraph. Look, uh, please call me right away. I'm hoping you know how to reach Peter Joe, maybe he's even with you now. It's urgent I talk to him. I have some news about his godfather, Chief Jeddore. Tell him investigators from the Ministry of Environment are on their way to the Sweet Bounty mine right now. Tell him they're checking out exactly what I told him, that the mine is responsible for his godfather's death. 364-6311, extension 25. Call me." He hung up.

Now, he'd just have to wait. He sipped his mocha, turned to his computer, and began typing the first words of the story that he was sure would rock front pages everywhere – the story that would move him up to one of the biggest presses in Canada, right where he was sure he deserved to be.

## Chapter 10

Except for a school of dolphins bow-riding our wake out of Bay L'Argent, the ferry ride had been an uneventful three hours of sun and salt air. At Rencontre East, Anna and I rejoined for a walk up St. Aubin Hill, one of Rencontre's harbor-mouth guardians, during the half-hour layover.

She had been unsuccessful at finding the van drivers. "Everyone looks the same," she complained, "all dressed like common Newfoundlander folk! I did not even find five people conversing together!" She had eavesdropped on their conversations, too, hearing no clues about official government business in any of them.

But then she grinned widely with self-satisfaction. "However, Peter, I did go below deck, and I got these!" She handed me her business card. I turned it over to find she had written five license plate numbers on the back. "When I return to Corner Brook," she said, "I will report them, and then they will be – how do you say? – in the poop?" At that, we both had a good laugh.

When the ferry docked at Pool's Cove, the vans were first off and we were last – we lost them again before we even got started. The next 70 kilometers of our highway journey turned, dipped, and crested us past spruce and birch-lined, waterlogged bottomlands, and through highland barrens with brilliant ocean vistas. We came at last down the final hill of Route 365 into Conifer and stopped in the parking lot for the Conifer Medical Centre, the very spot where my godfather and I were picked up by the helicopter. A crowd of women had gathered there, centered about a woman of stout build, our tribal Puoin, Mary Benoit. Anna parked and turned off the motor, and I felt home once more.

Mary recognized me immediately as I stepped out of the MG, and she hurried my way. Like the other women now behind her, she was wearing a full-length woolen skirt and the distinctly-Mi'kmaw peaked cap of broadcloth. Both were hand-made, bordered with embroidery, beadwork, and colorful ribbons. This was traditional Mi'kmaw dress now reserved for special occasions, brought out now for Salite, the celebration of my godfather's life.

Mary was a proud and morally strong woman, well respected among the Mi'kmaq for her knowledge of ancestral medicine. For as long as I can remember, she had been a caring and tempering force among The People.

"Kwe', Pie'l, kwe'!" she said, greeting me with an embrace. Mary was of medium height, and I bent down to receive her. At 59, she was still physically strong and carried thick black hair, braided to her waist and only slightly grayed.

"Me' talwele'in?" she added, asking how I was.

"Kwe', Ma'lij. Wela'lin," I said, returning her greeting. "Wele'i ... aqq mu weleyiw," I added with a tone of sadness – I was well, yet I was not.

She tightened her embrace with a motherly "O', Pie'l," offering what comfort I might accept, then broke the embrace and stepped back, holding my hands in hers. "Wen net a't kitap?" she asked, letting her eyes drift to the woman standing next to me.

"Teluisit Anna," I replied. Then, turning to Anna, I said, "Anna, this is Mary Benoit, our Healer. Mary, this is Dr. Annamarie Chartier. Anna is helping me discover how Godfather Abraham died."

Mary's full, round face smiled and she offered her hand to Anna. "Hello, Anna, you are welcome here."

"It is my pleasure," Anna replied, accepting the handshake.

"Pie'l," said Mary turning back to me, "how long will you stay?"

"Several days, it may take some time to find what I came to discover. And the ceremony?"

"Tomorrow," Mary answered. "We will count on you to be part of it. Abram spoke fondly of you often, even in his last days. His spirit will rest well if you are there. Where will you stay tonight?"

"With whomever will have me," I said. Mary caught the humor in that and laughed.

"Of course, you may stay with my husband and me," she said, still smiling. Turning, she said "Anna, I will talk to the women – I am certain any one of them would be pleased to have you in her home."

"And the others, Mary, how are they?" I asked.

She grew solemn, and her eyebrows arched in solicitude. "Oh, Peter," she said. "Many are not well. They suffer with tremors and speak in babble, and my medicine does not help them. I offer them comfort, but it is little. I have never known such a sickness. Many believe the mine poisons our water and our salmon."

"Whatever it is," I said, "the evil in it has taken one of us already. I will not let it take more."

She gave me an approving look and wished me well, told me to arrive at her house in time for dinner, and excused herself to attend to matters of the burial. Before leaving, she returned to the other women to ask if one of them would take Anna in for a few days. A widowed woman of about 80 leaned out around Mary and waved – it seemed Anna would have a place to stay tonight.

With that, Mary signaled for Anna to follow, and Anna said "Au revoir." Mary, Anna, and Widowed Woman went off together, and I left to find other members of my Tribe. I determined to also visit my godfather's house. If there were any clues to his death there, I would have to find them before his belongings were buried with him.

\* \* \* \*

Later that evening, after dinner at Mary's, I took a solitary walk, wanting to fill my senses with the memories of this place. Under a full moon, brilliant white and setting in a clear sky alive with stars over the southern Newfoundland coast, I threaded my way on a dark path through trees and brush to the shore of Black Duck Cove on Pjila'si Bay. The moon laid an intensely bright and undulating path across rippling water directly to my feet, giving me false warmth against the chill of the night air. Save for the occasional whistle of a loon and the gentle lap of the waves, it was stone quiet.

I sat cross-legged in the grass at the edge of the Bay and reflected how the stresses of the last few days were giving way to the uncertainties of the next. The stillness brought a sense of calm to a mind still grappling with conflicting assertions. Everything pointed to the mine being the culprit in my godfather's death, yet Anna's experience said it could not be. If not, then what? I could conceive of no other cause. I closed my eyes, letting the night diminish my questions, awaiting a vision of answers.

Just then, my eyes opened. It was a barely audible snap, like a twig breaking under the weight of a cautious footstep. I slowly turned my head in the direction of the sound, keening my ears and stopping my breath.

There, again. I turned fully around and listened hard. Again it came, but now there was faint motion, a subtle movement in the trees. I strained my eyes to see. *Was that the silhouette of a man?*

Then came the slap of a branch against fabric.

"Ow!" I heard. It was unmistakably a feminine voice with a French accent.

I released my breath in a sigh of relief. "Anna?" I called out.

"Peter? Where are you?"

"Straight ahead. Come toward the moon."

A few more snaps, then the rustle of shoes in the grass, then the figure became the gray-white outline of a woman. Unable to see me against the backlight of the moon, she was almost on top of me when I spoke again. "Here, Anna," I said.

"Oh!" she startled. "There you are!" She sat down in the grass beside me and we both turned to face the Bay.

"It is beautiful here, Peter. It seems you love it so, yes?"

"It holds pleasant memories for me, Anna, more than I can describe. I was born here, raised here, lived the best 15 years of my life here. I hand-lined many salmon from this very cove. My footprints live deep within the grass beneath us. This place brings me great peace. It reminds me of my godfather, it reminds me of what it means to be Mi'kmaw. Yet, it angers me too. It reminds me he let me be taken from it."

She probed my eyes – I suppose she didn't know how to respond to that. Then she broke the silence with "Blue eyes are not Mi'kmaw, Peter."

"My father is Mi'kmaw," I answered. "Or was – I don't even know if he's alive. He left my mother and me before I was born. My mother is French Canadian. When I was 15, she moved us to Montreal where I spent the next 19 years of my life. I learned to live there, work there, study there, I have friends there. But my heart is here. This place will always be home for me."

There was a long pause, and I could see a moonlit contemplation overtake her expression.

"Peter," she said slowly, "if you never learn how your godfather died, can you live with that?"

My mind snapped at that and I scowled inwardly, for I knew I would find the reason. The knowing was within me as strongly as the knowing of my own will. As I realized she was only expressing what she knew to be within the white man's realm of possibilities, I relaxed.

"I am part Mi'kmaw," I answered calmly, " yet I am full Mi'kmaw. I am ready to accept what is to be. But, in here," I said, putting the flat of my fist to my heart, "I believe I will discover it."

"Belief without basis is false hope, Peter. What cannot be proved cannot be."

*An absolute*, I thought, and I suddenly found her awareness to be so very limited. By her white education, perhaps, just as I found my education in the white world to stifle my own worldview.

"Munmkwej," I said in return.

"What, Peter?"

"Munmkwej. The Woodchuck."

"I don't understand."

"When I was a boy, " I explained, "my godfather told me the stories passed to us by the Old Ones. Each one was a message about how to live.

"One morning, two old women found a dead woodchuck lying outside their wigwam. They were hungry, and thinking it would make a good breakfast, they brought Munmkwej inside. They skinned and gutted him, cut him up, and put the pieces into a pot to simmer over the fire.

"Suddenly, as the water began to boil, Munmkwej came back to life. He put himself back together, leapt from the pot, took his fur coat from the tanning frame, and ran from the wigwam into the woods laughing."

She looked puzzled. "I still don't understand, Peter," she said.

"It means be careful what you assume – things are not always what they appear to be."

She seemed to contemplate that for a while, and I decided it was time to tell her about my meeting with the Minister. "While I was in St. John's, I spoke with Minister Winslow," I said.

She turned her head my way. "Oh? And what

did you learn?"

"He's a pompous, arrogant, demeaning and power-hungry man with a self-inflated ego," I began. "I could go on ..."

She laughed. "Yes, that he is. Anything in addition to his personal traits?"

"He's hiding something, Anna, and I don't trust him. The more I probed his involvement with the Sweet Bounty, the more he stonewalled. Jimmy thinks he was bribed to approve the mine plan knowing it was a fake. When I confronted Winslow with that, he became livid with anger and ordered me out."

"Well, Peter, you may answer that question tomorrow afternoon. If you accompany me to the River, you may see for yourself that everything is as it should be."

I nodded, intending to do exactly that after the funeral.

A solitary loon whistled from across the bay, breaking our momentary silence, and I listened intently. It always seemed such a wild, haunting cry – performed tonight, I thought, to remind me the Great Spirit Creator is forever close in this place. I was soothed by its presence. Then, as if satisfied I had heard its message, it ceased its lonesome call, leaving us in our silence once again. I began to tell Anna about my other discovery.

"I found something very strange at my godfather's house today," I said.

The look on her face asked me to continue. "A plate under the steps to his front door," I added.

"A plate? How do you mean, a dinner plate?"

"Exactly, but that's not the oddest part of it," I said. "The plate held melted candle wax on top of a handful of black dust with white crystals in it, like salt.

There were straight pins encased in the wax, as if the pins had been stuck into the candle before it burned down onto the dust."

She screwed up her face, as if this was just too queer a story to be believed. "What does it mean?" she asked. "Something your godfather created in a state of feeblemindedness? A child's prank?"

"I don't know. If it was a prank, it was not like any prank I ever learned. And the plate did not match any I found in his house."

Another silence rose between us as we both tried to attribute some significance to this. When it seemed that neither one of us would be able to, I turned to her and changed the subject.

"What about you, Anna? I know almost nothing about you."

She sighed quietly and became distant, as if she were being transported to some other place and time. She absentmindedly twirled her fingers in the grass.

"I come from a place as beautiful and simple as this, a tiny village in the south west of France. L'Aiguillon-sur-Mer it is called, near the Bay of Biscay.

"My father was like most other men there, a fisherman of oysters and mussels. My mother was a homemaker, helping to make ends meet by selling bread at the market. We were quite poor. My brothers grew to be fisherman like my father, but I was determined to do better for myself.

"I always did well in school, well enough to earn a full scholarship to University of Picardie Jules Verne at Amiens. I earned my doctorate and held a post-doctorate position in environmental chemistry there. Through a close friend, I learned of a position as assistant professor at Sir Wilfred Grenfells College. I was lucky to have been chosen, and began there eight years ago.

"An associate professorship became available not very long ago when the department chairman passed away. He was a charming man, but it was so very unfortunate – he smoked himself to his grave years before his age would have dictated. I was lucky again to follow into the position of the man who succeeded him."

She suddenly shivered and pulled her sweater tight around her shoulders.

"You're chilled, Anna," I said. "Perhaps we should be getting back. We will have another long day tomorrow."

She nodded and shivered again. We rose and slowly made our way along the dark, wooded path back to town.

## Chapter 11

I did not sleep well last night, my mind restless with thoughts of today. I had no wish to bury my godfather, to say the final goodbye, but that is what must be. I comforted myself with the knowledge he would live in my memories, yet I could not stifle the fear I would forget him. And I still felt the twinge of anger at his leaving me for a second time.

Mary Benoit stood at my side as I turned to face the throng behind me. More than 300 had turned out here at the powwow grounds – tribal members, relatives and friends of my godfather from the Reserve and from distant places, some I recognized, most I did not. There were many women dressed as Mary was, with peaked caps and full-length, embroidered woolen skirts. There were men wearing leather coats with tall, embroidered collars and long epaulets covering their shoulders and chests. Like me, they had blackened their faces and un-braided their hair in mourning.

There were children, too. The oldest ones stood silent, as though instructed to set the example for their

## The Sweet Bounty

younger siblings. Little ones clung to their mothers' skirts, and a few of the impatient ones played hide and seek among the trees of adults to stem their boredom.

Heavy, gray stratus had overtaken the morning skies. A cold, damp wind shivered the crowd and whipped at unbraided hair. I was loaned a frilled buckskin jacket with fur collar and caribou antler buttons, a little short in the sleeves but warm.

I turned back around. The white birch casket, resting on an altar of stone, lay open no more than ten feet before me. The interior of the domed lid had been inlaid with the birch-bark images of leaves. Sacred Eight-Pointed Stars and Crosses, fronds of sweet grass, and images of Muin the bear and Qalipu the caribou, hand-carved in relief and stained with red and yellow ochre, ringed the outside of the casket at two levels.

Inside the casket, my godfather had been laid upon a bed of caribou furs. A shroud of birch bark had been placed over him, and upon it lay strands of brightly colored beads with feathers of eagle and great auk tied in.

Beside the casket stood a platform of lashed birch poles that would serve to elevate the Kinap, our spiritual healer, as he gave his oration.

My godfather had been embalmed by modern methods, but I reflected how the ancients had embalmed their dead in a way that would today seem as barbaric as cannibalism. Had his death occurred even 200 years ago, appointed members of the Tribe would have carried his body off to a remote location. There, removed from the mourning family, these men would have dismembered the body, removed the bones and entrails, cut the carcass into pieces and dried them over an open fire. Then, having sewn the pieces back together, they would have wrapped him in the best animal skins and furs available and returned with the shrunken likeness of the deceased to the tribal burial grounds.

The Kinap stepped onto the platform and we looked up. Framed by a full head of long, white hair whipped back by the wind, the creased and sea-weathered face of a 75-year-old man looked back at us. An ample coat of white, fur-lined caribou hide, closed by whalebone skewers from collar to thighs, covered his lean and agile frame and flapped open below his knees.

A wind growled through the structure, as if delivering the Kinap's wordless command for silence. A hush fell suddenly on the crowd. Then, as if it had known its task was finished, the wind calmed. My godfather's funeral, a blend of ancient custom and Catholicism, the faith of most Mi'kmaq even today, was about to begin.

The Kinap held out an open palm to Mary, signaling her to smudge this occasion and all its participants before his benediction. She stepped forward and lit a tightly braided bundle of sage and sweetgrass, protecting it against an unwanted breeze with her back and shoulders. She held it smoldering before her, and, with an open hand, wafted the smoke toward herself, entreating it to cleanse her spirit. Guarding the delicate heat with a curved hand, she walked slowly around the casket and allowed the smoke to drift over and around it.

The Kinap stepped down from the platform and stood before Mary with a lowered head. After she smudged him, she turned to me and the three other pallbearers and smudged us as we, too, lowered our heads. Then she turned to the assemblage, held the bundle high, and allowed the smoke to drift over it. Hordes of cupped hands reached into the air as if to draw it downward. She finished by placing the bundle in a small bowl within the casket where it would continue to smolder, driving out any foul spirits that might inhabit my godfather's body. Then she returned to her place beside me, and the Kinap returned to the platform.

Facing the crowd, he held his hands high, palms upward, and looked to the sky. He beseeched the blessings of Kji Niskam, the Great Spirit Creator, and the spirits of the ancient Mi'kmaq. Drawing his hands back in front of his face, he leveled his eyes and made the Sign of the Cross, saying "Ta'n teluisit Wkwisitniskam, Ewujjitniskam, aqq Wejiliwiniskam." The crowd answered its Amen in unison with a humble "Na tliaj."

It was the custom to revere a personage of importance by a recitation of the deceased's lineage, a heralding of heroic deeds, and the telling of a relevant legend. In a booming voice, the Kinap pronounced how my godfather had descended from proud Jeddores and Joes who had been Chiefs of the Mi'kmaq for as long as my ancestors had lived in this place. He described how he had served as Traditional Chief with great honor, like the many great Traditional Chiefs before him – William Joe, John Jeddore, Pie'l Jeddore, Joe Jeddore, Antle Joe, and many others, all the way back to the Great Chief Maupeltuk who, upon his baptism by the French in 1610 at 100 years of age, took the more well-known name of Henri Membertou.

"Since Abraham Jeddore was a boy," he said, "the Elders would talk. They said 'He would be Saqamaw one day.' They said 'He was more Mi'kmaq.'" Heads nodded in agreement. It meant my godfather never had to say he would be Chief, people just knew.

Now he recited the legacy of this modern day Warrior Chief, and there were many valorous deeds to his credit. "We remember Chief Jeddore led us in the marches for respectful treatment as a First Nations people, and how he inspired us to confront the government against one-sided policies of economic development and baseless claims of sovereign rights over Mi'kmaw territory.

"We will remember he returned to us the old spiritual ways which the Catholic priests had taken from us many years ago, and that he restored peace among our Band after years of internal strife. We will remember he guided us to be self-sufficient, and how we now turn away government handouts. And we will remember he fought to preserve our lives and livelihood against this latest menace of industry from the shores of a foreign nation.

"Let us remember he died putting his beloved people first. You, and you, and you," he said, singling out a random few with his finger, "and me." He placed the palm of his hand on his chest. "We were always first in his heart."

At each pause in his delivery, the crowd grunted its approval with a boisterous he'he'he'.

The Kinap concluded his oration with the legend of Elder Brother Kluskap, noting this most famous of Mi'kmaq legends was also the most appropriate for Chief Jeddore. "Just as Kluskap taught the Mi'kmaq about the world," he said, "Chief Jeddore taught us about ourselves and our worth as a First Nations People. He helped us remember the old ways. He made us once again proud to be Mi'kmaq!" The crowd ratified his words with shouts of agreement.

## The Sweet Bounty

Then he folded his hands, bowed his head, and instilled a solemn air with the Lord's Prayer. "Nujjinen wa'so'q epin jiptek teluisin," he began softly, and we lowered our heads to pray with him.

With the end of the Lord's Prayer came the time to move to the Kutudakun, the traditional burial grounds. As the Kinap closed the casket, the three other pallbearers and I took our places, I at the front right corner.

The casket had been placed upon a broad sling of tanned and hand-sewn caribou hides with two stout birch poles projecting from its pair of sleeves. At the Kinap's signal, we reached down, simultaneously hoisted the poles onto our shoulders, and began the laborious, slow march to the burial ground in practiced unison. We trudged a tedious uphill path to the plateau overlooking the Bay. There, near the center of the plateau, amid the tombs of other great Chiefs, lay the open grave where this Chief was soon to be buried. My body ached with each step, but a weight one hundred times more would not have surpassed the heaviness I felt in my heart.

With great care we set the casket down beside the grave and the Kinap opened it for the last time. Mary had followed closely behind us, and now she removed the still smoldering bundle from its bowl and waved the smoke over and around the grave.

Now the drummers arrived and set their drum within a circle of stools beside the casket. They sat and played and chanted while mourners filed by, paying their last respects and placing in the casket trinkets, gifts, and the personal belongings he would need in the Next World. Hundreds passed before him. Some with faces streaked with tears. Some only pensive-faced, having already accepted his passing. Others portraying ire, perhaps at the needlessness of his death. Mary smudged each one, and with the passing of the last mourner, she smothered the bundle and returned it to its bowl.

The Kinap closed the casket for the last time. As he stood back, four men threaded two sturdy ropes between the sling and the casket. They carried the rope ends and walked with us as we lifted the casket on the sling and moved to the grave.

We held the casket there, momentarily suspending it over the empty, brown hole. Then, slowly, we lowered it, transferring our load to the ropes. Against the casket's imposing weight, the rope handlers braced and heaved away from the grave as we removed the sling from under the casket.

Then, visibly straining, they cautiously lowered their burden. When it rested at the bottom of the hole, they pulled the ropes from under it and moved aside. The Kinap then approached the grave and gave his final Sign of the Cross.

Workers now began to fill the grave shovel by shovel. I stood for a moment as they worked, observing the other tombs. This area of the burial grounds was reserved for Chiefs, and their tombs were different from the simple graves of common folk. Tradition called for earth and sod on a rectangular pyramid of interlaced poles to be built over a Chief's grave. Such pyramids surrounded me, and I could not help feeling a swell of pride at this vivid reminder of the many centuries my people have thrived in this place. His body would rest among honorable company.

When the earth was mounded well above the grass, the workers began to erect the pyramid.

## The Sweet Bounty

Beginning at the foot of the grave and from opposite sides, two men jammed the sharpened ends of two poles into the ground at their feet, leaning the tops forward over the grave until one rested in the notched end of the other. To hold them temporarily in place, a third worker met the mated poles with the first of eight end poles that would close up the foot of the pyramid.

They took up a second pair of poles and laid them up snugly beside the first, repeating this act with more poles until they arrived at the head of the grave. The natural taper of the poles created a leaning-in toward the center. End poles were then erected to close the pyramid and hold it permanently in place. Earth and sod were laid upon it until the pyramid became the gray-brown of fall grass. In spring, a lush green would veil its newness and it would become as the others, taking an honored place among tombs already hundreds of years old.

The burial was now complete. The Kinap turned and raised his palms high to the crowd for the last time. Without a word, the drummers ceased their activity and all became still – so still I could hear my own breath.

"Saqamaw Abram Jeddore," his voice boomed again, "our Great Chief, has taken the path of Great Chiefs before him. Skidekimuchute has taken him to Kji Niskam! From this point forward, we shall no longer speak of him as Saqamaw Abraham Jeddore, but he shall have a name of great honor among the Family of the Mi'kmaq! He shall be called ... Godfather!"

He paused, allowing these words to flow over the crowd. It took only a split second for what he said to register and my eyes shot up at him almost involuntarily. His eyes met mine with a brief and barely discernible smile and nod of his head. That he would be known hereafter as Godfather was a great honor for me, too.

His attention returned quickly to his audience. "It is done!" he called out. "May the Spirits of the Ancients welcome him, and may God bless him ... forever!"

In the vacuous silence that followed, his words reverberated in a temblor of finality. That silence lingered no more than a heartbeat, for when he dropped his hands, the drummers and dancers and singers and onlookers broke suddenly into riotous celebration, as if linked together by supernatural cue. Whoops and yips, calls and hollers, singing and shouting and booming drums ensued. They would continue this joyful ruckus through day and night until exhausted of all human energy, too spent to go on. Tomorrow, we would find many of them collapsed into the sleep of a fall-chilled dawn on the very place they had danced their last step.

Coincident with this jubilation would be the Salite, a sacred tradition in which we assist my godfather's passing into the Next World, a great feast that given by us as thanks for sharing his life with us.

Thus was the celebration of life at death.

Skidekimuchute. The Spirit's Road. The Milky Way. The silver path of stars to a life forever in the Next World. The image lingered within me, tormented me. Such departures were so completely unchallengeable. A lonely anger grew in my chest and I stormed off into the trees, refusing once again to believe what I knew to be true. *How could he do this to me?*

A murmuring wind twisted the yellowed leaves around me. 'Accept what is', it said, 'it is the Mi'kmaw way'. But I rejected those words and strode faster, as if I could outpace the wind, outrun my conflicted head and heart. I stopped, shouted out in anguish my godfather's name at the skies, and asked why. No answer came, save the murmur on the leaves. 'Accept what is,' it said again. Tears welled in my eyes and I fell to my knees in grief.

I knelt there for long minutes in my solitary despair. Gradually, my darkness at what I could not change subsided and I calmed. A lighter heart grew slowly within me. I stood and turned back to rejoin the others.

Then I saw it.

It was on a commoner's grave. A red clay pot, like the kind one might plant graveside flowers in, but it held no flowers. As I approached it I noticed a second pot on another grave. I stopped and looked around. There, another. My head continued its arc. Another, then another. I counted nine in all.

What were they? What place did they have on these sacred grounds? They were no part of Mi'kmaw custom I could recall. And why had I not seen them before?

I stooped beside one for a closer look. It held dirt and a partially burned candlewick. I poked at it. The dirt was oily, and when I brought my finger to my nose I detected the faint smells of burnt cooking oil and pepper. Beside the pot was a divot where someone had removed soil from the grave, and a coin had been placed in the divot.

I lifted the pot with both hands and looked beneath it. Nothing there. I held it over my head. Was that writing on the bottom? An inscription? I brushed off the clinging grass and dirt to see it better.

It was faint, but the first letter was clear. It was

a capital A, taller than those which followed. The next letters were hastily scribbled, but I recognized a b, the next were indecipherable, then an h and an m. Then another capital, a J this time. Then a d. No, two ds. And the last three letters – what were they – o-r-e?

*Could it be?* I quickly checked another pot, then another. They were all the same, the same contents, the same coin, the same scribbling on the bottom.

*What sickness is this? My godfather's name?* I suddenly fumed. Now I knew the plate I discovered earlier was no child's play. These were intentional pranks at best.

Then, instinctively, my mind raced through the accumulated facts of my anthropological studies at Concordia. I couldn't yet be certain, but the obscurity was starting to acquire a vague familiarity. I hurried back to town, carrying one of the pots with me. I had to find Anna and I had to make a phone call. A textbook from the Webster Library would confirm my suspicion.

# Chapter 12

I found Anna at the Amanda Joe Building. She was putting something into the MG's open trunk when I approached her from behind.

"Oh, Peter!" She jumped as she straightened and turned around. "I did not hear you!"

"Anna ... you're packing?"

"Rearranging, Peter, I will need my analytical equipment handy where we are going. It is nearly noon and we have a long day ahead of us, remember?"

"Anna, look at this." I handed her the pot.

"A pot of dirt. What is it?"

"Smell it."

She held it to her nose. "Burnt something. And pepper?" she asked. "I don't understand."

"I didn't either, at first. Now I think I do, I just need to confirm it. I found eight more just like it in the burial grounds, each one on a grave. Look at the bottom."

She lifted it over her head and tipped it away. "It's writing ... a ... b .. h ... m ... j ... dd ... o ... r ... e. abhm jddore" she attempted. "Abraham Jeddore? My word, Peter, your godfather's name?" She screwed up her face again, just like when I told her about the plate. "This is very strange, Peter. What is it?"

"I'm not sure yet, but I think it's a Santeria curse on my godfather."

"Santa what?"

"Santeria. La Regla de Ocha, Macumba, Candomble Jege-Nago, it has many names. It's a syncretism of African folk religion and Catholicism, started in the Caribbean by African slaves in the 1500s. The Cubans forced them to accept Catholicism against their will, so they hid their native Yoruba and Bantu religions behind an apparent worship of the Catholic Saints. Trance possession, sacrifice, curses, magic. It thrives in the Caribbean, Puerto Rico, Central and South America, even the States. It's the Americas' brand of Voodoo."

"But, Peter, this is maritime Canada. There is no Voodoo here," she said.

"That's what I thought, until now," I answered.

"And why your godfather? Why here in this tranquil little place in Newfoundland?"

"That I don't know, but I intend to find out."

"You think this is what killed your godfather? Peter, think sensibly. Voodoo? Curses? Magic flower pots? It is all so ... how do you say ... hocus-pocus, so ... unscientific! Surely you do not believe this!"

"Anna," I said impatiently, "history is replete with examples of religious belief taking profound control of people's lives. The 30 Years War, Bohemian Rebellion, Crusades, Islamic Jihad. Visions of the Virgin Mary in Bosnia-Herzegovina, Zeitun, Guadalupe, and Lourdes. Countless miracles, unexplained healings, salvations, and works of evil. All on the strength of undying faith. And though it isn't written by the white man, I can assure you similar things occurred in First Nations history. Belief is the most powerful of spirits.

"Besides," I continued, "it doesn't matter whether you or I believe it. What matters is whether my godfather believed it."

She looked stunned. Her mind seemed to weigh my words, though she said nothing. She turned away, then back again with a look of exasperation in her eyes. "We should be leaving, Peter. Can you be ready soon?"

"I need to make a phone call first. Five minutes?"

"Of course, Peter. But please hurry. I must complete my work before dusk."

I went into the Amanda Joe Building and asked to use a telephone. A nurse led me to a vacant desk where I dialed my officemate at Concordia.

The department's electronic receptionist answered. "Departement de Sociologie et d'Anthropologie ..." it began. I interrupted the message with his direct number.

His voice mail answered. "Halloo! This is voice mail for Donnan McAdams," it said in a lilting Scottish timbre. "If I get a name, number, and a message, I'll call you!"

"Mac, it's Peter Joe. Do me a favor? The Webster Library has several volumes on Santeria I'd like you to check out. I need to know about a curse. See if there's anything about clay pots left on gravesites, oil, pepper, and a coin left on the grave, maybe as payment for a soul's deed. And a plate with black dust – probably coal – salt, and candle stuck with pins like a Voodoo doll. I don't have time to explain, but it's important. I'll be out of touch the rest of the day, I'll call you tonight.

Thanks, Mac." I hung up and went back outside. Anna was already in the MG, motor idling, ready to go. I climbed in.

We drove the first 50 kilometers saying almost nothing, I lost in my thoughts, wondering how my godfather could be the victim of a Santeria curse, Anna wondering I don't know what, maybe planning her work, maybe thinking I'd become a lunatic. I had to admit, death by magic would be a stretch to most, but, according to Anna, so would death by mercury. The way I saw it, everything was uncertain and nothing was out of the question. I intended to follow every lead to its end.

\* \* \* \*

We were in the barrens plateau now, tundra to outsiders. Had I not known this country, we could have been almost anywhere in the vast and uninhabited center of Newfoundland – scrub grass, ground-hugging shrubs, and scant anything over two feet high.

Soon we descended into lowlands. Here, the brush and trees were thick and tall. Ponds, wetlands, potholes, lakes, streams, all draining to the same place. This was Conifer River headwaters country, and what didn't go directly to the Conifer would get there eventually.

This was also my childhood playground and I knew it well, at least as it was 19 years ago. I privately hoped the wildness of this place, still sacred in my own mind, hadn't changed.

The motor whined as Anna geared down and we slowed, crossing a bridge over the Conifer. The river flowed wide and full below us. With the melt of new

## The Sweet Bounty

snow two seasons coming, it would top its banks. We stopped on the far side of the bridge with two wheels in the grass at the right edge of the road.

"Let's start here, Peter," said Anna. "We are about one-half mile from the mine. This will be a good place for our first samples."

We climbed out of the MG and I watched as she went to work. She opened the trunk and removed a flat metal platform with two wire hooks on one edge and two small posts with rubber feet on the opposite corners. It reminded me of the kind of tray a waitress on roller skates would have hung on your window glass at a drive-in diner. Then she removed a black vinyl case, a laptop computer, and an unfamiliar-looking, briefcase-sized apparatus and set them on the ground.

She closed the trunk and hooked the platform on the hinged edge of the trunk. The platform covered nearly the entire surface of the trunk lid and the rubber feet rested neatly on it, making a flat working surface. She set the laptop, the apparatus, and the vinyl case on it. Then she went to the cab, returned with a pair of fishing waders from behind the driver's seat, and put them on.

She opened the vinyl case. It contained an array of wide-mouth glass bottles with black lids cradled in rigid foam. She removed a bottle about the size of a canning jar and a small vial no larger than my thumb and pushed them into the wader pockets. Then she climbed down the bank, turned to face upstream, and waded into the river. Water rose to the tops of her knees. When she had her footing, she carefully dipped the large bottle into the water, mouth downstream, and filled and capped it. On her way out, she did the same thing with the vial, except that she dipped it all the way to the bottom and filled it with sediment.

She returned to the MG, wiped down the bottles with a hand towel, and set them on the platform. She removed her waders, shook the water from them, and returned them behind her seat. Then she opened the laptop, connected it to the apparatus, and turned both of them on.

"What are you doing, Anna?" I asked out of curiosity.

"I'm preparing to analyze for mercury and other metals," she answered.

"You can do that here in the middle of nowhere? No Bunsen burners or test tubes or chemists in white lab coats?"

"Yes, Peter, with my laptop and this." She pointed to the apparatus. "It's called a Laser-Induced Breakdown Spectrometer. It fires a pair of short, powerful and perfectly timed laser bursts at a droplet in the sample chamber. The energy of the laser vaporizes the sample and breaks down the water and all its contents into plasma, a gas of elemental ions at temperatures in the thousands of degrees. As the plasma cools, each element radiates a particular combination of light frequencies, or colors, called a spectrum. By analyzing the spectrum, one can determine which elements are present in the sample. The spectrometer reads those colors and sends data about their intensity and wavelength to the laptop. Special software interprets those signals and displays them as a series of vertical lines on the monitor. It's very reliable and it all happens in the matter of a few seconds."

"Hmm, and you said my pot was hocus-pocus," I said.

"Yes, Peter, I suppose it seems that way," she said seriously, her attention focused on her work. "But I can assure you it is all very real."

She opened the sample door of the spectrometer and a small, motor-driven tray slid part way out. With an eyedropper, she removed a droplet of watery sediment from the vial and placed it into a shallow well in the tray. As she closed the door, the motor pulled the tray back inside.

On her laptop she clicked an icon labeled Spectra. The monitor flickered momentarily and displayed a faint rectangular graph of intersecting vertical and horizontal lines. Across the top of the screen were the words SPECTRA Ready.

She turned to the laser spectrometer and pushed Start. A red light flashed on then off within the span of a second. At nearly the same time, the monitor said Receiving, which changed to Analyzing almost immediately. A few seconds later, the screen filled from left to right with dark vertical lines of varying height. Anna examined them carefully.

"Most interesting," she said with surprise.

I bent over and peered at the monitor. "What's interesting?"

"I'll show you," she said, and with the touch pad of the laptop she drew a box around some of the lines. "Mostly what I would expect," she said as she worked, "the usual naturally-occurring minerals, of course." She double-clicked the box. The lines within it magnified and became a row of needle-like spires, wide at the bottom and tapered sharply to their tips. Some of the spires were wider or taller than others. The rest of the lines disappeared. "But then there is this group here, Peter." She ran her finger across some of the spires.

"Quite unexpected," she said.

"What's unexpected?"

"These are what we call heavy metals ... they are metalloids and transition metals, really. Some are present at higher than average levels, but that is to be expected in a mineral-rich area like this. That is why the mine is located here. But this element," she continued, leaning forward to touch the tallest spire, "this one is much higher than I would have expected."

"What element is that?"

"Well ..." she hesitated, as if she didn't want to say. "Mercury," she said finally.

"Mercury? But didn't you say ...?"

"Yes, I did, Peter, but this seems to say otherwise."

"What does it mean?" I asked.

"I don't know, Peter, it is too early to say. It may be what your godfather feared could happen has happened, but one must question why mercury is the only one elevated, and why it is so highly elevated. If the mine were releasing contaminants to the River, I would expect many elements to be elevated in this sample." With great concern in her eyes, she looked up at me. "We must get closer to the mine."

I nodded, but my mind was focused on 'what your godfather feared could happen has happened.' The words rang like the clapper of a church bell. Yesterday, it appeared I would be pressed to find even a single cause of my godfather's death. Now, I seemed to have two. Which one killed him? Alongside my thoughts about Santeria magic, my conversations with Jimmy Nolan and Minister Winslow once again raced through my mind.

## The Sweet Bounty

Anna stashed her equipment into the trunk and we drove northward. We had gone barely a quarter mile when an imposing chain-link fence appeared on the right. It was at least eight feet high with razor wire across its angled top, like prison fence. But the razor wire was on the outside – clearly intended to keep people out, not in. Between every other pair of posts hung yellow Keep Out signs, though they were, in my view, superfluous – the message of the razor wire was perfectly clear.

Another quarter mile brought us to what appeared to be the mine entrance, a wide, graveled road on our right leading straight back from the highway. Anna slowed as she passed it, swung around to the other side of the highway, and came to a stop in the grass directly across from it.

The road led to a guard shack about 100 yards distant, then disappeared around a bend behind a cluster of trees. It was flanked at the highway by a pair of yellow signs with bright red letters that read 'No Trespassing – This Means You!'

The razor-wired fence converged on the entrance road from the north and south, traveled along both sides of it, and terminated at a gate beside the guard shack. But there was no sign proclaiming what this place was. Apparently, someone didn't want anyone to know.

As we took in this scene, the gate opened and a white van began to move in our direction. The driver stopped at the highway and examined us for a few moments. The van was armor-plated, with Ceborro Minerals Company, USA painted on its side. It lumbered onto the highway as if heavily loaded. Then the driver turned north, apparently satisfied we were harmless.

With the van on its way, our visual path to the guard station cleared and we now saw the figure of a man standing beside it. He looked directly at us and raised a hand-held radio to his mouth. Anna and I spoke no words as we looked at each other, but we both knew it was time to leave. She engaged first gear and we drove back the way we came.

We stopped at a location a short distance beyond where we first encountered the fence. I waited in the MG while she took out her vinyl case, donned her waders, and walked to the river. She filled another pair of bottles just like she had done at the bridge.

She had removed her waders and was stowing her equipment when I heard the sound of tires on the highway. I turned around in my seat for a better look just as Anna closed the trunk. The vehicle approached us from behind, slowed at the edge of the highway, and stopped directly behind us.

What I saw gave me good reason to step outside the MG. Anna and I exchanged wide-eyed glances. The hunted had just come to the hunter – it was a dark gray van bearing the Newfoundland and Labrador Coat of Arms. We froze.

The doors opened and two figures stepped out. Brown work boots appeared below the driver's door, black loafers below the other. As they came from behind their doors, I saw the driver was a pale, stocky man about five-feet-eight with closely cropped, brown hair. He wore a gray coverall unzipped to his waist over a gray cotton T-shirt. An insignia on both shoulders of his coverall matched the one on the van. There was an unnatural bulge below his left armpit, and I wondered if he carried a shoulder holster.

Above his loafers, the other man wore black polyester pants and a pressed white shirt. He looked oddly out of place here.

Wears Loafers appeared to be in charge and approached us first. He walked with a swagger, and when he halted in front of me he propped large, intimidating hands on his hips. Like a bodyguard, the driver stood behind him.

"And who might you trespassers be?" he demanded. He had a Latin-sounding accent, and it was far more an accusation than a question. His tone dared us to answer. He tossed a stern look at Anna then back at me.

Anna's feistiness drove her to answer first. "You ran us off the road yesterday!" she fired. "It was a rude and dangerous maneuver which nearly killed us. I intend to report you to the authorities!"

Wears Loafers moved to confront Anna. He towered a good nine inches above her. "You have the wrong man, sweetie, and you didn't answer my question."

Anna only glared back.

When she didn't respond he moved back to me. "What about you, Indian Boy, you gonna answer my question?"

I ignored the slur and forced a stern calmness. "Peter Joe. Who's asking?"

He turned and smirked to the driver. "So, this is the famous Peter Joe we've been hearing about," he said. Then he turned back to me and replaced the smirk with a scowl. "You're trespassing on private land. What are you doing here?" he demanded.

"Tell us who you are first. Then maybe we'll answer," said Anna from behind him. There was her feistiness again.

He moved again to confront her, closer this time, almost breathing down into her face. "That's none of your business, sweetie, and frankly, I don't see that you're in a position to be asking the questions. This is my land and you're on it."

Something at Anna's feet caught his attention and he looked down. "And what might these be?" He bent down and picked up the sample bottles. She had forgotten to stow them in the trunk.

Her eyes darted at me then back to Wears Loafers. "It's river water and sediment," she said nervously. "I am ... a biology teacher. It is for a class demonstration on aquatic biota," she said.

He held the bottles up and examined them. His hands shook when freed of his hips and he was unable to hold the bottles steady.

"Hmmm. Labeled nice and fancy-like, too." He turned to the driver. "Biota," he smirked again and then turned back to Anna. "They look pretty clear to me, honey. Seems your biota are still in the river." He handed them to the driver. "Take these with us," he ordered.

I stepped in front of Wears Loafers, cutting him off from Anna. "Look," I said, "I don't know who you are, but give the lady her bottles. Neither of us knew this was private land, we're outside the fence. It's just for a middle school biology class."

His scowl intensified. "That's right, Indian Boy, you don't know who I am. But I say you're trespassing and you'd better leave before I radio the Constable and have you both locked up."

I looked at Anna with resignation. It was clear we weren't going to get anywhere with Wears Loafers and I decided we could get another sample later when he wasn't around. "Let's go, " I said to Anna, "we can get river water somewhere else."

Anna was about to send him another salvo, but he clipped her short. "Better listen to Indian Boy, honey." He rapped his knuckles on the trunk of the MG. "I'd hate to see this sweet little car end up as a heap of scrap."

Anna relented and we climbed into the MG. Spinning tires threw gravel as we hit the road. A laser-like glower in her eyes burned holes in the windshield as she jerked hard into second. "The bastard has my samples, Peter," she said.

As we drove away, through the side view mirror I saw Wears Loafers and the driver turn back to the van. A hundred yards later, they and the van disappeared from view.

\* \* \* \*

"What now, Sir?" the driver asked as he and his passenger settled into their seats.

The passenger leaned down to pick a stone out of his loafer. "Back to the assay lab," he answered. "Biota, my ass. I was warned about Peter Joe. He's up to something. It's time to have those bottles checked and make a phone call."

The driver started the motor and engaged the column shift. "Right, Mr. Ceborro." He made a U-turn on the highway and returned his passenger to the mine.

## Chapter 13

Less than a mile later, without warning, Anna geared down, slowed to the right edge of the road, and accelerated out of a U-turn into the northbound lane.

"What are you doing?" I asked.

"We have been duped, Peter. At what other time have you met an impeccably dressed guardian on one of the most remote parcels of the Queen's land with instructions to intimidate visitors? We were not trespassing, Peter, we just let a complete stranger bully us out of our mission. But he has a reason for being a bully, and we're going back for the samples we came for. Maybe they will help us understand what he is hiding."

I had to agree with her and I nodded. "But if we're really going to find out what's going on there, we need to get a lot closer than the boundary fence."

"What do you mean?" Anna asked.

I pointed up the road ahead of us. "Watch for an old birch snag on the right, looks like a caribou skull. It marks a seldom-used service road, probably well grown-over by now. Turn there, and stop behind the snag."

A short while later, Anna slowed again and turned off the highway. The grass had grown thick and tall, but there beneath it was the aged and broken tarred macadam of the old road. She drove slowly though the grass to a small clearing, well hidden by the tall brush that had grown up around it. She stopped behind the snag, turned off the motor, and looked at me with what-now in her eyes.

"Get your things," I said.

We climbed out of the MG. While Anna went to the trunk, I brushed up the laid over grass with a branch to cover the MG's tracks.

When I returned, Anna had just closed the trunk and was holding her waders and four more bottles. "Follow me," I said. "I think we're about a quarter mile downstream from the fence."

For ten minutes we fought our way through the woods in waist-high grass and thick brush to the Conifer River. There at its edge, just as I remembered it, was an old gauging station once used to measure the Conifer's depth and flow.

The station was a small, one-cot log cabin, and beside it stood a tower of heavy timbers. The cabin was now ramshackle and partly covered with brown moss and climbing plants. But the tower had fared better against the onslaught of time and nature – its timbers looked strong and sound. We stood within what had also been a clearing, but now it, too, was overgrown with a shamble of brush and weeds.

Both the gauging station and the tower were completely enclosed by a six-foot, chain-link fence. The gate was chained and padlocked, and it bore a weathered, rectangular sign with the words 'Canadian

Geologic Survey.'

A stout cable of twisted steel extended across the river from the top of the tower, and a hand-powered cable car, anchored in place by a hook and chain, hung from the cable over a platform beside the tower. The cable car was an open-top box of steel, with iron struts suspending it at its corners from a pair of iron pulleys standing on top of the cable. A crank wheel hung below the cable between the pulleys. The cable terminated at an identical tower on the far bank, exactly where I wanted to go.

"Now what, Peter?" Anna asked.

"When you were taking your samples, I noticed the fence spanned into the River from both sides, but not all the way across. There's an old deer trail on the other side of the River that will take us to the fence. We can wade around it and you can get as close to the mine as you want." I looked up and pointed to the cable car. "And that is what will get us to the other side."

"You are scaring me, Peter. You are teasing, yes?"

It occurred to me she might be right – I hadn't stolen a ride on that car for 19 years. But I saw no other way to get there. "No, Anna," I said, still looking up, "I can't think of any reason to tease you about something that scary."

She rolled her eyes and rattled the gate against its chain. "And what about this?" she demanded.

I walked a few steps to a tree on which was nailed a small survey plaque announcing our longitude and latitude. I reached up and felt behind its top edge. A broad grin swept my face as I realized it was still there – a key, which I proudly held up for Anna to see.

"Peter!" she scolded. "This is trespassing, and dangerous trespassing at that! We could be arrested. I could lose my career!"

"Only if we're caught," I said, still grinning.

I unlocked the gate, pocketed the key, and stepped onto the tower's ladder. I turned to Anna who was still outside the gate. "Coming?"

Sighing her resignation, she draped the waders around her neck and came to the ladder. I climbed and Anna followed closely behind.

I stood on the platform next to the cable car and reached down to help Anna up. Once on the platform, she climbed into the car while I steadied it. Then I climbed in after her.

I pulled us toward a timber with my left hand while I loosed the anchor hook with my right. I released the timber and the car swung and creaked about its pivot. Anna stiffened and instinctively grabbed one of the struts.

I released the wheel brake and we rolled along under the cable, slowly at first, then gaining speed, until we reached the middle of the River. There we slowed and stopped, our momentum insufficient to carry us up the incline to the other side.

The rush of water roared in our ears and dragged the air above it downstream, creating an artificial breeze in our faces. It was an unsettling feeling, hanging and rocking there, supported only by the tenuous mercy of wood fibers and twisted filaments of wire.

There was a mild fear in Anna's face and she tensed her grip on the strut. "Peter," she said, "this is not a comfortable place for me. How do you plan to get us the rest of the way?"

I peered over the edge of the car and down at the dark green River. I guessed it to be five feet deep at this point, and it hastened by only two feet below us. I looked back at Anna. "Can you swim?" I asked.

"That's not funny, Peter. Stop teasing me!"

I stowed my grin and reached up and folded down the knurled iron handles of a crank wheel that would power us to the other side. It squealed as I cranked, but within a few minutes we bumped the other tower and Anna, more comfortable now that she was no longer dangling over open water, reached over the side of the car and hooked the anchor chain to it. I set the brake, and we stepped over the edge of the car onto the platform and climbed down the ladder.

We found ourselves almost at once on the old deer trail, the same trail my godfather and I had walked, beside the same waters we had fished, many times before. The comfort offered by this place seemed nearly ancient.

My godfather and I had often skewered and spit-roasted our catch over a fire ring we had built only a short way off the path. The rock ring, the spit, the stump chair I sat on while my godfather told me the stories of the Old Ones – all were still here, as if they had been used only yesterday. I squatted and laid my hand on the stones, wanting them to be warm, wanting to feel those experiences, wanting to be here with him, once again. Maybe, I hoped, my godfather had still come here long after I moved away.

The timber grew thicker on this side of the River, but the well-used trail allowed us a quick pace and it did not take long to reach the boundary fence. The deer were barred here from continuing on the old trail, and I wondered if the new trail they made alongside the intruding fence would take them where they instinctively wanted to go.

The fence was identical to the one on the highway side of the River – chain-link, eight feet high, and topped by the same razor wire. Keep Out signs were attached here, too. It was clear Wears Loafers didn't look kindly on errant intrusions from any direction, and I wondered again what he didn't want us to know.

Anna was about to don her waders when something caught my attention, something odd about the fence line. I moved closer.

"Anna, over here," I said.

She turned. "What is it, Peter?"

"Come see for yourself."

My discovery was immediately apparent when she arrived.

"Someone has cut the fence!" she exclaimed.

"Yes. And these," I said, pointing down at the ground between us. There, waffled boot prints had been cast into the now-hardened mud. They were small, like a young woman's. I found no other tracks around us and thought it odd a young woman would venture into this country alone.

I moved to the fence for a better look. It would have taken a strong shear to open this hole. This was no casual breach – Young Footprint Woman had gone to a lot of trouble to bring along the right tool.

I knelt down and from one of the sharp ends of fence wire I picked a bundle of frayed, black threads. Rolling them absentmindedly between my thumb and forefinger, I mused out loud. "It seems we're not the first to wonder what's beyond this fence."

I stood up and dropped the threads to the ground. "Well, I see no reason to break in when we have an invitation to use the front door. Do you?" I pulled up one side of the split, opening a shoulder-high, inverted V in the fence. I bowed from the waist and ushered the way with a sweep of my free hand. "Ladies first, Mademoiselle."

Anna's face acquired a sultry look. "Ah, mai oui et merci, Monsieur," she said, and, flinging a wader leg across her shoulder as if it were a fur stole, she sauntered to the fence like a model on a fashion show runway.

"Now you're teasing me," I said and I followed her through.

On the other side, Anna collected her first pair of samples and set them beside the hole in the fence to be picked up on the way back. She removed her waders, shook them free of water, and hung them around her neck once more. We were ready to continue on.

We had walked only a short distance more when we came to Pie'lik, a small brook that merged with the Conifer. It had always been too wide to jump across here, and my godfather and I had adzed a log flat on one side and laid it across this tributary to make a crossing. But it was gone now. High water must have washed it away in the intervening years. Close by, though, someone – Young Footprint Woman? – had narrowed the gaps between scattered boulders with piles of rock, making a less stable but usable path across. They ground under our weight as we hopped them over the stream.

I guessed the distance from the fence to the mine road would be about the same as we had discovered along the highway earlier. This part of the

## The Sweet Bounty

trail had not been used since the fence was built, and the brushy re-growth made the going slow. I heard the sound of a light truck on a graveled road some distance ahead of us, but the trail and the River diverted eastward before we encountered it. Though I could not see it, I presumed the gravel road must be the mine entrance, just beyond the trees on the other side.

As I recalled, the River would begin to narrow and deepen soon. Eventually, kilometers from here, it would diminish in breadth and depth as it divided into its myriad sources of streams, ponds, lakes, brooklets, and springs in the barren tundra uplands.

I was prepared for a long walk, but I was not prepared for what I heard and saw next. The trail, the trees, and the riverbed abruptly disappeared. No more brown, earthen path, no green forest crowns, no rippling, rock-strewn spawning grounds – they were simply and plainly gone. In their places, a large concrete canal in the shape of a broad U, wider than the riverbed at its base and with sides at least eight feet high, spewed the River toward us and blocked our way. Too stunned for even a single word, Anna and I exchanged looks of incredulous disbelief.

We eyed the outer sides of the canal where they angled upward at a gradual slope to a flat top. Though we said nothing, both of us knew instinctively what we would do next. Anna slid the waders off her shoulders and onto the ground. We scrambled up. At the top, we lay prone and inched forward to the edge, our legs still on the slope. What I saw when we got there shook the very core of my being.

A tamed and docile Conifer River flowed toward us within a smooth concrete canal. Within this man-made constraint it moved in silence, robbed of its wild undulations and its waves and eddies and pools, bereft of the random clash of turbulence and stillness that always was this river. Imprisoned in the unrelenting sameness of concrete, this once magnificent creation flowed with a sad, resigned apathy.

Anna nudged me. I hadn't noticed she had been looking through a small pair of binoculars the size of opera glasses. She must have stashed them in a pocket when I was covering the MG's tracks.

"Peter," she said, "this is not supposed to be!" She handed me the binoculars and pointed beyond the canal. "Look!"

The binoculars magnified for me an even greater shock. Thousands of acres before us were laid barren, stripped of soil and life. Where tundra grasses and shrubs had not yet been scraped away, they were charred to the ground. Every tree had been upended and burned, and blackened piles of them still smoldered, lending an acrid, burning stench to the air. The old riverbed was empty and as dry as scorched earth. Upstream, the canal forced the River around the devastation in a wide, unnatural bend.

Within those barren acres lay a great, gaping hole, a quarter-mile or more across. Within the hole, machines with giant, rotating wheels gouged and clawed at the earth and spilled their winnings onto the beds of huge trucks waiting in long lines. Our ears were filled with the throaty, rumbling strain of improbably powerful diesel motors and the squeal and groan of hardened rock resisting hardened steel – the sounds, I imagined, of the proverbial encounter of immovable object and unstoppable force.

Surrounding the hole, enormous half-mountains of earth, tops shaved like flattop crew cuts, obscured

## The Sweet Bounty

the horizon as far as we could see. Ant-like silhouettes of the same trucks worked in rows on top of them.

My heart sank to the depth of my gut and my spirit faltered – this desecration, this assassination of memories recalled here, struck hard within me. An unwelcome image of Wears Loafers beset me and I cursed him under my breath. *So this is what you hide.*

I lowered the binoculars to scan the ruins with my bare eyes, thankful my godfather was not here to witness this enraging scene. For here was the cause of his crusade, laid out before me as far as I could see.

"Anna, what the hell is going on here?" I asked.

"This is an open pit mine, Peter, and those flat-top mounds are the leach heaps. But this is not supposed to be an open pit, it is supposed to be an underground mine! Someone has changed it, or lied about it, or maybe no one knows about this. Could the Ministry know? I don't know, Peter, but this is wrong, this is so very wrong!"

"So, Jimmy's right," I said with anger beneath my words, "the mine plan is a fake after all. I wonder what else about this operation is a lie. Jimmy was sure someone in government was paid to keep this quiet, and now I see why. He just couldn't prove it."

"But who, Peter? It would not be so easy to hide something like this, it must be someone very high."

"Someone who craves power," I said. "Someone who thinks he ought to have a lot more than he has. Someone who's arrogant enough to think he can pull it off. Winslow comes easily to mind, if you ask me. He certainly seemed to be hiding something. Jimmy thought so too."

"But he could not hide something like this by himself, Peter, other people would have to know about it. The Minister of Mines must also approve the plan."

"Maybe both of them were bribed," I answered. "The cost of buying silence would be petty cash to an operation this size. Or maybe Winslow paid the Minister of Mines to keep it quiet. Once a man sees his way to take the money, the motive is there to protect it. Either way, it seems that the Minister and our bully friend Wears Loafers are well acquainted.

"Anna, Jimmy Nolan needs to know about this. Someone needs to expose what's going on here. This is criminal and someone needs to set it right, especially if this is linked to my godfather's death."

I suddenly noticed the shadows were long with the lowing sun, and I checked my watch. It was 6:15 p.m. "We'd better be going," I said. It's getting late and I've seen enough for one day. If we stay any longer, we'll be crossing the river in the dark."

I could see the anger in Anna's face. None of this was right by her either. "Very well," she said with frustration, "but I must have one minute before we leave, please."

We slid down the concrete slope on our backsides. Anna put on her waders once more and collected another pair of samples. Then she returned the waders to around her neck and nodded her readiness. "OK, let's go."

"Peter," she said from behind as we began our way back, "I want to take these to Grand Falls-Windsor tonight. My Department has a laboratory there for water quality studies on the Exploits River. It has everything I need. If you are going to give Jimmy Nolan a story, you should give him the evidence to go with it."

## Chapter 14

At 5:15 p.m., Minister Winslow's telephone intercom button flashed, just like it always did when his secretary buzzed him.

"Sir, you have a call on line one," she said.

A particularly troublesome matter distracted him, and he didn't notice she hadn't identified the caller for him, nor did he have the presence of mind to ask. Just three minutes ago, he had received an internal memo. It said the Premier had opened an investigation into the rumors and allegations of bribery surrounding the Sweet Bounty and no government official would be held harmless.

Minister Winslow's life had just become more complicated, and his blood pressure rose four points. He cursed out loud. Soon, some nosy legal beagle would be sniffing around his personal matters. He worried a lot about that, especially since that someone would be in a position to do something about whatever impropriety he found.

Fortunately, the transfers were going to an account under a false name. That would make things tough for the investigators, but he wondered if he had done enough. It didn't matter whether or not the money could be traced to the Sweet Bounty. Once it was discovered he had access to unexplained deposits, the politics of coincidence would see to the rest of his fate.

*What's the big deal, anyway*, he wondered. *What's a little $25,000 here or $50,000 there?* Had not the people of Newfoundland vested in him the right to govern as he saw fit? Of course they had. So who were these damned investigators to question the integrity of a man in his position?

Still, what if the investigators caught up with him? What would he do then? Could he claim he was hung out to dry for political purposes? Maybe that was it – he was only the scapegoat, the patsy. The real corruption still ran thick under the Premier's nose.

Or could he take someone down with him? But who? Maybe that damned Ceborro.

Without thinking, he told her to put the call through, and, when line one lit up, he punched the speaker button and gave his usual greeting.

"Office of the Minister, Minister Winslow speaking," he muttered.

"Ah, Winslow, how nice you're there," the voice said pleasantly.

It sounded familiar, but his distraction prevented him from identifying it.

"Who's this?" he growled, his attention now focused.

"Why, Winslow, I'm surprised you don't recognize the voice of your benefactor by now."

*It's Ceborro,* he thought. *The damn cocky son of a bitch. Just the man those investigators should really be after!*

"What do you want, Ceborro, I'm busy."

"Ooooh, Winny, that's a rather nasty attitude. All that cash I've been depositing in your bank account ought to have bought a little respect by now, wouldn't you say?"

The Minister audibly blew an impatient breath through puffed cheeks. "Alright, Ceborro, I'm all ears. How may I help you?" he said with feigned courtesy. He wished Ceborro would just leave him alone right now.

"Much better, Winslow. Try to remember this pleasant attitude for your next important caller.

"I had a visitor today," Ceborro continued. "Peter Joe came to see me."

"Peter Joe. What did he want?"

"I don't know exactly, but I'm sure he'll make trouble. The guard spotted him and a lady friend snooping around the entrance road. I found them at the south boundary fence, poking around the River. Collecting aquatic biota for a biology class, she said, but it was a lie. I took her bottles to the assay lab and had them checked out. Plain old river water and sediment except for one thing – acid. Lab says the bottles were spiked with acid, says that's protocol for metals analysis. My guess is Joe's trying to find out whether Jeddore was right about the mercury, and the lady is some chemist he brought along to do the testing.

"Any idea who she is?" he went on. "She wouldn't tell me. Short dark hair, athletic-looking woman with a smart mouth. French accent and drives a red MG."

The Minister paged through his mental Rolodex for a dark-haired French woman with a red sports car. The description was vaguely familiar. Yes, now he remembered. He met a professor like that three years ago. It seems his department had hired her to review the Sweet Bounty plan. He couldn't remember her name, but he knew he could find out later.

"Sorry," he answered quickly, "don't know her."

Paul Ceborro chuckled at that. "Too bad, Winslow, if they come up with something, it's gonna make you look real bad, giving the OK to a shoddy operator like me." Now he laughed out loud.

"Just remember," he continued, "your government won't pull the plug on my operation while I'm paying all that lovely extraction tax. But they'll pull the plug on you as soon as it's revealed you're on the take. Which, by the way, would be the last you'd hear from me. No more payola. It'll be bye-bye Minister. And you know they'll never trace any of it to me."

The Minister fumed and his nose began to run. He sniffed some of it back and wiped off the rest with his cuff. Ceborro had the upper hand again and he hated that.

"By the way, Winslow, you're investigators are doing a fine job here. They're leaving no stone unturned. Seen any results yet?"

"Field tests say you're clean, Ceborro," the Minister answered with a scowl in his voice. "We're still waiting for confirmation from the lab, but at this point you have nothing to worry about."

"Very good. I'm confident you'll ensure the final results corroborate that," Ceborro responded.

"Well, I gotta go, Winslow. It takes a lot to keep a shoddy operation like this running in the black. Keep up the good work." He laughed again and hung up.

Minister Winslow punched Speaker Off and swiveled his white, leather, executive chair to face the

## The Sweet Bounty

window. He leaned back, clasped his hands behind his head, stretched out his legs and crossed his ankles. He smiled. It was clever of him not to tell Ceborro he knew about Peter Joe's professor friend. With just the right help, she and Peter Joe could be Ceborro's undoing. The Minister had enough experience with field tests to know they could be devilishly uncertain. *How unfortunate*, he thought with a grin. He was sure the right words and a small tithing to the lab director could tip the results of those confirmation samples in just the right direction. He could gain the upper hand again.

But something Ceborro said worried him and now he needed to think. Staring out at the Atlantic helped him do that. Did Ceborro already know about the bribery investigation? Could the Premier already have released that information to the Telegraph? If word about it got out in the press, Ceborro would cut him off in a wink. He was sure of it.

A quick phone call to the Premier's office would tell him if the Telegraph had been notified. If it had, the very first thing he'd have to do is make sure Jimmy Nolan didn't write that story.

He frowned while he dialed the Premier's secretary. This would be yet another upset in the order of his life, and he didn't like the messy business of thuggery. That was work for scoundrels and lowlifes, not fitting for a man in his position.

\* \* \* \*

As Paul Ceborro hung up, something told him he could no longer trust the Minister, and he wondered if Winslow had told him the truth about anything. He knew Winslow was motivated by how much he had to lose. He certainly didn't trust Winslow to take care of Peter Joe and his friend, whoever she was. That he would have to do himself.

He could take care of Winslow later, he decided. Peter Joe was the worry now. Joe snooping around made him nervous – there was no telling what his father would do if he let someone stir up more of Chief Jeddore's kind of trouble. *Best to end it before it starts*, he thought, *and to keep Sir out of it.*

He rose from his office chair and tugged at the cuffs of his poplin dress shirt. He threw his Hugo cardigan sweater over the back of his shoulders and lightly tied the sleeves across his chest. He liked how that made him look like a tennis pro.

As he left for the day, he remembered he had purchased a special gift for the Orisha after Jeddore died. He grinned widely. It was time to use it.

## Chapter 15

"Damn! Does it have to bite them in the ass?" Realizing he had cursed out loud, Jimmy Nolan scolded himself for being so vocal around the others. Mostly, he hoped Beverly hadn't heard it. The Matron General would have chastised him heartlessly in front of the others with an eloquently delivered tongue-lashing solely for her own entertainment. And once she got going, there was no stopping her. One could only wait it out.

Jimmy Nolan was frustrated beyond measure. Right under everyone's eyes unfolded a human tragedy, a classic environmental crime hidden by its perpetrators behind the trite and all too transparent veil of progress and what's best for the economy. His editor had put his stories on the wire, but none of the big presses picked them up. Not even the CBC showed an interest, and that confounded him. *Didn't they care? The depravity was so obvious!*

His wooden swivel-chair squeaked as he sat forward at his desk. He pinned down the newspaper with his elbows and rested his cheeks on his fists.

Beneath the desk, his right knee bounced like a sewing machine. He had read his latest piece three times since it was printed, looking for the flaw he couldn't see. Now he read it again.

MINE'S LINK TO DEATH PROBED

St. John's –

Following the death of a prominent Indian rights activist, the Ministry of Environment began a long-overdue investigation into the operation of the Sweet Bounty, a gold mine in south central Newfoundland. Rumors abound high government officials were bribed to approve the Sweet Bounty three years ago. Now, the mine is alleged to be operating in violation of all its permits and discharging toxic waste to the Conifer River, threatening the lives of a nearby Indian community.

The Sweet Bounty of Newfoundland fell under suspicion when the St. John's Telegraph learned Saqamaw Abraham Jeddore, Chief of a small band of Mi'kmaq Indians, died of suspicious causes two days ago. In critical condition, Jeddore had been evacuated by air ambulance to St. John's General Hospital where he died almost immediately.

Jeddore was an outspoken opponent of the mine, and claimed the government of Newfoundland ignored the threat it posed to the Mi'kmaq of Conifer and to Pjila'si Bay. He frequently cited the damage methyl mercury would do to the Tribe's salmon aqua farm, a main source of jobs and income, and the direct threat it posed to the lives of his people.

## The Sweet Bounty

Jimmy began to fiddle with a wooden pencil while he read, unconsciously bending it with his thumbs and index fingers.

Jeddore's death remains a mystery, but sources who wish to remain anonymous point to methyl mercury poisoning as the likely cause. Ores of the Sweet Bounty mine are known to contain high concentrations of mercury, and the community of Conifer and Pjila'si Bay lie just 50 kilometers downstream from the mine. Natural bacteria in the aquatic environment convert mercury to toxic methyl mercury.

The Telegraph has learned other Tribal members have developed symptoms similar to those suffered by Jeddore.

Environment Minister Albert Winslow ordered the probe yesterday. Though he predicted the results of his Department's investigation would exonerate the Sweet Bounty, he swore to investigate every allegation without regard to source.

"Not a single citizen will be harmed by any operation under the jurisdiction of this Department while I'm on watch," said Winslow.

Salmon are known to accumulate methyl mercury from their food chain. The Provincial Poison Control Centre warns about ingesting methyl mercury, a deadly neurotoxin.

Results of the investigation are expected soon.

The pencil snapped, skittering a piece of lead across his desk onto the floor. He leaned abruptly back into his chair and it squeaked again. He threw the broken pieces of pencil onto the newspaper and sighed through pursed lips. Just like the other times he read it, he just didn't see what was missing. How many Indians would have to die before this atrocity garnered the national attention it deserved? And how much longer would he have to wait to break out of this small town rag?

"Jimmy!" A woman's voice woke him from the sulk of self-pity. "Jimmy! Fax for you!"

It was Beverly. He raised his head in response to her call and rolled his eyes. She annoyed him, and he wondered how such a lazy and self-righteous person ever got a job there. But he rose from his chair anyway and strode the seven steps to her desk.

She was standing, already holding out the fax for him, when he arrived. He reached for it, but when he did she drew it back. Bewildered, he looked up, and that was his mistake. Her eyes were waiting for him and they had that look – the look that said he was in for it.

"Watch your mouth, young man," she chided. She scowled like she had been rudely awakened from a blissful dream and poked a finger into his chest. "This isn't a locker room. You'd do well to remember you're in the presence of a lady." Then she held out the fax again.

He was stunned. *She couldn't be done already*, he thought. *Just 22 words and not even loud enough to draw attention. Maybe she's ill.*

He reached for the fax, expecting her to draw it back again, expecting her to continue. But she didn't. She released it to him and wordlessly turned her attention to something else. Astonished, he took advantage of that rare opportunity and wheeled toward his cubicle.

## The Sweet Bounty

*You'd do well to remember you're in the presence of a lady,* his mind replayed. God how she annoyed him!

He sat down at his desk. The fax machine must have been near the end of its roll because the paper curled in his hand. He pulled it over the edge of the desk to flatten it, laid it out before him, and began to read.

Government of Newfoundland and Labrador

Office of Willy Daniels, Premier

For Immediate Release

Attorney General to Investigate Bribery

Premier Willy Daniels today asked the Minister of Justice to investigate allegations by the St. John's Telegraph that government officials accepted illegal payment to approve the Sweet Bounty mine.

"I will not allow a pall of deceit and corruption to hang over this office," said Premier Daniels. "The citizens of Newfoundland and Labrador can expect the official business of their government to be conducted in a manner conspicuously above reproach. Therefore, I today asked the Minister of Justice in his capacity as Attorney General to appoint a special prosecutor to investigate these allegations."

A number was given for more information. Jimmy's day was suddenly brighter and he grinned widely. *Thank you, Premier Daniels! You just added legitimacy!* Maybe the plight of the Mi'kmaq would be heard after all. Maybe he'd only have to wait a little longer for his deliverance from this place.

    He slapped the press release onto the lower left corner of his desk, sipped a warmed-up yesterday's mocha, turned to his computer, and began to tap out his next piece. Later, he'd try to reach Peter Joe again and tell him the good news.

# Chapter 16

In the small town of Hermitage, on the eastern shore of Hermitage Bay, Paul Ceborro stood before the picture window of his living room and gazed out at the fading, red-orange sunset of a Newfoundland evening sky. As he watched it darken, he ran his fingers through his hair and thought about how much he resented being there.

His crisp, Italian cotton shirt tugged across the back of broad shoulders as he drew the curtain closed. He slipped off his black Salvatore Ferragamo loafers, placed them neatly against the wall beside the window, and turned to face the room behind him.

Except for the marbled apothecary table and a Harmon-Kardon audio system, the living room was vacant. *No place for worldly furnishings in a sacred Igbodu*, he had reasoned. *I must have a proper room.*

Now, in the center of that room, he carefully positioned a ceremonial mat, and upon the mat, a tiered, wooden altar. Atop the altar he had placed the images of Olodumare, the giver of ashe, the spiritual energy of the universe, and Chango, the ruler of lightning and thunder. On the level beneath them were the images of the three Orisha to which he would pray tonight – Elegua, the keeper of the doors to the divine world and the medium between the Orisha and humans; Ochosi, the protector of warriors; and Ogun, the only Orisha with the power to control life and death.

With tremoring hands, he chose a finger-size vial of azogue – heavy, shining, liquid mercury, his insurance against the meddling of unwelcome spirits – and unsteadily shook tiny droplets around the altar. He closed the vial and set it on the bottom level.

Over the crate of roosters, he draped three cloths dyed in the sacred colors and placed the crate on the mat as the centerpiece of his offering.

He filled his mouth with the potent, distilled juice of sugar cane and spat it all around him as a blessing. At the entrance to the room, and at the four corners of the compass, he spilled his bottled brew of water, sugar cane, and carojo butter. With a humble request that they confer their powers upon him, he raised it up in prayerful offering to the all-powerful Orisha and drank it empty.

Kneeling before the crate, he folded the colored cloths one by one and placed them neatly on the mat. He worked his hands into a pair of thick leather gloves. Carefully, he opened the crate and removed a single rooster. It pecked at his gloves and flailed its wings violently, seeming to know its fate. "Yakina, yakina," he said to it calmly, repeating the centuries-old words of the Santero priest before the blood offering.

He held the rooster with his right hand at the base of the neck and trapped its struggling body under his right arm. Then, with a sudden and practiced jerk of his left hand, he pulled its head sharply. For a while, it fluttered and clawed at his arm involuntarily, as if defying death. But the audible snap and the now lifeless form in his hands told him it had died humanely. He congratulated himself on a killing well done.

With a sacrificial knife, he slit the rooster's carotid artery and spilled the blood into one of the ceramic basins containing the sacred stones. Some of the blood sprayed onto his face, and the sweet smell piqued his senses as he smeared it off with the crease of his elbow. He performed this sacrifice three times until the stones of each basin were well saturated. *Blood favors the Orisha and makes them powerful*, he reminded himself.

Now, with eyes closed, he sat cross-legged on the floor before the altar and silently thanked his godfather for sponsoring his initiation into the Santeria religion so many years ago. He snickered to himself, certain no one suspected he possessed the skills he was about to exercise. *This is good*, he thought. Had they been asked, the people of this quaint and peaceful town would have said he attended mass regularly and seemed like a good Catholic. That was the masquerade he had been taught to practice so carefully since adolescence, the same masquerade begun in the 16$^{th}$ century by African natives captured and sold to Puerto Rican and Cuban slave owners by the Spaniards. He grinned broadly. Keeping this outward showing alive would assure him being above suspicion should a mysterious and unfortunate event befall Peter Joe.

He ran through his mental checklist, making certain all was ready. Everything had to be perfect – there was no room for error. He could not tolerate the passing of months as he had with 'that sack-a-maw

Jedder.' Justice must be swift this time. Peter Joe must die before he caused any trouble, before word of any trouble he might have already caused trickled back to the home office or, worse, to his father directly. His ulcer throbbed as he thought about how his father would demean him.

But he had another problem, one that now caused him great worry. Of the Orisha he needed today, two preferred to be summoned on a Tuesday, and the other preferred the third day of the month. Today was neither of those days. As a Santero priest, he knew the Orisha were particular. If they were displeased he summoned them on the wrong day, they might unleash on him some terrible wrath. But Peter Joe had pressed him for time, and Paul had to choose between keeping this Peter Joe trouble quiet and dealing with displeased Orisha. He could only hope he had offered the Orisha enough to humbly redress his imposition.

He exhaled audibly. It must be now, he decided.

He placed the bembe recording into the CD slot of his music system, pressed Power On, and turned up the volume. He sat bolt upright with his head back and hands folded anxiously in his lap. Slowly, the rhythm drew him in. He closed his eyes, drew in a long breath, and exhaled with deliberate control. He chanted and rocked, obediently letting the crescendo of drums overtake him. The drumming grew louder and stronger. He undulated left and right, left and right, moving unalterably into the manic state of the possession trance.

Then, suddenly, he felt their presence, and now they stood before him. They circled the altar three times. He felt their pleasure with his gifts and he smiled unconsciously.

## The Sweet Bounty

He threw back his head and his mind swore its allegiance . "I am ready!" he cried out.

Abruptly, Ogun was on him. Paul Ceborro shuddered and shook. Now Ogun was in him, in complete control of his body and mind. Paul gasped at the air and fell completely to the floor. He convulsed uncontrollably, writhing and twisting and curling in the pain as he gave himself completely to Ogun's will. *What joy in this anguish!*

Then, as suddenly as they began, the convulsions ceased and Paul Ceborro lay deathly still. The possession was complete. His body relaxed and he was calm once more. They were as one now. He and Ogun.

\* \* \* \*

It was dusk and becoming foggy as we drove back onto the highway on our way to Grand Falls-Windsor and I was puzzled by more questions. Who was Young Footprint Woman and how did she know about the gauging station? How did she find the gate key? I know this country, there is no other approach to that side of the Conifer for more than 100 kilometers in any direction. What did she want badly enough to carry a shear all that way? And what did she discover?

Why was the mercury in Anna's first sample not proof enough the mine had already contaminated the River and poisoned my people? What else did she need to know? Why go all the way to Grand Falls-Windsor to analyze the other bottles, why not just use the laser device?

I had to start with the questions I knew I could get answers to.

"Anna," I began, "why are we going to your Grand Falls-Windsor lab, why not just use that laser ... spec ... thing in the trunk?"

She answered with a matter-of-fact "Laser-Induced Breakdown Spectrometer" and turned on the headlights at the same time. The motor hummed us along at a brisk 65.

"Yeah, that," I said.

"Well, Peter, if you recall my earlier explanation, I said the laser breaks down everything in the sample well into its basic elements. They become plasma, a soup of ultra-hot ions. Nothing survives in its original form. The spectrometer can tell me what everything inside it is composed of, but it can't tell me what it used to be. Those elements, like carbon, hydrogen, oxygen, and the metals, could have come from anything in the water, including the water itself. Dirt, bacteria, insect parts, whatever – there is no way to trace it back. It is far more enlightening to know what they were before they were torn apart by the heat of the laser."

"I follow that," I said, "but then why use it at all?"

"Because while metals like mercury are elements, too, they are also ... how do you say ... a different beast? Geologists have characterized much about the minerals in earth's crust. Their presence in a mine waste stream is a bit like the code to a combination lock or a fingerprint. They mimic their source, and, when they are known, the source can be identified.

"In the lab, we perform tests which preserve the form of matter present in the sample. We can identify the original compounds and they, too, can help us to decipher what has happened in the environment where the sample was taken.

"If you recall my description of the chemistry of the leach heaps and holding ponds, you will know what other key compound I would expect to find if the mine were already contaminating the River, yes?"

"Cyanide?" I answered.

"Precisely, Peter. That will tell me if the ponds or leach heaps are leaking prematurely. But since it is a compound, the Laser Spectrometer would break it down into its elements. I would no longer recognize it. So I must analyze for it at the lab.

"Besides," she added, "you will want to give Jimmy Nolan flawless evidence if the mine is at fault. The Laser Spectrometer is well suited for field tests, but its results do not yet survive well in the courtroom. Someday perhaps they will. But at the present time, lawyers and judges want evidence that has been corroborated by the more traditional methods we perform in the lab, especially when those methods are prescribed by regulation and customary procedure."

\* \* \* \*

The Ogun-Ceborro rose from the floor and broke into exuberant dance, a warrior's dance, across the Igbodu and around the altar. It screeched war cries and flailed a machete at imaginary trees, clearing a path for imaginary warriors to follow.

It demanded rum, which Elegua poured liberally onto the altar. Spontaneous flame instantly erupted and engulfed it completely. The Ogun-Ceborro swung the machete high over its head with both hands and spun through the flames unharmed. It ran and leapt high into the air, machete behind its head and knees drawn to its chest. It gave a threatening cry and brought the machete down with fearsome power into a perfect, three-point, squat landing on feet and blade of machete. It turned its head and growled to any enemy that might be foolish enough to threaten an Orisha warrior.

Now, the Ogun-Ceborro ceased its dance. It jerked the machete blade out of the floor and rose fully upright. Slowly and deliberately, it turned the machete on itself. Without warning or emotion, it thrust the machete into its abdomen. It gave no cry of pain. It twisted and withdrew the machete and spilled no blood.

Elegua and Ochosi watched all of these antics with amusement.

Then all became quiet as the Ogun-Ceborro moved to stand beside Elegua and Ochosi at the altar. With both hands on the hilt, it planted the tip of the machete on the floor between its feet. A clear, deep voice came forth. Paul's mouth formed the words, but it was Ogun who spoke.

"Ikú oro, ikú eléyà ni Peter Joe máa kú!" The words of the ancient Yoruba deity reverberated within the walls of the Igbodu. Paul's body jostled with laughter as Ogun declared Peter Joe would soon die. It would be a horrible, bloody death, one befitting a worthless human being, he had said, and he gave Paul explicit instructions for the curse. Paul Ceborro was pleased.

Then, as suddenly as he came, Ogun sprang from Paul Ceborro's body to become pure Orisha once again. Paul's body shuddered, then collapsed and fell to the floor like a marionette suddenly freed of its strings.

## The Sweet Bounty

And there it lay in a formless, crumpled heap.

*　*　*　*

"So," I asked, "if mercury is in the ore, and you found it in the water, isn't that enough to say the mine is already polluting the River and poisoning my people? It seems pretty obvious to me."

The fog thickened and it began to rain. Several heavy drops bounced and disintegrated on the illuminated roadway before us. Her answer was momentarily interrupted by a few loud plops on the ragtop and large splatters on the windshield. She flipped on the wipers to clear it and slowed for the fog.

"Well, that may prove to be the case, Peter, but just as important as what I found is what I did not find. The ores of the Sweet Bounty also contain iron, sulfur, zinc, copper, and nickel, to name a few. I found none of them above ordinary background levels. Nor did I find gold. That is why I am wary of making the seemingly obvious conclusion. Remember that cyanide and sulfuric acid are not selective. If one metal from the ore is present, others should be there too."

"But if the mercury didn't come from the mine, how did it get there?"

"A very good question, Peter, and one I may not be able to answer. If it is from the mine, the lab analyses will confirm that. But if it is not, then we must determine its source by other means."

I pondered that but I was frustrated. Every answer seemed no more than the beginning of another question. I distracted myself by staring out my window.

We had just crossed the Northwest Gander River. The highway was typically empty tonight – we neither saw nor passed another vehicle in the last 50 kilometers. This had always been a seldom traveled road, especially at this time of day. We were 130 kilometers from the communities around Pjila'si Bay, and there were few reasons to travel this way unless you were fishing the Northwest, hunting for moose, or on your way to Grand Falls-Windsor for supplies.

But tonight the road seemed particularly isolated. Fog, a clouded, moonless sky, narrow shoulders with heavy timber close along the roadsides, and the monotonous thump of heavy raindrops seemed extraordinarily confining.

\* \* \* \*

Long minutes passed before Paul Ceborro regained consciousness. He uncurled himself, pushed up onto an elbow, and scanned the room as he waited for his mind to clear.

The altar was still there. The Igbodu was undisturbed. He sat upright on the floor, shook his head, and rubbed his face. He stood.

He saw no sign the Orisha had been there, yet he clearly recalled every moment of the evening. He remembered the pain and elation he felt as Ogun mounted him. He remembered the dancing and the flames. He remembered piercing himself with the machete, but, when he checked his own abdomen, he found no wound. He smiled. *What magic they bring!*

Now his mind regained clarity, his thoughts jelled, and he remembered the instructions Ogun had given him. There was no time to waste. He went immediately to work.

## The Sweet Bounty

He moved to the marbled apothecary table in the corner of the room, the table he reserved for the preparation of spells and curses. He chose a scrap of brown wrapping paper and wrote the name Peter Joe on it nine times. He wrapped the paper around nine boneset roots, carefully tied it with braided cat hair, and placed the bundle at the bottom of a red, clay pot.

To the pot he added nine peppercorns and nine pinches of sulfur and red ochre, then nine pinches of dirt he had collected from the graves in the Mi'kmaw burial ground.

He chose one of the clear plastic boxes from the corner of the table and carried it with the pot to the kitchen. He measured out two cups of cooking oil into a cast iron skillet, placed it on the range, turned the gas burner to high, and waited. When the oil smoked with the heat, he opened the box and dumped the mail-order scorpion into the oil.

The oil popped and spattered and the scorpion writhed in the sudden agony, stinging at the oil in frantic anger. Its body crackled and bounced in the heat until, scorched and lifeless, it could squirm no longer. He watched as the carcass sizzled and turned in the boiling currents of oil until the scorpion had completely dissolved. Then he turned off the burner and waited again.

When the oil cooled, he poured the contents of the skillet into the pot, took it back to the apothecary table, and inserted a wick. Then, with the pot cradled in his left arm, he turned off the lights and left the house.

It was only four minutes to the Hermitage cemetery. He walked casually, but he looked around frequently to see if any locals might still be sitting on their porches or watching through secretively parted curtains. Since first living there, he had convinced himself that small town people were notoriously nosy, and the magic of Santeria was one secret he wanted to keep to himself.

He climbed the slope out of the cove to the small plateau where the cemetery was located. Now above the rise, a damp, cold breeze blew in his face, and he could just make out the cemetery gatepost lamp, its old, dim bulb making a frail beacon against the moonless night.

He walked deep into the cemetery. From between trees in an obscure corner, he scanned the dark horizon, looking for a yard lamp or porch light, any stray light that might give him away. When he was certain he could not be seen, he placed the pot gently on the ground, knelt beside it, and performed the last of Ogun's instructions – he lit the wick with an ordinary kitchen match.

He stood, planted his hands on his hips, and grinned with supreme pleasure as he watched the mixture burn. He had followed Ogun's instructions to the letter. Very soon, Peter Joe would be dead, he was sure of it. He need only wait for news of the tragedy.

Still smiling, he looked to the night sky and gave thanks to the Orisha.

* * * *

Suddenly, it began to pour great sheets of cold rain. Thunder shook the air. Curtains of wind-driven water pounded the MG. Instant rivers flowed heavily on the road and viscous fog cut visibility to just a few car lengths. The reflection of the headlights off the fog blinded us and Anna switched them off in favor of the road-hugging yellow of the fog lamps. She slowed as quickly as prudence allowed, trying to avoid hydroplaning on the slippery flow of road water. We shouted over the deafening torrents just to be heard.

She flipped the wipers to high, but the narrow wands of clear glass they dragged behind them quickly blurred again in the relentless onslaught of rain. It suddenly grew very cold. Rain seemed to pour in under the ragtop and stream down the inside of the windshield. Our breath condensed onto every window. We wiped them with our hands but it re-condensed only seconds later.

I wiped my side of the windshield again. It was then I saw them.

"Anna, there!" I shouted and pointed, but it was already too late. The eyes reflecting an eerie yellow glow would be on us faster than I could brace for the impact. Anna turned the wheel in a desperate attempt to avoid them. We spun immediately into a circle, gaining speed in a hydroplane as traction abruptly gave way to momentum.

There was no sound of an impending collision, no squeal of tires on the road, no gasp of breath before impact – there was no time. There was only silent, inexorable motion lasting fractions of a second, like a frightful, carnival-ride nightmare. The brown figures couldn't scatter and we were sliding too fast to miss them.

The spin threw me hard into the windshield. The collision slammed me backward. Nkekkunit Abram wrapped me in his arms. I blacked out.

\* \* \* \*

As Paul Ceborro walked in through his front door, he felt a fleeting, unanticipated moment of joy. He stopped with his hand still on the knob and wondered if something had already happened to Peter Joe. He smiled again. *No matter*, he thought as he continued inside. He would hear something soon enough. That's how word traveled in this country.

He closed the door behind him and turned on the lights.

## Chapter 17

Jimmy Nolan was doing something tonight he rarely ever did. He was working late. He wanted to finish his piece about the Premier's bribery investigation before he went home so he could present it to his editor first thing in the morning. This was hot news and he wanted it in print as soon as possible. He long suspected payoffs were involved, he just couldn't prove it. Now, it looked like the Premier would do that for him. All he had to do was get it on the front page when the proof came.

He looked at the clock over his door, then dug for the Metrobus schedule in his top right drawer, the same drawer where he kept take-out menus and scraps of paper with phone numbers. He found it at the very bottom. With the schedule on his desk, he flattened out the wrinkles and ran his index finger down the Water Street column to the first scheduled stop after 8:35 pm.

The Number 5 ran every half hour on the half hour at regular quitting time, but at this time of night it ran only once an hour. Checking the times, he back-calculated that he could get it at Prescott and Water, his usual corner, at 9:08. Allowing seven minutes to walk there, he had 26 minutes for a final proofread and a phone call to Peter Joe. And he could still be home by 9:40.

He shoved the schedule back into his desk drawer, turned his eyes to his latest draft, and read it for the last time tonight.

PREMIER EYES MINE BRIBERY CHARGES

St. John's –

Yesterday, Premier Willy Daniels ordered a special investigation into charges officials high in his administration were bribed to approve the Sweet Bounty Mine in south central Newfoundland. The Minister of Justice in his capacity as Attorney General will appoint a special prosecutor.

This investigation comes on the heels of a separate investigation opened only one day earlier by the Ministry of Environment after allegations the same mine violated its permits and discharged toxic waste into the Conifer River.

Both of these investigations were preceded by the mysterious death of Abraham Jeddore three days ago. Jeddore was Chief of the Mi'kmaq Indian community at Conifer and a vocal opponent of the mine. He campaigned vigorously against the mine over concerns mercury released by the mine would create methyl mercury, the same toxin that killed hundreds of Japanese at Minimata in the 1950s. Though the cause of Jeddore's death has not been officially determined, knowledgeable sources claim his symptoms at death were classically those of methyl mercury poisoning.

## The Sweet Bounty

Since first proposed four years ago, the Sweet Bounty has been surrounded by controversy. Rumors the Provincial government purposely overstated job and economic benefits and ignored probable environmental and human health threats surfaced early. Suspicions high government officials were bribed to expedite approval and bypass public review arose in the media soon afterward.

The latest investigation is to begin immediately. Said Premier Daniels, "I will not allow a pall of deceit and corruption to hang over this office. The citizens of Newfoundland and Labrador can expect the official business of their government to be conducted in a manner conspicuously above reproach."

Neither the Premier's office nor the Justice Ministry gave any indications when the investigation would be complete.

*Perfect*, he decided. He printed it then placed it in the center drawer of his desk. Now to reach Peter Joe and Dr. Chartier.

After his last attempt to call Dr. Chartier, he had transferred her number from the paper scrap to a sticky note, which he had then stuck on the top right corner of his monitor for easy finding. Now, he dialed as he read Dr. Chartier's number.

He was again given immediately to her greeting. "Bonjour," it said, "you have reached the Department of Environmental Chemistry ..."

*Damn*, he thought, *cell phone's off again*. He waited impatiently for the end of the greeting. "Au Revoir!" it said finally, and he left his second urgent message.

"Dr. Chartier, Jimmy Nolan again. St. John's Telegraph? As soon as you get this message, it's extremely urgent I talk to Peter Joe. There's been another development. The Premier ordered an investigation into the bribery allegations I told Peter about, in connection with the Sweet Bounty Mine. Appointed a special prosecutor and everything. It's gotta be Winslow. Anyway, I'm getting that piece out right away, it'll be in tomorrow's evening edition.

"I'm getting closer to the truth every day here, and when I get it, his godfather's story will be read all over Canada. Hell, it'll make news all around the world. So I really need to talk to him and find out what he knows as soon as possible. Gotta keep the momentum going and ..."

He was interrupted by a beep, signaling he was almost out of time. "Shit," he muttered. Then, realizing he was still being recorded, he calmed and apologized into the phone. "Sorry for that little indiscretion, Dr. Chartier. Please call me, it's urgent." He left his number again and returned the handset to its cradle.

"Well, feck," he said out loud. That was the second time in as many days he tried to reach Dr. Chartier and all he got for his efforts was 'nobody's available' with a French accent. Jimmy was frustrated. Things were happening fast in St. John's, and he needed whatever Peter Joe knew right now. *Where the hell was he? Why didn't she answer her cell phone, or at least call back?* He concluded there was nothing he could do but wait, as if he hadn't already been doing just exactly that.

He sighed as he checked the clock. It was 9:01. *Might as well go now,* he thought. He grabbed his mac off the side chair, threw it over his shoulder, and left

## The Sweet Bounty

the room. He was two steps beyond his door before he remembered to turn off the light. He stepped back, flipped the switch, and continued past Beverly's desk toward the main entrance, turning off the other lights as he went.

\* \* \* \*

A heavy drizzle fell through the fog and the diffuse light of a lamppost on the other side of Duckworth Street. The man in a black oilskin coat leaning against the building behind it raised his head. His right hand tipped back the brim of a sou'wester hat while his left hand flicked a cigarette ash into a puddle on the sidewalk. The last light in the Telegraph building had just gone out. He pulled down the brim of his sou'wester and lowered his head again.
*Soon*, he told himself.

\* \* \* \*

Outside, the foggy drizzle caught Jimmy by surprise as he turned left onto the Duckworth Street sidewalk. The sky had been clear earlier today when he grabbed a fast takeout at the Casa Grande, but the chilling night air after a warm, clear day often brought fog and a drizzle on the coast this time of year. He slid the mac off his shoulder and put it on, then flipped the collar up and pulled it tight around his neck as he walked. It would be a soggy wait for the Metro.

EW Finke

* * * *

The man in the sou'wester hat dropped his cigarette to the ground and quietly snuffed it out with a soft-soled boot. He stepped away from the building and crossed the street, hands in his pockets, hat pulled low and head down. His target was half a block ahead. If he kept to the shadows and walked at just the right pace, he would catch him at the second corner.

* * * *

It struck Jimmy how empty Duckworth was tonight. Except for a man he had seen by a lamppost across the street from the Telegraph, there was no one. Offices, cafes, and coffee shops all were closed. Most of the tourists had gone home by now – just a few optimistic gift shop owners stayed open this late in the season, and even they were closed for the day.

The dense fog and intervening buildings muted the horn of a tug and the clatter of a crane in the Harbour. Here and there burned the yellow and curtained lights of a few second-story, row house flats. Jimmy passed by an empty parked car and glanced back over his right shoulder. Even the man by the lamppost was gone now.

But that was okay with him, he felt unexpectedly elated to have the whole city to himself tonight. He was confident the two investigations would prove him right about the Sweet Bounty and Chief Jeddore. With Peter Joe's first-hand report, he would have a story to beat all stories, and Peter's being the dead victim's godson would hold spellbound the hearts of millions of readers.

## The Sweet Bounty

Things were going his way now. Soon, the Telegraph would mete out justice and shape public sympathy like the big presses did, and soon he would be moving up to one of them. He smiled at his sudden good fortune as he walked. Prescott was only one block farther.

\* \* \* \*

A sound came from behind and the man in the sou'wester hat ducked quickly into the sheltered entryway of a cafe. He turned his head and looked behind him. It was nothing, he determined, or maybe it was a cat. He eased his head out of the entryway and re-located his target. Whatever it was, it didn't matter – the target apparently didn't hear it. He stepped back onto the sidewalk and continued his pursuit.

\* \* \* \*

Jimmy finished the second block on Duckworth and rounded the corner onto Prescott. Though indistinct with the fog, the intense lights of the Harbour made him squint until his eyes adjusted to the sudden brightness. A few seconds later, a flashing yellow light moved across his view from right to left in the distance, and a muted horn sounded again.

*A tug*, he thought and he smiled again. Except for the rag, he liked it here, especially downtown, close to the romantic sounds of the Harbour. They reminded him of home – Kinsale, County Cork – smaller than St. John's but a lot like it.

His eleventh step on Prescott was interrupted by something at his shoulder, something pulling it back. He turned his head to see what it was. The gloved fist came hard and fast, giving him no time to react. In his remaining half-second of consciousness, the Harbour lights reflected the man he had seen by the lamppost. Then, he staggered back, his legs gave out under him, and it suddenly became dark everywhere. Jimmy Nolan collapsed into a sprawl on the sidewalk, and the rain soaked his face.

In a low crouch over the body, the man in the sou'wester hat took careful notice of his surroundings. When he was certain no one had seen, he turned back to the red-haired man lying motionless on the sidewalk before him. He looked into the young, wet face and shook his head. *Practically a kid*, he thought.

But $500 was $500 and he undertook to finish the job he was given. He grabbed the limp body under the armpits, dragged it to the edge of the sidewalk out of the rain, and leaned it against a cold, stone building. Then, just as he had been instructed, he took an envelope out of his pocket and shoved it inside the red-haired man's coat.

After a second look around, the man in the sou'wester hat continued his stroll down Prescott and disappeared into the fog.

## Chapter 18

Something punched at Jimmy Nolan's foot and a voice shouted at him. His willed his eyes to open but they fought to stay closed. He realized he was very uncomfortable, and his first thought was to raise his cheek off the cold, hard sidewalk. Sluggishly, he pushed himself up enough to prop onto an elbow.

Slowly, his mind let in the noises of a city beginning to stir. When his eyelids at last began to open, he raised a hand to shield his eyes from the morning sun. His vision was blurred and his face throbbed everywhere. His whole head ached.

From his nearly horizontal position on the sidewalk, Jimmy Nolan squinted up at the voice. Through puffy eyes he saw the fuzzy vision of a man in a black leather jacket, shin-high, boots and a black helmet with a tiny brim. One hand held what looked like a small, black baseball bat. The other held little ropes tethered to the mouth of a large, four-legged animal that swished its tail and snorted. *A horse,* Jimmy decided, *and the man must be a Constable.*

He was right. Again the Constable jabbed at the sole of Jimmy's shoe with a billy club and shouted. "You there! Be no sleepin' on the sidewalk, we run a respectable town here, right? Drunk and been here all night, I 'spect. Best you be movin' on 'fore you find yourself in the lockup."

Jimmy tried to speak, but it hurt to move anything on his face. He tried again, this time slowly and deliberately, and the words came out in barely audible mumble. "Howw'd ... I ... get ... here?"

"What?" The Constable furrowed his brow and squatted to hear him better. He studied Jimmy's face. "Well, now," he said finally, "that's quite a bruise you're carryin', son."

Deciding at last that Jimmy was not there by choice, the Constable holstered the billy club. "I hope you got in a few good licks," he said, "'cause by the looks of things it was the other fella got the best punch." He grabbed Jimmy by the upper arm and pulled him up. "Come on, get up. Let's get you somewhere you can clean up and tend to that jaw."

Jimmy wobbled as he stood and had to lean into the Constable to get his footing. When it seemed Jimmy could stand on his own, the Constable took him by the upper arm again, turned him around, and slowly walked him up Prescott Street. Jimmy's eyes were still not able to focus through the swelling, and he stumbled here and there as he walked. With the reins held at the small of the Constable's back, the horse dutifully clopped along behind them.

The city began to come alive as they rounded the corner onto Duckworth. Vans and panel trucks blocked lanes with their deliveries, and important-looking people in suits bustled by. A man in coveralls grabbed a tool belt from the bed of a small truck and went into a café not yet open for business. An attractive, middle-aged woman in a red dress approached Jimmy from ahead and they exchanged glances. But her eyes darted quickly to front as she passed by and she paled, as if she had just seen the Elephant Man. "Where do you want to go, son?" the Constable asked.

Jimmy turned his head back to the Constable. "I ... wwwork ... at ... the ... Tele ... graph," he mumbled, but at the ph a sharp pain shot through his jaw and he winced. He made a mental note to not make that sound again.

"What?" the Constable asked again.

Jimmy halted and the Constable and the horse stopped with him. Still weak, he slowly unbuttoned and reached into the top of his mac for one of the business cards he kept in the inside chest pocket. But his hand stumbled onto something crisp, and he wondered what it was. He was sure he hadn't put anything there when he left the office last night. He pulled it out.

It was a sealed manila envelope, slightly larger than standard-size. He flipped it over and found nothing written on the outside. He transferred it to the other hand, then continued to fish for a business card.

"... Hhheere ..." he said, and he gave the card to the Constable. As he did, a little drool escaped from the edge of his mouth, and he gently wiped it off with the back of his hand. He pushed the envelope into the torn, outside waist pocket. Whatever was inside it, he could find out later when his face didn't hurt so much.

The Constable studied the card as they resumed their walk. "So, you're a reporter," he said at last. "Well, that explains a lot, doesn't it? My guess is somebody didn't like something you wrote. Thing is, I don't know any Liberals with the gumption to actually slug a reporter." He grinned widely and turned his head to face Jimmy. "So it had to be a Conservative, right?" Now he laughed.

Jimmy didn't laugh. Not that he would have if his face didn't hurt, he just didn't think it was funny.

The Constable must have taken the hint because he stopped laughing and cleared his throat. "The Telegraph, right?" he said more seriously. "It's just ahead. If I get you there, will there be someone to help you take care of that jaw?"

"... Yeahhh ...," Jimmy answered, but as he did an abrupt fear caused him to frantically check his watch. 6:59 it said. He relaxed and breathed a sigh of relief when he realized Beverly wouldn't be there for another hour. He was sure she would be merciless about this.

Two blocks later, they arrived at the Telegraph building. At the main entrance, the Constable released Jimmy's arm and stepped back. "Alright, here you are, son. I'd get some help with that jaw right away, if I were you."

With that, the Constable turned away and pulled the horse to a stop alongside him. He laced the reins over the horse's neck and put his hands on the horn and cantle. "Hoah, Townshend," he said in a low voice, and he slid a foot into the stirrup and pulled himself up.

The saddle leather creaked when he turned to face Jimmy from atop the horse. "In case you're wonderin'," he called back, "I'm not gonna report your little sidewalk infraction. Seems to me you have enough trouble already." He touched the brim of his helmet as if to tip his hat, then turned away for the second time and lightly nudged the horse in the flank with the heels of his boots. The horse answered the command with a snort, the saddle creaked again, and the two of them clopped down the street.

"... Thhaaankth ..." Jimmy tried to call out, wondering if the Constable could hear him. He drooled again and dabbed it with his sleeve.

Jimmy turned, climbed the two steps to the door, and let himself in with a key. Thankfully, he would have enough time to ice his face and swallow a handful of Tylenol before Beverly or any of the first floor people reported for work.

On the second floor, he walked past Beverly's desk, turned right, and headed for the lunchroom at the end of the hallway. It was small and bright pinkish, a color chosen by a loose, self-appointed quorum of office secretaries on a pre-Beverly day when they had grown tired of the bland white it had been before. Arguing the need for a morale perk, they managed to convince an office manager to let them paint it that color one Saturday afternoon.

The room was just large enough to hold a refrigerator and a four-foot counter with a sink basin, a ten-cup Mr. Coffee, and a microwave. Above the counter was a plain, open shelf with 11 unmatched coffee mugs brought in by people who had no interest in keeping them for themselves, and a small mirror one of the secretaries kept there in case the washroom was occupied. A partially used roll of paper towels stood on end by a corner of the sink.

At the refrigerator, he opened the freezer and removed a try of ice cubes. He cracked them free onto a hand towel taken from the door handle, slipped his palms under it, and raised it up. He immersed his face into the ice.

"Aaaaahhhh," he breathed with relief, loudly enough someone down the hall would have heard him had anyone been there. A welcome cold surged into the hot, swollen tissues of his cheeks, drained out the ache in his jaw, and swept around his eyes. He doubted anything else could have felt that good at that particular moment.

A full minute passed before he lowered his hands. He stripped a paper towel off the roll, patted his face dry, and looked into the mirror on the shelf. He gasped at what he saw. A deep blue color, flushed pink on the surface by the ice, imbued the entire left side of his face. His eyes were little more than slits, and his jaw was fat.

He pressed the fingers of both hands onto the skin of his face. It felt cold and stiff, and parts of it had no feeling. *Feck*, he thought to himself. It could be weeks before he looked even somewhat normal again.

He extracted a second tray from the freezer and cracked the cubes onto the towel. He gathered the edges into a makeshift bag and carried it to his office. He turned on the light, set the towel of cubes onto his desk, and threw his mac over the side chair. Sitting at his desk, he shook six Tylenol from a bottle in the top right desk drawer into his hand.

*What in God's name brought this on?* he asked himself. He didn't know the answer to that question, but he knew this was an experience he did not want to have a second time. He carefully washed the Tylenol down with rest of a day-old mocha.

Still wondering how he came to be in this predicament, he slouched into the swivel-chair. His eye caught the corner of the envelope sticking above the

## The Sweet Bounty

pocket flap of his mac, and he turned his head to look directly at it. *The answer had to be inside*, he surmised. *Why else would it be there?*

He leaned to the side, pulled it from the pocket, and held it before himself, squeezing it between his fingers. The contents were pliable and fat. He slit open the top with a letter knife and peeled the halves apart. What he saw caused him to bolt upright in his chair.

It was money. Brand new bills and lots of them, bound under a folded sheet of paper with a rubber band. He slipped off the band, set the paper aside, and didn't stop counting until he got to 30.

Thirty crisp, red-backed portraits of William Lyon Mackenzie King, Canada's tenth and arguably greatest Prime Minister. He held his breath while did the math in his head ... *30 times 50 ... Sweet Mother of Jesus!* One thousand five hundred dollars, cash money, right there in his hands. He would have whistled if he could.

He mentally summarized the last 11 hours. He had been mugged by an unknown assailant on a dark street, left unconscious on a sidewalk for an entire night in a cold rain, and now he found himself in possession of a small, unexpected fortune. Someone really wanted his attention. He picked up the paper, hoping to learn who as he unfolded it and read a typewritten message addressed to him.

My Dear Mr. Nolan:

By now, you will have experienced a generous sample of my sincerity. I trust my friend was not too harsh, and I pray the contents of this envelope are adequate compensation for your inconvenience.

It will be most apparent I have taken a great effort to make my point, and you may ask what I seek for my trouble. Very little, Mr. Nolan, very little, indeed. I ask merely that you heed this simple advice:

DO NOT PUBLISH THAT STORY.

And that is all. Quite uncomplicated, don't you agree?

One last thing, a word of warning. Should that story appear against my advice, I shall insure you have the pleasure of my friend's company once again. Am I clear?

He read it again, then flicked the note onto the desk and ran the words through his head. *I seek merely that you heed this simple advice. Do not publish that story.* That was it – no name, no signature, no details.

Who sent it, and which story did it mean? His assailant could not have been so tardy as to deliver a note meant for a story already published, could he?

Then Jimmy remembered the piece still in his drawer, the one about the bribery investigation he planned to give his editor this morning. It had to mean that story, he decided, but how did his assailant, or, rather, the person who sent him, learn of it? Jimmy didn't know the answer to that question either, but he was pretty sure people didn't assault reporters unless the stakes were very high.

*Let's think this through*, he instructed himself, *narrow it down. Except for the Premier himself, who else could have known about the bribery investigation? The Premier would have announced the investigation to trusted staff before issuing the press release. Word of mouth takes time to filter down in government circles.*

## The Sweet Bounty

*For the assault to have taken place so soon after the press release, it had to be someone who received word of the investigation early – maybe the Premier's immediate office, or the Minister or Deputy Minister level, but probably no more than one level below that. It also had to be someone worth bribing in the first place, someone highly influential or someone with direct authority to approve or disapprove. That narrowed it to one of the Ministers or a highly trusted advisor to the Premier.*

But that was as far as he could go, and he let out a frustrated sigh. He reflected that all that deductive reasoning hadn't helped. He had always suspected it was the Minister of Environment, and there he was right back where he had always been. How could he prove it was him? How could he flush him out?

Then it suddenly occurred to him, a way to do just exactly that – flush him out. It would take a small stretch of the truth, but it could work. Gleefully, Jimmy penned a simple addition to the end of the very last sentence of his piece. That sentence now read:

Neither the Premier's Office nor the Justice Ministry gave any indications when the investigation would be complete, but both offices hinted investigators were following a strong lead in the case.

With a renewed energy, he gathered up the press release, his piece, the note and the money, and left his office.

On the third floor, he approached his editor's office and peered in from the hallway. *Good*, he thought, *no secretary yet*. He passed by the secretary's desk and saw his editor was in. He rapped on the door jam.

The editor was occupied with something going on outside the window at street level, and he stood with his hands on the sill and his back to Jimmy. "Come," he said without turning around.

Jimmy entered, placed his things on the corner of the editor's desk, and stood quietly beside the guest chair.

His editor turned casually, then froze. He screwed up his face in disbelief. "Jimmy?"

Jimmy nodded.

"What on earth happened to your face?"

"I ... was ... assaul ... ted," Jimmy replied.

"What?" The editor furrowed his brow and leaned closer to hear him better.

Jimmy rolled his eyes, then grouped together the thumb and first two fingers of his right hand and wiggled them over his left palm. The editor acknowledged the request with a nod, then pushed a pad and a pen across the desk. The editor sat down.

Jimmy sat, too, and he slid the threatening note and money toward the editor. When the editor seemed to grasp what they were, he wrote, "I was assaulted. Please listen carefully," then pushed toward him the pad, the Premier's press release, and his latest piece.

Then Jimmy spoke slowly and deliberately for a long time. He knew the editor had read all his other pieces, but this was an important opportunity to tie them all together for him. He described how Chief Jeddore had been killed by methyl mercury and that the mercury had probably come from the Sweet Bounty mine. He explained how the Minister of Environment had lied to the people of Newfoundland about the jobs the mine would bring, and how he had approved the

## The Sweet Bounty

Sweet Bounty knowing it would do harm to the Mi'kmaq community of Conifer and the Conifer River itself.

Jimmy described the Ministry's investigation into the Sweet Bounty's permit violations and toxic waste releases, and how he suspected that investigation was just a deception by the Minister to divert attention away from himself. He added how he had enlisted Peter Joe, the godson of Chief Jeddore, and Dr. Chartier to help him get the truth about the Sweet Bounty and prove how Chief Jeddore died.

Then Jimmy explained his plan to expose the Minister – the man who was probably still taking bribes for the cover up, and the same person he suspected was responsible for the assault. His editor was to publish his latest piece, and Jimmy would take the money and disappear for a few days. During that time, the Minister was sure to reveal himself, and Jimmy would find Peter Joe with his proof mercury from the Sweet Bounty mine had killed Chief Jeddore. He finished with how he would lay open the whole fraudulent mess in the Telegraph for a public inquisition.

Jimmy sat back and waited for his editor's response. The editor folded his hands on a bulging abdomen and squinted his eyes at Jimmy, thinking long and hard before answering.

Then he sat forward. "It's risky, Jimmy," he said at last. "The odds of you being able to prove all this are slim, you must know that. And it all might just backfire. The last thing we need here is a slander suit."

His eyes went back to the note and the money. He absentmindedly drummed his fingers on the edge of the desk while he thought some more. Long seconds passed before he looked up and sighed as if he might regret what he was about to do. Then he spoke again.

"You'll need a car that can't be traced to you, I'll talk to the motor pool. Don't use any credit cards, they can be traced, too. I'll get Finance to advance you $1500. You are to contact me and only me, and I want to hear from you every day. In the meantime, I'll see if I can get a friend at the RNC to slip me a few bank records."

Jimmy nodded, but he would have grinned from ear to ear if he could. He was being given his first assignment as an undercover reporter, but "... Thankth ... very ... mmmuch ..." was all he could muster. He stood to leave, and, in his excitement, overturned the chair. He righted it, apologized with an embarrassed "... Sorry ... " and another " ... Thankth ... " and headed toward the door.

As he was leaving, his editor called him back. "Jimmy, do you have a gun?"

Jimmy hesitated, then turned back and nodded a yes.

"Take it, just in case. Who knows how serious your Minister might get when I print this."

Jimmy nodded again.

"And get someone to look at that face, will you? You don't want that kind of thing to become permanent."

## Chapter 19

It had been light only a few hours when Jimmy Nolan disembarked the Number 5 at the end of its run by the Village Mall, having slept the night in his office with a now well-entrenched instinct for self-preservation. He entered his third floor apartment and turned up the volume on the police scanner, just like he always did when he came home. He'd be leaving for a few days, but a reporter could never have too many leads, and maybe he could compose a piece or two while he was in hiding.

He listened while it scanned, but it seemed the airways were giving up no communications tonight so he turned it off. He rewound the auto-recorder and pressed Play, hoping the scanner had picked up something while he'd been away. He cranked up the volume and resumed the task he had come home to do.

In his room, he pulled a tattered, hounds tooth travel bag from the closet floor and threw it onto his bed. He went to his bathroom, downed another five Tylenol, and went to work. Somewhere between packing socks and the third pair of underwear, his ears heard what he thought was 'Chartier.' Immediately, he stopped and cocked his head to the words emanating from the recorder.

It was RCMP, a Constable's voice. The signal was faint and cluttered with bursts of static, but he deciphered enough to learn a man and a woman had been taken by ambulance to a hospital in Grand Falls-Windsor. The woman would be treated for internal injuries, but the man was not expected to survive. Dispatch asked him to repeat the names, and this time Jimmy was sure he heard the words 'Peter Joe and Annamarie Chartier.' Dispatch acknowledged the names then closed the communication. Static filled the frequency and he heard the familiar click of the auto-recorder pausing itself while the scanner searched for another live signal.

"Hohy theck!" Jimmy said out loud, his jaw still swollen. *This can't be! Not now!*

An all-consuming anxiety overtook him. Everything Jimmy had worked toward was suddenly evaporating before him. The plans he laid out to his editor, bringing the Minister to justice, exposing the Sweet Bounty, his first undercover assignment – gone, wiped out, just that fast. Without Peter Joe, he could never piece together the evidence he needed!

Unexplainably, the thought of Beverly's reaction to this misfortune flashed through his mind. *My God*, he thought, *I could be at the Telegraph forever!*

Quickly, Jimmy pushed Rewind on the auto-recorder. He listened intently while it replayed the transmission. *How did the Constable say it just then?* Jimmy replayed it a third time.

The Constable didn't say 'dead,' Jimmy discerned, he said 'not expected to survive.' *Could he still be alive?* Jimmy's mind raced through the math. This was Friday morning. The counter told him the transmission had taken place sometime Wednesday night. That was nearly a day and a half ago.

The odds Peter Joe was still alive weren't good, but he decided to play them anyway. He phoned the hospital, identified Peter Joe and Annamarie Chartier as his friends, and inquired about their condition. The receptionist passed him to an attendant at the admissions desk, who told Jimmy they were both there, but said privacy laws prohibited him from saying more on the phone. Jimmy hung up and breathed a cautious sigh of relief. *Thank God, there was still hope!*

Hastily, he shoved the remainder of his clothes into the bag. It was almost completely zipped when he remembered his editor's advice, and from his closet shelf he snatched the .22 caliber Ruger Bearcat and a half-empty box of Federals. Wishing he were more skilled with it, he blew the dust off the Ruger and shoved them both into the bag. Just for good measure, he threw in a survival knife, too, then zipped the bag closed and dragged it from the bed on his run to the door. He flipped off the lights, let the locked door slam behind him, and leapt down the three flights of stairs two steps at a time. He threw the bag into his car, jumped in beside it, and started the motor.

*To hell with the motor pool*, he thought. In his own car, he could be there in a little over four hours. Maybe Peter Joe was going to die, but maybe Jimmy could get there soon enough to learn what he knew.

\* \* \* \*

*But was he dead?* That was the question Paul Ceborro was asking himself. Sitting with his elbows on the desk, he peered over folded hands at one of his drivers standing on the other side. He forced an outward calmness as he asked the driver why he waited so long to tell him, but he boiled inside. His eyes threw a steely glower.

The driver shrugged. "Didn't think it was important," he said.

Paul looked at the driver with an air of intimidation even his father would have been proud of. "Didn't think it was important ... Sir," he corrected.

"Yes, Sir. I didn't think it was important, Sir," the driver responded nervously.

Paul Ceborro dismissed the driver from his office with an insolent wave of his hand. *Incompetent fool!* Just exactly when had he told his people they were paid to exercise judgment? He was sure he made it clear he wanted to know everything that went on here. Maybe it was time for a little group discipline, something to remind them they were to do only and precisely as he said. He leaned back in his chair as the door closed and cursed the driver under his breath – he had been waiting nearly a day and a half for this news.

It had been after 11:00 p.m. when the driver was on his way back to the mine. His headlights caught something alongside the road, almost in the river. It was a red sports car and it was totaled, he had said. It looked like it had been hit from behind by something – another car, maybe a truck – which was nowhere to be seen. There was a lot of blood and the people inside were not moving so he called 9-1-1. He had waited until the RCMP and an ambulance arrived, then watched as the ambulance loaded a man and a woman and whisked them back the way it had come. He then inquired with the Constable, having recognized the sports car as the same one sitting outside the Sweet Bounty's gate as he left to deliver a load of ingots to Gander International Airport. He had learned the woman was alive and would be treated for internal injuries, but the man, an Indian, had bled profusely, was comatose, and was not expected to survive. Satisfied he had been a Good Samaritan, the driver had continued on his way.

Paul Ceborro fumed again. Ogun had promised a bloody, ignoble death, and had that driver been just a little more thorough, Paul Ceborro would have had the confirmation he had been waiting for. But he hadn't been, and now Paul had to go out of his way to find out if Peter Joe was dead. He loathed doing someone else's work.

It wasn't difficult to figure out where they had been taken. Grand Falls-Windsor had the closest hospital for most of south-central Newfoundland, including the Sweet Bounty. Standard company protocol demanded that company telephones be programmed to speed-dial 9-1-1 and the numbers of the closest hospital, fire department, and air ambulance. Paul lifted the handset of his desk phone and stabbed at the key labeled 'HOSP.'

A hospital receptionist answered and connected him to the admissions desk. A man came on the line, and Paul asked about the condition of his dearest friends Peter Joe and his wife. "They were admitted together on Wednesday after a most unfortunate accident," he added.

"Yes, there it is ... Wednesday night ... Peter Joe and Annamarie Chartier," the man said. "I can tell you they're here, but anything more requires approval from the higher-ups."

Paul said he understood what the man was up against, what with all the red tape and regulations about privacy these days, and said he would probably visit them later today anyway. Sensing empathy, the man launched into an exchange about how he had to agree with that, and he wondered out loud where this country was headed. Paul played along hoping the man would let slip a little more information, which he did, eventually saying both of his friends were doing better than expected.

Paul's thank-you dripped with graciousness, but he slammed the phone down when he hung up. He stood and pounded the desk with both fists. *How was it possible Indian Boy could escape so certain a death as one orchestrated by an Orisha warrior! It never happened!* He paced the floor and punched at the wall.

Reminding himself that rage only obscures a man's thinking, he sat down and forced himself to calm. He closed his eyes, inhaled deeply, and breathed out slowly and deliberately through pursed lips, mimicking his preparation for a possession trance. After all, he reasoned, the man was in a hospital. He had bled profusely and had not been expected to survive. He's alive, doing better than expected, but he has to be just hanging on. So, probably, was the woman. What was her name again? Chartier, he remembered.

Abruptly, he began to see this whole unfortunate situation in a much more optimistic light. He opened his eyes and grinned. He sat upright, dialed his secretary, and told her he would be out of touch for a while. Then he hung up and laughed quietly.

He could be at the hospital in an hour and a half, but there was no need to rush. Like leashed dogs, they weren't going anywhere. And it would be an easy job to finish them off himself.

## Chapter 20

Albert Winslow stood behind his desk and cursed. He kicked at the chair and squeaked out a whimper. He paced. His reputation, his authority, everything he valued – threatened! What would people say if they discovered it was him?

There it was, laid out on his desk. There in the bold, black letters of the early edition, and on the front page, no less! PREMIER EYES MINE BRIBERY CHARGES. Who could miss it? And they had a strong lead, it said!

Obviously, Jimmy Nolan was more reckless than he had first judged. He decided he must ask his friend to be more convincing next time, but what he needed right now was a plan, something to keep his cover and protect his position.

A diversion? Maybe that was it – shift the spotlight to someone else. And who better than that bastard Ceborro to take the rap. If he handled this right, he could make it appear that it was he himself who had saved the Indians from the mine. He'd be their indignant champion, and they'd christen him their savior. They'd probably even give him an honorary chiefmanship, or whatever they called it.

Fortunately, he already had half the plan. The College President had hesitated at first, but the promise of a hefty research grant, the threat of losing the standing analytical contract, and a few thousand for himself had brought him around very nicely.

*How unfortunate for Ceborro*, he smirked. The College's confirmation tests would prove the field results to be wrong, and, much to everyone's surprise, mercury, coming from the Sweet Bounty of course, would be found in the Conifer River. His Department would have no choice but to act. He'd banish this atrocity against human life and shut down the mine himself. He'd be everybody's hero.

Sure, there would be plenty of screaming from the House of Assembly – it wasn't everyday such a lucrative tax project was jerked out from under them. But one of Canada's finest First Nations People, he would say, had already died, and others would too if they resisted. The Department's report would prove it. No assemblyman would want that on his hands. They'd follow him like the children of Hamelin had followed the Pied Piper.

And that lady scientist – Chartier, was it? She would be given the lead role. She, who had given the Sweet Bounty her professional approval three years ago, would be the one to confirm the final, irrefutable evidence that the mine had contaminated the River, poisoned the Mi'kmaq, and killed Chief Jeddore after all. He smiled at the irony.

As for himself, he'd say Ceborro had deceived him, and he would expose the mine plan for what it was – a fraud. Once the Department's report was out, Ceborro could squeal as loud as he wanted. No one would believe a word.

But the business of the bribery investigation still ate at him. What if the diversion wasn't enough? What if the investigators kept coming? Cleverly, and unbeknownst to her, he had deposited the money in an account under his ill and elderly mother's name, but a thorough investigator might still trace it to him. Even the remotest connection to it could be a huge problem. At the least, he'd have to come up with some convincing explanation. At the worst ... well, that was unthinkable. He could lose everything!

He sat down, swiveled his chair to face the Atlantic, crossed his ankles, and clasped his hands on top of his head. He needed a plan. Whatever he did, he had to do it quickly, before the investigators got too close. His left foot tapped nervously against his right.

And then it came to him. He decided the money and the account would just have to disappear for a while. Alas, his dear, doddering mother, once remarried then divorced again, had no one else in this world. Her youth long spent, by an unfortunate turn of fate her illness would be diagnosed as rare and fatal. Power of attorney would place her future in the hands of her devoted son and caretaker, Albert Winslow. Social medicine would fail to cover the cost of experimental treatment and the expenses would drain her account. Tsk, there would be nothing else he could do.

With that, he sat upright and smoothed an unruly strand of hair across a high, bald forehead. Only a few things remained to be done. The first was to order his investigators to hold Ceborro until the RCMP could lock him up. The second was to get the incriminating test results into a press release. The third was to empty that account.

He lifted his phone to call his secretary in. While he waited for her to answer, he congratulated himself with a smug, jowly grin. At last, this would be the end of that cocky, Puerto Rican bastard Ceborro.

## Chapter 21

"He seems to be coming around now, doctor," I heard. I blinked open my eyes in time to see a blurry white uniform step out of my view.

I found myself in a small room lying on my back in a bed with silver rails all around. My arms rested at my sides on top of a sheet that covered me to the chest. A clear plastic tube ran under a side-rail and disappeared under a swatch of tape on the back of my left hand. A padded collar constrained my head and facial bandages blocked my peripheral vision. A long wire ran from the clip on my right index finger to something behind me, and a rhythmic 'beep' kept perfect time with the throbbing in my head.

Into view at my feet came a dark-skinned, thirty-something man in a blue scrub jacket. He was tall and gaunt with large, bony hands and lanky arms. Here and there unruly sprigs of coarse, black hair burst free of the thin, blue cap unable to hold them in place. With his hands on the foot rail, he leaned into locked elbows, letting the ends of a stethoscope dangle freely in front of his shoulders. Angular features carried a friendly smile.

"Welcome to the living, Mr. Joe," he said. "I'm Doctor Garrett. For a while there, we thought you might leave us."

Something clicked behind my head and the beeping stopped. I inhaled to speak and felt a stinging pain in my chest. I winced and quickly released my breath.

"You had a nasty accident," he continued. "You'll recover very nicely, but you gave us all a fright."

I struggled to remember. "Where … am … ?"

"Central Regional Newfoundland Health Care Centre, officially. Grand Falls-Windsor hospital. RCMP found you and Ms. Chartier 37 hours ago, off the road about 15 kilometers south of here beside Great Rattling Brook. Nearly in it, I'd say. Lucky you weren't, you'd both have drowned. The car's a mess. Back end's all bashed in."

"Thirty seven hours … what day is it?"

"Friday, about noon. Ambulance brought you in Wednesday night."

"Wednesday night …" I fought to remember, but the images weren't coming. Then, unpredictably, a solitary recollection flashed. "Anna," I asked, "where's Anna?"

"Ms. Chartier? In another ward, and faring rather well, actually. She suffered a broken femur and some internal bruising, but we patched her up yesterday. She's been motoring around in her wheelchair all morning, the nurses can't seem to keep her still."

I tried to sit up but I felt that sting in my chest again and I was weak. I relaxed back into my bed with a grunt.

"Easy, Mr. Joe. You're not in a condition to be going anywhere on your own yet. Your CT scan says you sustained two broken ribs and a head injury, you've been comatose since the accident, and facial bleeding caused you to lose a lot of blood. We stitched you up and you'll heal in time, but we need to keep a close eye on you for a few days. And you need rest.

"The cervical collar is a precaution against whiplash," he added, "it seems you sat a little taller than the headrest. If you're feeling no neck pain by this afternoon, we'll take it off and the nurses will help you out of bed for a little stroll around the room."

Just then, he turned his head toward the door. He rose up to his full height and looked back at me with a broad grin. "Well, speak of the devil. You have company, Mr. Joe," he said and he stepped aside.

A leg, cast to the hip in white plaster and jutting horizontally, entered my field of view from the right. It was followed by a woman who turned her wheelchair to smile directly at me. It was Anna. "Bonjour, Cher Peter!" she exclaimed, "I was informed you were awake and I decided I must see this for myself. I was frightened I might not see you again!"

As the doctor left the room, a few random memories of the accident began to trickle back. "Anna ... it's nice to hear your voice. I ..." But before I could say more, there was a rap at the door, and Anna turned to look.

"Mr. Joe? Ms. Chartier?" asked a male voice.

"Oui?" responded Anna.

"Constable Pierce, RCMP. I was told I might find you both here. Would you mind answering a few questions for my report?"

## The Sweet Bounty

Anna looked at me, awaiting some signal this would be OK. I nodded that it was, and she motioned for him to sit in the chair beside the foot of the bed. I turned my head as best I could to see a man dressed in the traditional Scarlet Serge, replete with the Boss-of-the-Plains Stetson. He was older and slightly overweight, with closely cropped, mud-colored hair graying from the temples to behind the ears.

"I won't take up much of your time," he began as he sat down. He removed the Stetson and hung it on his knee, revealing a high forehead and a buzz cut. He flipped open a small, black notebook and removed a pen from the fold, leaned slightly forward with the pad on his lap, and poised his hand to write. "Now then," he resumed as he looked from Anna to me and back again, "can either of you describe the other vehicle?"

Anna's brow rose and her eyes widened. A smile took her face. "You are joking, are you not, Monsieur? There was no other vehicle," she said.

Now memories of the accident began pouring in. "She's correct," I said. "It was a thunderstorm, a flash flood, and caribou."

"I swerved to miss them," added Anna, "but there were too many. We spun backwards and collided with them in reverse."

"Caribou and a thunderstorm?" he quizzed.

"Yes," said Anna, "a whole herd of them. It rained so hard we did not see them until we were already too close. So many it was not possible to miss them."

He stopped writing and gave us a puzzled look. "Thunderstorm and caribou," he repeated.

"Yes, sir," I responded.

He sat back in his chair and looked at us in silence for a moment. His face acquired the accusing look of an investigator confronted by suspicious facts.

"You must know how unlikely that sounds," he said finally. "The herd stays well south of here this time of year. We might get three thunderstorms in an entire year in Newfoundland, and the season for them is long past. No reports of caribou in the area, no signs of them were found at the scene. No rain of any sort in the weather reports."

He took a long pause to size up our tale, as if trying to decide whether we had something to hide. Then, apparently having decided we didn't, he suggested, "Perhaps you imagined them? Sometimes our minds play tricks at night."

Anna and I exchanged glances again. She was incredulous, but even I would have questioned the story I heard us tell him.

"But that is what happened, Monsieur," Anna confirmed with assurance. "I saw them." She turned to me. "We both saw them."

"The evidence at the scene points to a hit and run." he said. "Our best guess is you were struck from behind at high speed by a larger vehicle. No sign it slowed down as it approached. It probably sustained only minor damage and was able to continue on. We're looking for such a vehicle now."

"That cannot be, Monsieur!" Anna protested.

The accident was one more strange addition to a long course of equally strange events – the plate of wax and ash, the pots bearing my godfather's name, the encounter with Wears Loafers, Young Footprint Woman – and I was beginning to wonder if they were all pieces of the same puzzle. I decided it was best to not challenge the Constable's assertion until I knew more. "Anna, "I said, "maybe the Constable is right. It was late and we were tired. Maybe we did imagine things."

Anna shot me a scorching look, and she was about to unleash her contempt when I winked. I worried whether she would take the hint, but I was rewarded when her face relaxed, though suspicion remained in her eyes and she hesitated. "Yes ..." she said cautiously, "maybe the Constable is correct." Slowly she turned her head toward him, her eyes lagging behind, still trying to see the intention behind my words.

"Will that be all?" she said, her eyes now focused on him. It was more a declaration than a question.

The Constable reinserted his pen into the fold and closed the notebook. "Yes ma'am," he said, "I believe so. May I call you later if I have any other questions?"

"Oui, you have my number?"

"Yes, I retrieved it from your cell phone when looking for identification."

"Very well, then I have a question for you, Monsieur," Anna said. "I carried some valuable belongings in my car. Did any of them survive?"

"Oh, yes, I nearly forgot," he said, and he bent to retrieve some articles from a large, black plastic bag. "Only these." He held up a purse that Anna recognized as hers, then proffered her waders and a dented, black vinyl case. "I'm sorry, everything else of value was destroyed."

Anna reached for the case, placed it on her lap, and opened it. Her eyes grew wide. "How very strange,

Peter. Look." She tilted up the open case for me to see. "Our samples, they are intact."

"Well, if there is nothing more, I'll take my leave," the Constable said and he nodded to each of us in turn. "Mr. Joe ... Ms. Chartier ... good day, and thank you for your time." He returned the Stetson to its customary place and rose. Anna nodded back, and he left the room.

As soon as he was gone, Anna snapped her attention back to me. Her eyes glared. "And what was that about, Peter?" she scolded, referring to the sudden change of story.

"About the supernatural," I answered.

"What?" Her curiosity got the best of her ire, and her face relaxed a little.

"Think about it, Anna. What happened to us would sound preposterous to just about anyone but us. The Constable was right. Caribou rarely stray from their seasonal range, especially as a herd, and Newfoundland rarely sees a thunderstorm, especially at this time of year. Maybe it really did happen just as we remember it, but to anyone else it would be a stretch.

"The plate of wax, the pots in the burial ground – maybe they're why my godfather died and the other tribal members with the same symptoms are still living. Were we the victims of a something supernatural, too? I don't know. It's all too surreal to believe, but it's too coincidental to ignore. I only know that history abounds with events that rational people can't explain. Who can say ours wasn't one of them?"

Anna screwed up her face again, and I could see she was having difficulty with my line of reasoning. "You mean the evil santa-whatever forces caused our accident and wiped away all the evidence, don't you,

Peter?"

"Santeria," I corrected, "and yes, I do."

"And do they make you imagine the pain in your ribs, the bandages on your face, this cast on my leg?" She rapped on it with the knuckles of her right hand. "These are real, Peter! I believe what my senses tell me, and they tell me it is far more likely the caribou were off track and we experienced a freak thunderstorm!"

I was about to elaborate on my own senses when a robust-bodied nurse with a square face and short, graying hair appeared at the door. "Time for our bath, Mr. Joe," she said in a gruff but musical voice. She presented Anna with a lingering smile that insisted on privacy. It didn't occur to Bath Nurse she might be interrupting something.

"I was just leaving," Anna said hotly. She pulled her purse, the waders, and the vinyl case into her lap and wheeled herself out of the room.

With Anna's wheels barely through the door, Bath Nurse closed it behind her, turned to me, and clasped her hands in front of her chest. "Well then, Mr. Joe. Are we ready?"

\* \* \* \*

Dr. Annamarie Chartier rolled herself down the hall to her own room and stopped beside her bed. She offloaded the belongings returned to her by the Constable and sighed deeply. She was frustrated by Peter's fixation on the supernatural, but she decided to deal with that later when her reaction was not so visceral. Right now, she wanted to focus on what she understood well, and that meant getting those samples analyzed as soon as possible.

She removed the cell phone from her purse, flipped it open, and held *End* for the required three seconds. After its pre-programmed interval, it chimed its welcome and notified her she had missed four callers and had an equal number of new messages waiting.

She didn't recognize the second and third numbers but noticed they were the same. The first was her office – probably wondering when she'd return – and the fourth was Christa calling from the Exploits River water quality lab. She wondered why Christa would be calling at all.

Christa was a transplanted California girl who sought something a little more rugged and self-enriching than Burbank. She was freshly out of a Master's program, but she was both a highly experienced chemist and a capable equipment technician who solved her own problems quite well by herself. She was a little too flamboyant and casual for Annamarie's taste, but that was a small price for such a rare find.

Annamarie Chartier cleared her missed messages and autodialed her voice mailbox. She keyed in her password and listened.

The first message was indeed from her office, her Department secretary to be exact. It said she would take notes for her at Monday's staff meeting if Annamarie wouldn't be back in time ... again. Annamarie caught the sarcasm in the 'again' and decided she owed her secretary lunch or maybe flowers. Then she pressed *7* to erase the message.

The next two messages were from Jimmy Nolan, trying to reach Peter. The first one said the Ministry had just launched a surprise investigation at the Sweet Bounty mine, something about permit violations and waste discharged to the Conifer River. The second told her the Premier ordered an investigation into the bribery surrounding the Sweet Bounty and it was probably Minister Winslow taking the money.

She stopped to think about both of those messages. They confirmed for her what she had seen with her own eyes, and she now realized just how well deceived she had been. Her self-assuredness flagged. How could she have been so naive three years ago? She wondered if the heap liners had failed prematurely, or if maybe there just weren't any liners at all. Whatever the situation, she was thinking Jimmy might be right about the mercury all along, and it now seemed more important than ever to have those samples analyzed.

Which took her to Christa's message, the one she worried about most. It told her that Christa had been called back to Corner Brook for some unexpected work. Some last minute, rush analyses, she had said, by order of the College President. She would be gone for a week and worried the Exploits River samples would exceed their holding times. She asked Annamarie to call her as soon as she could.

Annamarie deleted that message, but she was troubled on two counts. If the Exploits samples exceeded their holding times, they would, in analytical terms, expire and have to be collected again. That meant more expenses against an already over-budget grant and a serious delay on the final report. She would have to call the grantor with an unwelcome explanation for a second time this month. She dreaded that call.

But it also meant there was no one at the lab to analyze the Conifer River samples. They had a holding time, too, and two of those days had already passed. How long would Christa be gone? A week, she remembered, and she quickly checked her call log. Christa left her message on Wednesday. Today was Friday, and that meant Christa would be gone at least five more days.

She did some quick math. Still plenty of time left, she determined, but only if Christa returned on time, and only if everything went perfectly at both labs. If Christa ran into equipment problems, and they were the norm in these days of tight university budgets, that would be it – she would have to collect the Conifer River samples all over again.

She? Who was she kidding? She, Annamarie Chartier, would crank herself across the Conifer in that rocking, tipping, swinging cable car, walk the mile and a half to return with new samples, then cross the Conifer again? She with her acrophobia, she with the smashed up MG, she with a leg in a cast? Her throat tightened and pushed out an uncomfortable squeak.

She was just about to call Christa when the phone rang in her hand. The tiny screen identified it as the Exploits lab. She held it to her ear hopefully. "Christa?"

Yes, it was Christa. Annamarie listened as Christa explained how she had enlisted the help of three other analysts to help her with the Corner Brook work, and how she talked one of them into coming back to Grand Falls-Windsor with her to help out with the Exploits samples, too. They had arrived an hour ago and had already fired up the lab.

"Oh, how wonderful!" said Annamarie. *Christa always finds a way*, she marveled with a smile. Then she added that she had a special priority request for her, and could Christa come get the samples right away.

"Sure, Doc. Where are you?"

"Central Regional Health Care Centre. Meet me in the lobby."

"You mean the hospital?" she inflected with surprise.

"Yes, Christa, I'll explain when you get here."

"OK, Doc. It was weird at the College this week, too. The Prez had a cat over this special job. See you in a frac." Then she hung up.

Annamarie breathed out a long sigh as she closed her cell phone. She was suddenly relieved, and she now felt she could talk to Peter about his fixation rationally. And she would tell him about the messages from Jimmy, too.

But there was one more call to make first, a call to Pierre Martin at the Centre for Chronic Disease Prevention and Control in Ottawa. It was time to follow up on that autopsy, time to learn if methyl mercury killed Chief Jeddore.

\* \* \* \*

I was cleaner and I felt better, but it had not been a comfortable experience. It was clear Bath Nurse didn't mind, but I didn't like being washed by a stranger. I wondered if I would have to endure that humiliation again before I left this place.

Glad it was over, I remembered Mac was still waiting for my call, probably worried why I hadn't already called him. I carefully leaned to the shelf beside my bed, pulled the telephone to my lap, and dialed my office-mate at Concordia. It was time to learn if Santeria curses killed my godfather.

## Chapter 22

Phhhhhhtt. The sound of automatic sliding-glass doors opening caught Annamarie Chartier's attention, and she lifted her eyes from the magazine in her lap. Dressed in a hospital robe and sitting in a wheelchair, she watched from across the nearly empty lobby.

An elderly man, hunched, thin haired, and using a walker, inched his way through the doors with leaden slowness. Close beside him walked a heavy woman of about the same age, the fluorescent lights reflecting back the pale blue of her over-treated gray hair. She mumbled something to her husband as they passed through the doors, and he stopped all motion as he turned toward her. Without being asked, she faced him directly and repeated herself, after which he gave a slow nod of his head and resumed his snail-like progress. Behind them, a young woman gave an impatient roll of her eyes.

Eventually, the elderly couple labored themselves to the right toward the reception counter. The young woman seized this opportunity and accelerated past them in a trot-skip.

## The Sweet Bounty

At five-feet-three, she was a slight, pixie-faced blonde of 26 years, wearing shortly cropped hair tipped in the colors of the rainbow.

"Nice wheels, Doc. What's up with the cast?" the young woman said with a broad smile.

"It's nice to see you too, Christa," said Annamarie, unfazed.

"Sorry. It looks serious."

"It was very serious. Peter nearly died. The MG is a complete loss. Sit down, I have a lot to tell you."

"Oh my gawd," said Christa. She dragged an end table to Annamarie's side, sat down on it, and crossed her legs in patamasana. She raised her eyebrows, gave a worried half-smile, and cocked her head.

Annamarie began with her first encounter with Peter Joe and how a simple friendly offer embroiled her in an elaborate search for the cause of his godfather's death. What she wanted was to simply drop him off at the Reserve and grab a few quick samples to squelch a reporter's rumor before it acquired a life of its own. What she got was a complex and dangerous journey that sent her to this hospital and exposed a lie she had held as truth for over three years.

"He's Indian?" interrupted Christa.

"Yes. His godfather was like a father to him, they were very close."

"Handsome, too?"

"Yes, Christa, he is an attractive man, but I'm only trying to help him."

"Not hookin' up, huh? Is he here, too?"

Annamarie ignored the first question. "Yes, but his injuries are more serious. He was in a coma, cracked several ribs, and he lost a lot of blood. He'll need to be in care here for several days more."

"My gawd," Christa responded.

Annamarie continued with her story. She described how a train of government vans ran them off the road and into the brush on their way to what she only just learned was a Ministry investigation of the Sweet Bounty. She told her about the strange plate and the mysterious clay pots which Peter claimed were spells put on his godfather. The unnerving encounter with a man Peter called Wears Loafers who seemed, strangely, to be body-guarded by an armed man from the Ministry. The surprising discovery of mercury in her first Conifer River sample. Finding the Conifer channelized in concrete, seeing the open pit mine, which was supposed to have been a deep mine, and the devastation raging in its wake. The crash, the call to Pierre Martin, and, finally, the unsettling realization the Sweet Bounty, the mine on which she had staked her professional reputation only three years earlier, might actually have killed Chief Jeddore.

"And that, Christa, is what's up with the cast," she finished.

Christa's eyes were wide with amazement and her jaw hung open.

"Which brings me to these," Annamarie continued. She lifted up the dented vinyl case and set it on her lap. "The special request I mentioned." Already getting the picture, Christa nodded as Annamarie opened the case.

"These are from the Conifer River. I want you to run tests for all the standard indicators of mineral extraction – cyanide, sulfite, metals, pH, conductivity, you know the drill. I want a complete organic scan, too. In particular, I'm looking for methyl mercury. I want the lowest detection limits you can get, and I need the results as soon as possible. As in yesterday."

Now Christa's face became serious, and she acquired a business-like mien. She didn't answer, but the distance in her gaze said she was already in the lab, planning extractions and digestions, juggling analytical sequences, squeezing detection limits, mentally scheduling everything for the quickest possible result.

"Okay, Doc," she answered finally. "Here's the scoop. The ICP is already up, so Randall can run the metals in an hour. I can run cyanide at the same time. Methyl mercury and the organic scan will take a bit longer, but the two of us working together can have them to you later today. Will that do?"

Annamarie smiled. "Yes, Christa, that will do very nicely."

"Which means," Christa said, straightening herself upright as she spoke, "I'd better get movin' if I'm gonna do what I just said." She uncrossed her legs, slid off the table, and took the case from Annamarie's lap. "I'll call you as soon as I get results, Doc," she said. Then she turned and moved quickly toward the door with the sample case under her arm.

"Good day, Christa," Annamarie called after her.

Now, confident she would soon have proof enough to shut down the Sweet Bounty and put bully-man Wears Loafers in prison, Annamarie felt herself relax. A sudden desire for sleep overtook her. As she turned to wheel herself back to her room, the hospital doors closed behind Christa's disappearing shadow.

## EW Finke

\* \* \* \*

I'm five, lying on my back, doing exactly what I'm told. "Close your eyes," he says, "and just let them light." I pinch my eyes shut. My arms lie stiffly by my side, my fists clench in anticipation, and the grin on my face is big enough to stretch across the Atlantic. I wait just as he said, barely able to contain myself.

Then they come – the flutter of papery wings, more a light brush of air than audible. The faint tickle of feet, curled tongues unfurling at eyelids and nose. I scrunch up my face and giggle. "Shhhhh, and keep your eyes closed," he scolds softly.

We had just left our favorite spring hole but our creels were empty. We stopped for a rest on our way back, and now we lay head to head, my godfather and I, in ankle-high meadow grass. We're surrounded by lupines, thrift, blue-flag iris, ox-eye daisies, asters, and brown elfin butterflies by the hundreds. I hear the assiduous drone of bees working the dog rose and clover not far away.

"Now, open them, slowly," he says, but I don't. I want to feel how many, and, in my private darkness, I count probing butterfly tongues. Now I feel the brush of wings. More are coming, I think.

"Peter ... open your eyes," I hear, but I keep them closed and feel the gentle sweep of wings again on my cheek.

"Peter ..." I hear again, more insistently this time. But it's not his voice. It's someone else. Bewildered, I open my eyes and turn my head toward it. I see the blurred image of a woman, and she's brushing the soft, warm palm of her hand gently along the side of my face.

"Peter, can you wake?" she asks, and I recognize the voice. A blink clears the fuzziness of dream sleep and at last I see her clearly.

"Anna ... ," I began, but pellucid thought did not yet come freely. Her touch reminded me the facial bandages, the neck brace, and the IV had been removed, and I was thankful for the freedom. Her eyes tried to look only into mine, but they strayed and I watched them rove the sutures which one day will be rivulet scars. There was a caring in her presence I had not felt before. My hand moved instinctively to touch hers, our fingers entwined briefly, and then she gently pulled hers away.

"Peter, I have some news about your godfather," she said.

"So do I," I said, but as I did my eyes fell on the young woman with the painted hair standing beside her. Anna introduced her as Christa from the lab. She seemed quiet and subdued as she and I exchanged silent nods. I returned to Anna.

"But I want to hear your news first," I said.

Anna nodded. "Well, Peter, it is as Jimmy described ... sort of," she began.

"What do you mean, sort of?"

"My hunch was correct, it was Pierre Martin whom your Doctor McGovern consulted about your godfather's death. Monsieur Martin informed me the autopsy found many bare and tangled nerve fibrils in your godfather's brain and nervous system. Blood, hair, and brain tissue tests confirmed mercury was indeed throughout his body. Monsieur Martin is certain methyl mercury was responsible for your godfather's death. But the rest is not as one would expect, Peter."

"Which means what?" I asked.

Anna turned. "Christa, please tell Peter what you found in the lab."

That was Christa's cue to come alive, and I quickly learned I was mistaken about her. She spoke with an animated exuberance.

"Well, I don't have all the results Doc wanted yet, but what I have is ... unexpected."

I decided Doc must be Anna.

"I analyzed three samples, right? One Doc took from the bridge, that one's the farthest from the mine. One she took at the fence. And one by the canal, that's the one closest to the mine."

I was with her so far, and she went on.

"Okay, the first run was unremarkable. But I knew Doc was lookin' for something special. So I recalibrated the ICP to cut the QL by an order of magnitude. And, voilá, there it was."

"Voilá there was ... what?" I asked, totally confounded.

Christa was deadpan, like I was the one who had just concentrated the ICP by the magnitude, or whatever she said, and should have known. "Why, mercury, Mr. Joe. There was mercury." Then she continued. "But it's weird 'cause there's mercury in two of the samples, but not the third."

"Mercury in two of them, but not the third," I restated, somehow expecting it to make sense if I heard it in my own voice.

"Exactly, Mr. Joe. And guess which one didn't have it?"

I wondered how I would have even the slightest notion which one didn't have it, so I blurted out the one I thought least likely to not have it. "The one closest to the mine?" I ventured.

Christa's face took on a look of disappointment, and she rolled her eyes. I was surely wrong, and I readied to accept my upbraiding.

"Gosh, Mr. Joe. How did you know?"

"What?" I turned to Anna. "How can that be? If the mine is the source, why doesn't the closest sample have mercury in it?"

"That is precisely the point, Peter."

"But yet there's mercury in the River, in the other two samples," I objected.

Anna nodded, but it was Christa who answered. "Right, Mr. Joe. And that's the riddle, see?"

"No, I don't see. What riddle?"

Christa began to draw a picture in the air with her hands. "Okay, the river flows from up here to down here, see?" She illustrated by moving a hand from above her head down to her knees.

"Here's the mine," she continued. She held an open hand high overhead and moved it in a tight circle. "And here's the sample closest to the mine, the one right next to the canal. Call it sample A." She placed her other hand just below the circle of her first and made a fist. "No mercury here, right?"

I nodded.

Then she moved her first hand down and made a new fist at chest level. "And here's sample B, the one by the fence. There's mercury here."

Then she moved her high fist down to her waist. "And here's the third sample, C, farthest from the mine, by the bridge. There's mercury here, too.

"So, the riddle is ... how did the mercury get to B," fist at chest high again, "and C," fist at waist, "if it didn't come from A," fist overhead. Then she waited.

I still didn't get it.

She rolled her eyes again. "Gosh, Mr. Joe, the answer is it had to come from somewhere between A and B. So, what's between A and B? What's between the canal and the fence?" She paused again.

I lowered my eyes, thinking, trying to picture it. Then it dawned. My godfather and I had crossed it hundreds of times, and Anna and I had crossed it just two days ago. My eyes shot back up at Anna.

"The creek , remember? Pie'lik, Peter's Brook. It flows in from the southeast. Only part of it is on Sweet Bounty property, but that's where it joins the Conifer. What does that mean – the mine has contaminated Pie'lik?"

"I think not, Peter. There's more," responded Anna.

"More?"

Once again, Anna deferred to Christa.

"Here's the kicker, Mr. Joe. The Sweet Bounty's a cyanide leach operation, right? If those liners are leaking, cyanide ought to be in the river, too. Without cyanide, the mercury wouldn't be there. Follow?"

I nodded again.

"Right," she continued. "Well, guess which samples had no cyanide."

My previous strategy having been a success, I went there again. "The one closest to the mine," I offered with shaky confidence.

Christa giggled. "The envelope, please," she mimicked. "I'm so sorry, Mr. Joe, that answer is not correct. The correct answer is ... none. None of the samples had cyanide. No gold either," she added.

"None?" I asked with surprise.

"Zip, zero, nada. Houston, we are not go for lift-off."

"Let me see if I get this," I tried to summarize. "Mercury in the two samples farthest from the mine, and no cyanide or gold in any of them. Does that mean what I think it means?" I turned to Anna again.

She nodded. "I believe so, Peter. The mercury which killed your godfather did not come from the Sweet Bounty."

I had already reached that conclusion myself, but I was stunned by the incongruity – what my godfather feared most about the Sweet Bounty had actually killed him, yet the Sweet Bounty wasn't the source. Christa had rendered the most patent conclusion impossible. Where else could it have come from?

And what about the Santeria? In my bedridden conversation with Mac, he confirmed my suspicion – I had indeed found the remains of powerful curses under my godfather's steps and in the burial ground. How were they part of this?

I knew how to find the answer to only one of those questions, and it didn't take long to decide what had to happen next. I slowly pushed myself up to a sitting position, threw back the sheet, and swiveled my legs off the bed. I winced with the pain in my chest, but I stood for the first time in two days.

"Peter?" asked a puzzled Anna. "What are you doing?"

"Ladies, if you will excuse me, I'll be getting dressed now. The Doctor promised me a walk and I'm going to take it. All the way to the caribou snag and Pie'lik."

Anna objected. "Are you crazy, Peter? You are not able to travel yet! Not to mention climb the tower and crank that ridiculous little tram across the River! And you have no car!"

But I was resolute. "Anna, if your Pierre Martin is right, I need to find the source of that mercury and stop it. He said it's already killed my godfather. It's killing other members of my Tribe and they don't even know why they're dying. If my godfather were here now, he would do everything within his means to protect them. But he's not, and they don't yet know how to protect themselves."

I was stopped mid-thought by my own words, their meaning just now comprehended. Suddenly, my godfather's death – his leaving – became crystal clear. He didn't leave *me*. As leader of his People, he lived for *them*, and it was now stunningly clear how much of his life he was willing to give them. In their cause, he made the greatest of sacrifices for a higher purpose!

A promise fatefully made near the very edge of memory flashed, and I sighed.

"My godfather told me I might one day be called to place the welfare of The People before my own," I explained, "and he asked what I would do. I was just eight then. Do you know what I said to him? I said 'Nkekkunit Abram, I would do the best thing, just like you would do.'"

"And ...," I stammered, stunned by the awakening, "it now seems exactly as he predicted. I am asked to do the best thing, just as he would have done. Someone has to help them, and right now ... I'm the only one who can."

As if she suddenly realized some things simply must be done, Anna acquired a resigned expression that told me she would be saying no more. Quietly, she wheeled closer, took my hand, and pulled me gently down. I crouched beside her. With her hands on my shoulders, she leaned over and kissed me lightly on the cheek. "Then you must go, Peter. But please be careful."

The warmth of her hand once again alongside my face held me fast. Only half aware, I asked Christa if I could use her car.

"Absolutely, Mr. Joe. I can use the college car for a few days," Christa answered as I turned my head toward her.

From her pocket she removed a string of bright beads in the shape of a rosary and just as long. At the end, where I might have expected a cross, hung a little Buddha and four keys. She removed one and presented it to me. Then she wrinkled up her nose. "The speedometer and the wipers are broke ... hold in the gear thingy on the uphills ... and, umm, steer left."

Her words drew an amused smile from me, and I thanked her.

Then together they left the room. As Christa closed the door after them I heard her whisper to Anna. "Not hookin' up, huh Doc?"

\* \* \* \*

On the fourth floor of the Confederation Building, East Block, a Department of Justice telephone rang. A tall, wiry man who had been leaning back onto the two rear legs of his chair sat suddenly upright, planting all four legs of the chair firmly on the floor. He pulled the phone toward himself and lifted the handset. "Justice. Special Agent Barnes," he said. His other hand readied itself to take notes.

Barnes listened as the caller, describing himself as an account manager at Bank of St. John's, said he had seen the Telegraph article about an alleged bribery.

"And?" said Barnes.

The caller told Barnes that a man, a Minister he recognized, had produced an irregular-looking power of attorney for his mother and asked for a certified bank draft in the amount of the entire account. "'For medical expenses', he said. The teller told him she needed a clearance first, then she notified me."

"How much?" Barnes pursued.

"$600,000 ... and change," the account manager answered. "Should I stall him?"

Barnes didn't hesitate. "I'll be right there."

## Chapter 23

Phhhhhhtt. The automatic sliding-glass doors of the hospital opened again, and in walked a confident Paul Ceborro. He stopped just inside and ran the fingers of one hand through his hair as he searched the lobby. His eyes finally settled on the admissions counter and he strode calmly to his right.

Occupied with some matter of paperwork he considered a senseless triviality, the man at the desk behind the counter didn't notice his visitor at first. The subtle clearing of a throat caught his attention, and he peered up dispassionately over his readers.

"May I help you?" he asked plainly.

"You may, sir," Paul Ceborro said pleasantly. "Where might I find my dear friends Peter Joe and Annamarie Chartier?"

"Name and address."

"Paul Ceborro, Hermitage."

"Spell, please."

"C-e-b-o-r-r-o."

"One moment."

The man began filling in the blanks of a blue slip

of paper, mumbling as he did. "C-e-b-o-r-r-o ... Herm ... see ... Peter ... Joe ... Annam ... Chartier."

Then he handed it up. "Sign there."

Paul Ceborro signed. The man took the slip and separated a yellow copy, which he handed back. "Keep that with you. The room numbers are there."

Without rising, the man leaned over his desk, stretched his right arm out to his side, and pointed. "Follow the signs to C Ward. Left, then right, another right, then left again." Then he sat back and returned to his paperwork.

Paul thanked him graciously and started down the hallway, smiling broadly as he went.

* * * *

"Doc ... Hey, Doc."

Annamarie Chartier stirred awake from the second nap of her day. Still dazed, she lifted her head toward the persistent voice beckoning her from the bedside.

"Wake up, Doc. You gotta hear this."

Annamarie settled back, her head falling deep into the pillow. "Ouí, I am listening." She rubbed the sleep out of her eyes as Christa began.

"Randall finished the rest of the tests and guess what. The mercury in those two samples? It's all methyl mercury, almost to the picogram. Just like what we expected, right? But get this. All the other organics were what I'd naturally expect to find in a river ... except one, and you'll never guess what it is."

Annamarie sighed quietly. She was neither in the mood nor alert enough for parlor games. "Christa, I'm ..."

## The Sweet Bounty

"Okay, I'll just tell you." Christa paused for a moment, allowing Annamarie to acquire the proper amount of suspense before revealing her news.

"Are you ready?" she asked.

Annamarie tiresomely closed her eyes. "Yes, Christa, I'm ready."

"Okay, this is it. Methyl cobalamin." She paused again, waiting for the surprise to appear in Annamarie's reaction.

The sleepiness in Annamarie's head was suddenly gone. She pushed herself up onto an elbow, and her eyes grew wide. "Methyl cobalamin?"

"It's a form of ..." Christa began.

"Yes, I know," Annamarie interrupted.

Annamarie suddenly looked puzzled. "Christa, methyl cobalamin would not be found in the environment, nor would it be found in a mineral processing waste. Are you certain about this? This is not a mass spec out of calibration, or a dirty chromatographic column?"

"Nope, already double checked that. It's the same pattern too. It's in the samples farthest away from the mine and not in the closest. Just how we found the methyl mercury.

"So I did a little research in the on-line catalogues and journals." she continued. "Methyl cobalamin is one of the pre-cursors for making methyl mercury. Care to guess what the other one is?"

Annamarie thought for a moment. "Works in plain water," Christa hinted.

Annamarie nodded as the chemistry came to her, but again Christa didn't wait for her to answer. "And yes, we found that in the samples, too," she said. "Presto change-o, methyl mercury. Exactly what killed

Mr. Joe's godfather."

There was a silence as Annamarie contemplated that, but it took her only a second to realize what it meant. The expression on her face told Christa she got it.

"You're thinking what I'm thinking, aren't you," Christa asserted.

"I believe so, Christa. Someone intentionally put them there. Someone may be intentionally poisoning the Conifer River."

"'Exactly, Doc."

Suddenly, Annamarie remembered something. Her eyes drifted downward as the mystery quickly took on greater proportions. "So that's why she was there," she mumbled to herself.

"What?" asked Christa.

Annamarie returned her focus to Christa. "The fence, it was cut when Peter and I arrived there. Someone had been in before us – small boot prints, like a young woman's, Peter thought. That must be why!"

Sinister extensions of those thoughts began to dawn. "Whoever planted those chemicals knew the mine would be suspect when methyl mercury appeared in the Conifer River and Pjila'si Bay. Surely that person knew about the Mi'kmaq salmon, and knew the Mi'kmaq fished the Bay. Christa ... is it possible that person *wanted* someone to die!"

"That's how I see it, Doc. Our person is making their own Minimata Bay."

"Yes," Annamarie continued, "and I expect our person will go to great lengths to protect that secret."

Then it struck her. "My God ... Peter!" she cried out abruptly to Christa. "What if he is discovered there?"

Just then, the door snapped closed behind them and they jerked their heads around. There, towering in front of it was Paul Ceborro, his menacing smile seeming to fill the room. Before they could react, he pulled Christa backward against his chest, locked her arms behind her back, and widened his hand across her throat, easily covering both carotid arteries with a thumb and two fingers. A simple, firm squeeze would halt the flow of blood and starve her brain of oxygen in as little as four seconds.

"And exactly *where* might Peter Joe be discovered, ladies?"

\* \* \* \*

Phhhhhhtt. The sliding glass doors admitted a young, fair-skinned and red-haired Jimmy Nolan. He searched anxiously for the admissions counter and rushed over when he found it.

The clerk sat with his back to Jimmy, prying at a recalcitrant file drawer with a letter knife. It snapped off at the handle while Jimmy waited for his attention. The clerk cursed out loud.

"Pardon me, sir," Jimmy said when the stream of obscenities stopped, surprised his own words came out so easily.

The man spun in his chair, nudged his readers back onto his nose with an index finger, and peered over them at Jimmy. "Damn thing's always jammed," he cursed. "I've complained, but nobody seems to care 'round here." He tossed the broken piece of letter knife into a trash can. "What's on your mind, sonny?"

"Peter Joe and Annamarie Chartier, are they here? Are they still alive?"

The man gave Jimmy a blank stare. "Well, nobody told me they stopped breathin'," he said dryly, "so I suppose they are. You a friend like that other fella looking for them? They seem to have a lot of friends. Sombrero, or Sebormo, maybe ... never heard a name like that around here before, have you?"

Jimmy shrugged.

"Well, whatever. Name and address."

"Mine?"

"Ain't no one else standin' beside you."

"Jimmy Nolan, St. John's."

The man filled out the blanks of another slip of blue paper and asked Jimmy to sign. He did, and the man separated the yellow copy and handed it to him. Jimmy examined it.

Without rising, the man stretched out his right arm and pointed as he had done earlier. "Keep that with you, it has the room numbers. Follow the signs to C Ward. Left, then right, another right, then left again," he repeated for the second time today.

Jimmy was quickly on his way when he called back to the man at the counter. "Thanks!"

A few minutes later, Jimmy poked his head out of the room and double-checked the number beside the door just to be sure he was in the right place. An obviously used hospital gown lay rumpled on the unmade bed, but the closet and bed were empty and Peter Joe was not there. *Had he been transferred? Discharged? Had he died after all?*

Jimmy snagged a passing nurse. "Ma'am, I'm looking for Peter Joe. Is this the room?"

The nurse nodded and stepped in. "Now that's very strange," she said with a bewildered look. "He was here earlier. No one told me he was to be discharged.

Wait here, I'll check the room roster."

Jimmy smiled but he didn't wait for her to return. He went instead to the other room number on his yellow slip of paper.

The door was closed and he knocked. He waited the polite interval, and then knocked again. Still no answer came so he cracked the door. "Hello?" he called as it drifted open.

The two bodies lay still and lifeless. He didn't recognize the one with the painted hair lying on the floor, but he was sure the other one, the one on the bed with half her face and hair buried in the bloody pillow, was Dr. Annamarie Chartier. He rushed to her and turned her head to see if she was still alive. His stomach squirmed nauseously as he peeled the pillow from her skin. She was still breathing, but her face was deeply bruised and caked with brownish, sticky blood. She had bled from a ragged gash running from the corner of her eye almost to her ear. She had been backhanded, he decided, or struck with something hard, probably more than once.

He quickly checked the lady with the painted hair. There were no obvious injuries and no bleeding, so he returned to Annamarie. He pressed at the call button for help, but it made only an empty click. The phone was dead, too, its cord ripped from the wall.

"Dr. Chartier!" He tried to rouse her. "Can you hear me?" He shook her shoulder. "Dr. Chartier!"

She stirred. "Unnngggh," came from her throat.

"Dr. Chartier, what happened? Who did this?"

"Mmmhh ... " she struggled, on the barest edge of consciousness. "... Man ... said ... he'd kill ..." Then she drifted away.

"Dr. Chartier, where's Peter?" he asked, but the question was too late. She was already unconscious again. As he covered her to the shoulders with a blanket from the foot of the bed, he heard a faint cough.

"He's ... gone," said a voice.

He turned to see the painted-hair woman trying to rise up onto an elbow. He knelt beside her and cradled her against his torso to a sitting position.

"What happened? Do you know where Peter is?" he asked.

She coughed again and rubbed at the soreness on her throat. She squinted to break the blurriness in her vision. "Yeah ... the mine," she said. She tried to clear the hoarseness from her voice, but the sudden rush of air rasped at her throat and she winced. She took a deep, slow breath.

"The creek inside the fence," she continued. "That's where it came from."

"Where what came from?" urged Jimmy.

"The mercury ... the mercury that killed Mr. Joe's godfather. I gave him my car ... he went there to find it. A caribou snag and a creek, I heard him say.

She drew in another breath and tried to drive away the dizziness. "That man, he said Mr. Joe was meddling where he ought not to be, like this Chief Jedder guy, and he ... was gonna find Peter and kill him. I told her not to tell him where Mr. Joe went, no matter what he did to me. Doc threatened to call for help, but then all I remember is ... I felt this pressure build in my head and everything got black. He ... he musta beat it out of her while I was passed out.

"He doesn't know ..." she wheezed.

"What?" Jimmy asked.

## The Sweet Bounty

"Mr. Joe ... he doesn't know that ... that someone is poisoning the river on purpose."

Jimmy eased himself up, helped her into a chair, and wrapped her with a blanket he found on a closet shelf. "Wait here," he said as he pulled it around her, "I'm going for help."

Christa nodded dizzily as Jimmy hurried out of the room.

A few minutes later, a team of doctors and nurses rushed in and began tending to Annamarie and Christa. But Jimmy wasn't with them, and he didn't come back.

\* \* \* \*

The faded-red, rusted out Stanza coughed and sputtered and climbed lethargically while I held the pedal to the floor and 'the gear thingy' in first as Christa had instructed. For a while, I didn't think I would top that hill, but I was well past the Sweet Bounty now and I prepared to turn off at the caribou snag. The motor popped and released a puff of blue exhaust as I backed off the pedal, then announced its further deceleration with a lingering gurgle. I turned into the grass, parked beside the snag, and turned off the key. The motor coughed two more times, then died.

I sat for a moment, bracing myself for the pain of getting out. After a deep breath, I decided it was time to try. Sliding the seat back as far as it would go, I lifted out my left leg first, then followed with my right. With a hand on the door and one on the jamb, I tipped my weight forward, leaning and pulling at the same time. It was arduous and my ribs ached with each movement, but I was standing at last.

After another deep breath, I started through the brush and grass. In ten minutes, I would be at the gauging station, ready to cross the Conifer once again. The worst pain was yet to come.

* * * *

As Special Agent Barnes led him from the bank in handcuffs, Minister Albert Winslow wondered what bases he hadn't covered. He thought about the falsified test results he wouldn't publish, the incriminating press release he wouldn't issue, the speech to the Assembly he wouldn't deliver, and the Mi'kmaw chiefmanship he'd never receive.

But mostly, he cursed that damn Puerto Rican bastard Paul Ceborro.

## Chapter 24

When my godfather and I had first discovered the key, it became my boyhood mind's assignment to wonder if it had always been there, and if anyone else knew about it. I never answered those questions, and at some point since then it no longer mattered. Until now, that is. Now, I found myself wondering how Young Footprint Woman had come upon it, and if she was the only other one who had.

A cold rain had fallen on my way to the gauging station, and I shivered under a sky of low, threatening clouds. Those two questions swarmed in my head as I unlocked and pushed open the gate. I had just slipped the key into my pocket when a limb rustled behind me. I turned in time to see a sparrow flit from its perch in favor of a higher branch.

"You won't mind if I ride along, will you?" I heard. It wasn't a question, and the voice was icy and haltingly familiar. I turned. There, beside the sparrow's tree, stood Anna's bully, Wears Loafers, with a wide, sinister grin on his face. His hand held a gun.

"Climb!" I was immediately commanded, and

he waved the muzzle like a threatening, metallic finger, exhorting me upward. For a fleeting moment, I wondered how broken ribs would fare in a contest with this man, but prior experience said he was no man to toy with, and the odds were definitely not in my favor.

Climbing the ladder sent waves of stinging pain across my chest, as if I had been shot with splintered glass, and I stopped and gasped for a miserly breath at each rung. More than once I felt the barrel jammed into my calf as he lost patience below me. "Move it!" he ordered.

After fifteen unendurable steps up, I stood on the platform and filled my lungs, thankful I had made it this far, but at the same time wishing I had never come back. I entertained the thought of planting my boot in his face as his head rose above the platform, hurtling him to the ground below. But he was adept at climbing one-handed and he kept the gun trained on me at all times. He ordered me away.

Inside the car, he leaned against the side opposite me. "Take us across, Indian Boy," he said.

It was a vile taunt, intended, I suppose, to instill fear. But I was determined not to be pulled into his game, and I drew in a long breath. I had to get past this encounter with Wears Loafers unscathed and find the mercury. But at this particular moment, I had no idea how I would do that.

I released the anchor hook and brake. The car swung free on its creaking pivot and rolled easily along the cable, coming to rest at mid-river just as it had done for me so many times before. But now the easy part was over, and I dreaded what was to come. I stalled for time, braced for new pain, and tried to fathom my captor's intentions. He stared back at me with a malevolent sneer, as if at last avenging some lifelong grievance, a look made even more disconcerting by our unsteady sway over the churning water below.

"Mind telling me what this is about?" I asked.

"When it fancies me," he simpered. "Crank."

Unable to stall any longer, I did as he said and reached up slowly to fold down the handles. I willed my arms to turn the wheel, but my chest rebelled again and I grimaced with pain.

He laughed out loud at my agony and taunted me again. "Shoulda died when you were given the chance, Indian Boy. You'd have saved us both a lot of trouble."

My heart rose into my throat. *Did he mean the collision? How did he know about it? Was I supposed to die then? Is that what this hijacking is about?*

"I said crank!" he shouted.

I turned harder against the uphill slope and the pain racked my body, as if every muscle worked to dismantle every bone. Slowly, the handles began to move in their engineered circle and we inched along. Excruciating minutes later, we bumped the other tower and I set the brake. I collapsed with the pain onto one knee, thankful the worst was over.

Wears Loafers climbed onto the platform and motioned me out, waving the muzzle again. "On the ladder, three rungs down, stop," he ordered.

He watched as I backed over the edge and stepped down to the designated rung. "Far enough," he said, and he held the gun at my head, point blank. "Not an inch either way."

I nodded my acquiescence, wondering what he would do next.

He turned to the car, released the wheel brake, and shoved it back across the river with his foot. I watched helplessly as it rolled almost to the other tower. There it stopped, swinging emptily in place, some protruding nub of cable preventing it from rolling back to the middle.

In that singular moment, a cold, foreboding wetness coursed over me and I shook uncontrollably, my fate suddenly understood. I was the caribou calf unsteady on new legs. He was the wolf in pursuit. Somewhere on this side of the river, he meant for me to die.

* * * *

Directly across from the birch caribou snag, a car slowed and eased off the road, rolling softly in the gravel as it came to a quiet stop. Jimmy Nolan turned off the motor. Behind dark sunglasses, he scanned the opposite side for signs of Peter and the man out to kill him. He could see no one, but it was clear someone had been there. The grass was flattened into narrow tracks on the old macadam, and unless he missed his guess he would find two cars parked beside the snag.

He pulled the .22 caliber Bearcat out of the bag on the seat beside him and turned it in his hand. It was such a small, light weapon, he noticed for the first time, not very threatening. But Peter's life was in danger, and if ever there was a time he would need it, this was it. He loaded the cylinder with six of the small bullets and clicked it into the frame.

Climbing out, he slipped the gun into the torn side pocket of his mac and started across the road. But he stepped back quickly, just in time to dodge a dark gray van bearing the Provincial Coat of Arms as it hurtled by. "Damn government people too feckin' much in a hurry to watch where they're goin'," he cursed as he resumed.

On the other side, Jimmy keened his eyes, searching the grass as it soaked his pant legs and shoes with the new rain. Half of him prayed Peter had outwitted the man who came to kill him. The other half expected to see Peter laid out in the grass already dead, and the very thought of it made him sweat. Everything he had worked for would be gone – his story, his future, everything.

At the snag, he peered inside a faded, rusty-red sedan to see the back seats cluttered with clothes, makeup, a half-consumed bag of Fritos, and a pair of old sandals. *The painted-hair lady's car*, he decided. Next to the sedan stood a white Ford F150 pickup that looked like it had been new only yesterday.

He saw no sign of a struggle, no blood or bodies, only a faint, freshly made path through the wet grass and brush leading to the river. He breathed a sigh of relief, and he broke into a run. At least, he thought, Peter wasn't already dead. But he had no idea how he would rescue him if they were already on the other side of the River.

Minutes later, he was at the old gauging station and he stopped to catch his breath. The gate was open, just as he had worried it might be. But there was something unexpected about the cable, and he climbed the tower for a better look.

"Holy feck!" he cursed in panic. The cable car, which by his worst fear shouldn't have been there at all, *was* there, dangling in the river's breeze about 25 feet away. He knew instantly that someone had shoved it back, and since Peter would have had no reason to do that, the man must have forced Peter across, then severed his way back. It confirmed for him that the man after Peter indeed intended to kill him on the other side.

He knew had to get into that car. But how? It wasn't far, but for all Jimmy Nolan could do from where he stood, it may as well have been a mile. He backed down the tower and searched frantically for a branch to snag it, thinking he could pull it toward him, but everything he found was too short or way too flimsy.

He went to the cabin and looked through a window beside the door, hands cupped around his eyes, straining to use the window's meager light and scanning for anything that could help. As his eyes adjusted, he saw a few metal tools hanging from the wall. Webs of dead flies filled the corners of the cabin, partially opened cardboard boxes were scattered on the floor, and dusty papers with curled corners littered an equally dusty desk beside a metal cot frame.

Suddenly his eyes fixed on something, and he wondered. Could he do it? It would be dangerous, something he had seen done only in a movie, but he was rapidly running out of time.

With a heavy, sharp-edged rock, he pounded at the padlock until the hasp broke free of the soft wood. The knob turned easily, but he had to shoulder the door to open it. Inside, he picked a rusted length of chain from the wall. Then he ran back to the tower.

Now Jimmy stood on the platform and carefully studied his next move. Gripping one end of the chain in his right hand, he let the loose end drop to his feet. He lifted his eyes to the cable overhead, then, in a wide and graceful arc, he swung the free end up and over the cable. But he had misjudged the chain's weight and swung too hard, and he watched in frustration as it wrapped itself whip-like around the cable. With a sigh, he pulled on the end still in his hand. It uncurled itself and fell back to the platform.

This time, he took the free end in his left hand and balled the rest of it in his right. It was heavy and awkward as he hefted it. He raised his head again, carefully weighed the distance, and heaved the balled chain upward. It rose into the slightest of arcs, rolled over the cable, then stretched itself out and fell in a neat, vertical trajectory. *Yes!* he congratulated himself. He grabbed both ends of the chain and tested it with a quick tug. The cable bounced in response. He was halfway there.

With his hands held high, he allowed the chain to ride loosely on the cable while he positioned himself with his toes precariously on the edge of the platform. Below him, the river roared over jutting rocks and churned in swirling eddies, distracting his focus, and he teetered. It suddenly struck him how ballsy this whole idea was about to become. But he steeled himself – someone had to save Peter from the man out to kill him, and it would be Jimmy or no one.

He stretched himself forward and shook the chain lightly, easing it toward the cable car. He tightened his grip and bent his knees. Then, with a hard swallow and a deep breath, he launched himself into the air.

At that very moment, all perception of the world around him vanished and all sounds muted, save the beat of his heart and the roar of his own breath. For that fraction of a second, he was completely weightless, bound by no law of motion or gravity, and time stopped. Jimmy floated in empty space for what seemed like an eternity, and he basked in the complete and utter tranquility.

Then, as suddenly as they disappeared, all earthly sensations returned, the chain went tight, the cable wowed, and his weight snapped him around like a pendulum bob. The chain vibrated in his hands as it slid over the twists of the cable, and the tail of his mac slapped in the wind of his motion. There he went – a fair-skinned, red-haired James Bond executing a daring and heroic rescue – and he was elated.

But his euphoria was soon overshadowed by a stark realization. Though he was sliding toward the car just as he had intended, he hadn't bothered to figure out how to stop himself, and it was only an adrenalin reaction that pulled up his knees and raised his feet in time. But both feet missed and went between the struts, and it was his buttocks and hamstrings that struck the car. It almost knocked the wind out of him and he grunted.

That his feet dropped down inside the car was a stroke of luck, because the transfer of momentum sent the car rolling, freed of the nub that had held it in place. Now, conjoined by serendipity, they careened along the cable as one.

His arms ached and his hands tired as they picked up speed. The car swayed and rolled, and the roar of churning waves grew louder as the sag of the cable brought him lower. That unnerved him, and though the river was still feet below him, he felt the unexplainable urge to raise his buttocks off the water. Abruptly, he realized why this trick was only done in the movies.

## The Sweet Bounty

Then, just when he thought he couldn't hang on any longer, he and the car slowed and came to a complete stop at mid-river. He would have breathed a sigh of thankfulness if he could, but his hands screamed with fatigue and he was too busy trying to figure out what to do before he dropped uselessly into the river below.

With his last burst of strength, he pulled his upper body toward the car in a sit-up motion and rolled the chain over the cable until his right hand was just below it. Then, in a final, desperate gamble with hands about to give out, he released the chain and lunged at the cable with his right hand, dropped the chain, and grabbed one of the struts with his left. The chain splashed into the river below as he pulled his torso into the car. He collapsed, relieved he could finally relax, and for a while he just laid there on the bottom of the car sucking in long breaths.

When at last he found the strength to rise up, he began to crank the car toward the other tower as fast as his aching, weary arms could.

## Chapter 25

At the fence, I saw once again the tracks Young Footprint Woman had made, though now they were mostly eroded away by the rain. They reminded me of why I came here in the first place. With a muzzle prod into my back, Wears Loafers issued a brusque reminder of why I was here now, and I wondered if I would live to see those tracks again.

His eyes set immediately upon the opening. "Nice work, Indian Boy. How long did it take you to cut your way through?" He lifted one side and waved me under it with the gun, then followed after me. I denied having cut the fence, but I stopped short of saying more. This was clearly not the time to admit that Anna and I had already been here.

At Pie'lik, I stopped again, wondering where he'd have me go from here. "Keep moving, we're crossing here," he said, and he pushed the muzzle at the back of my head. We waded across, ignoring Young Footprint Woman's piles of rocks only a few yards away.

We followed the trail Anna and I had taken a few days ago, and, before long, the canal appeared again, spilling the river toward us as if it had always been there. We slogged beside it through the bare, muddy earth in the wide swath cut by dozers and excavators. We climbed over downed trees, upended stumps, mounds of roots and dirt, and charred brush until we came to a bridge over the canal, strong and wide enough to carry heavy construction equipment from one side of the river to the other. We crossed it, then continued along a dirt road for another three hundred yards.

I was prepared to go farther when he stopped me in full view of the desecration Anna and I had seen from the top of the canal. "This is it, Indian Boy. A good place for a trespasser to die, don't you agree?"

The roar of diesel motors punctuated the air.

\* \* \* \*

Jimmy descended the tower and scoured the deer trail for signs of Peter and the man. It began to rain again and he pulled the collar of his mac tight around his neck. Fresh tracks led him upstream as fast as he could travel in the slippery mud.

\* \* \* \*

"Trespasser?" I repeated, not really believing what I just heard.

"Yes, quite convenient, don't you think? It isn't every day I catch one, especially one that refuses to leave after clear warning. I drove you off my land once already, and not long ago as I remember."

His gun hand began to tremor, like it did when he confronted Anna and me beside the road. But for the first time, it struck me how much it was like other hands – my godfather's hands – I had seen tremor only days ago. Could the mercury have poisoned Wears Loafers, too? And how? More to the point, how would I live to find out?

"It will be a simple story," he continued, "completely supported by the circumstances. The RCMP will hear that you became enraged when I asked you to leave the second time. You threatened me, charged at me, so, naturally, I defended myself. Which will neatly explain the bullet they'll find in your chest. And when they find that hole in the fence and the gate key in your pocket, they won't be asking me any more questions."

"Like I said, I didn't make that hole, and I don't know who did. But I see that doesn't matter to you."

It was raining again. Drops clung to my brow and ran down my cheeks, and I wiped them from my face with the sleeve of my jacket.

"You're smarter than I gave you credit for, Indian Boy." Then he paused for a second or two. "But perhaps I should call a dying man by his real name," he resumed. "Respect for the soon-to-be-dead, and all that. Mr. Peter Joe, I believe it is?"

"You promised to tell me what this is about," I said, ignoring the barb.

"You really don't get it, do you?"

"Maybe you'd better explain it to me." I tried to steal enough time to figure my way out of this.

He chuckled. "I guess Jeddore didn't pass to you Indians the wisdom of his dying words."

Suddenly, he had my undivided attention. "What do you know about my godfather?" I demanded.

A look of genuine surprise took his face. "Jeddore was your godfather? Oh, well done, Peter Joe!

## The Sweet Bounty

Here I was, thinking all along you were just another nosy eco-Indian poking around where you didn't belong. But now I see it runs much deeper than that. Godson and godfather, almost blood for you Indians, isn't it? Yes indeed, that does explain everything."

"Meaning what?" I demanded.

He looked puzzled. "Why you're here, of course." Then he stopped and jerked his head in the direction of the mine. "Look over there and tell me what you see."

Now the anger began to well up inside me. "I see rampant destruction, devastation, and ruin. The land of my father's fathers, and their fathers before them, defaced beyond recognition. A river once vibrant and alive now robbed of its soul. And I see a man who will spend the next 20 years of his life behind bars when he's found out."

He stopped me with his laugh. "How wrong you are, Peter Joe, on all counts! You allow a misplaced passion to muddle your thinking!"

He continued, as if correcting me. "Before you stands a highly advanced form of man's oldest endeavor, since the first discovery of flint, millennia before Christ. The boundless resources of the earth at man's behest. The very foundation of civilization! Imagine millions in taxes, profits and wages, wending their way through our societies, over and over and over, ever-widening the path of growth and progress. A sweet bounty all their own, if you don't mind the pun. You Newfoundlanders must accept that the cod really *are* gone. This is your *new* milk and honey. Gold is your future now." Then he sighed dramatically. "What a pity you won't be here to experience the glory of it all."

Suddenly, he became visibly shaken. "But Jeddore ... he would have ruined it! Would have ushered it all to crumbling bits! All that senseless drivel about mercury contaminating his aqua farm. Imagine all that fuss over a few mealy fish! I can tell you this ..." he said, pointing to the mine without turning, "they pale in comparison to what *that* will do for Newfoundland!"

Then he calmed as abruptly as he had become agitated. "And I couldn't let him do it. No, there was far too much at stake to let his outdated idealism stand in the way. Which of your countrymen would not choose prosperity over poverty? And the generations after them? I had no choice. I had to preserve the greater good.

"After that," he began again. He raised the gun at me and took it with both hands, as if to steady it for a shot. "After that, everything was under control again ... that is, until you came along. Now, I'm forced to visit this matter once again."

"*You* killed him? You *poisoned* the River with mercury?" I interjected.

He lowered the gun and laughed again. "Mercury? There is no mercury, there never was and never will be! The Ministry will give you its highest assurances. Why does that ridiculous notion persist?"

"I don't know," I said, surprised to hear the sarcasm building in my own voice. "Maybe it was the uncontrollable tremors or his incoherent babble. Or the tangled, distorted nerve fibers, and the mercury they found in his blood and his hair. Or maybe it was the way he writhed and died on a hospital bed after having done only good for a nation of people relegated to only afterthoughts by self-proclaimed messiahs like you."

The Sweet Bounty

"Ah, there's that uncontained passion again," he said easily. "I'm afraid you've been led astray."

"OK, let's say I play along with you. If mercury poisoning didn't kill him, what did?"

He shook his head in feigned disgust as his eyes drifted upward, and he muttered to the sky, "They have not learned the wisdom you teach, Orunmila." Then he looked back at me. "Why, it was nothing more than the most ancient and compelling force in all the universe, since before the very beginning of life and time."

The rain soaked his face and dripped from his brow and chin, but his eyes acquired an intense glee. He threw an open hand skyward. "Ogun, Ochosi, Elegua!" he shouted. "The almighty Orisha themselves have blessed me with their power!"

*So, that explains the tremoring hands!* Now it all made sense. Mac had reminded me about ritual mercury, how Santeros use it to ward off unwanted spirits. After years of inhaling the poisoned vapors of ceremonial candles and altar sprinklings, they became victims of their own medicine, quivering like the victims of Minimata, losing their sanity in the process. Now I knew Wears Loafers was the Santero priest, the man who had set the curses on my godfather.

But, even so, in what seemed to be the last moments of my own life, I found myself questioning once again how my godfather had really died. Had the power of his own spiritual beliefs made him vulnerable? Had the rest of my People come to believe it too? Had Wears Loafers cursed my entire Tribe? It seemed unlikely, but still ...

Or had Wears Loafers lied to me? Had he used ritual mercury to poison the Conifer in spite of what he said? My People tremored like Wears Loafers and my godfather. They babbled senselessly, Mary had said, just how Anna described the people of Minimata had done.

No, Wears Loafers would not have doomed his own undertaking, I decided. There had to be some other source for the mercury. But what? I only knew I had to survive this if I was ever going to find out. I wiped the rain from my face once again and tried to focus.

Wears Loafers calmed again. "And you ... you were to die, too. But you must be blessed," he said. "Contrary to my fondest wishes, you're still alive. Perhaps Ogun was displeased with me after all. Perhaps he even deceived me." He thought for a moment, then he shrugged it off. "Well, none of that matters now, does it?" He raised the gun again. "As you see, I have no compunctions about using a more contemporary power on you today."

"One more question," I said, still fighting for time. "How did you find me?"

He grinned, but he didn't lower the gun this time. "Sadly, it took a bit more persuasion than I had anticipated, but your lady friends eventually betrayed you. My advice to you is to look for more loyalty in your friendships."

"What did you do to them?" I demanded.

Suddenly his demeanor became deadly serious, his voice insistent and commanding. "No more diversions! Your time has come!" He cocked the hammer. "Do give my regards to your Chief Jeddore. Ódìgbòÿe o, Peter Joe!"

His hands tremored wildly, but at this range there was little chance he'd miss. I had to act fast. Bracing for the worst, I closed my eyes, sucked in my breath, and turned around. I began to walk away. If I gave him only my back as a target, maybe he'd realize he'd have no alibi, and maybe he wouldn't shoot. Maybe.

Blam! A bullet whizzed past my head. Blam! A pain seared at my left shoulder. I spun and dropped to my knees. Blam! Blam! I fell to the ground.

The shooting stopped as suddenly as it had begun. The side of my face pressed gently into a cool, wet softness, and I felt unexpectedly serene. I listened calmly to the staccato of raindrops on my jacket and watched the crimson blood drip from my shoulder.

Slowly, the sound of the raindrops faded. It became silent and peaceful. Nkekkunit Abram placed a Chief's robe over me, and I was warm. I closed my eyes.

## Chapter 26

Faintly, I heard a voice, then rustling in the brush nearby. It was a man's voice and it said, "Don't move."

I tried to awaken, tried to open my eyes to see where I was, but half of my world was dark. The smell of mucky dampness was close, and I realized the side of my face lay in the mud. I tried to lift my head, but I was stopped by an aching sting in my shoulder. The questions of where I was and what happened were being answered by rapid-fire memories of the last few seconds with Wears Loafers — walking away, four gunshots, falling to the ground.

*Four shots? But hadn't I been hit only once? Yes, I felt pain only in my shoulder. The rest of me was okay, I was sure of it. Could his aim have been so terrible?* My recollections were interrupted by the sounds of footsteps, and in my helplessness I began to panic. *Was he coming to finish the job?*

He stopped right in front of me, and I held my breath. I rolled my eyes upward, straining to see him, but all I could see was a hand carrying a sharply bowed branch. He knelt beside me, and I looked directly into his face. Uncontrollably, I groaned with relief – it wasn't Wears Loafers.

"Jimmy?" I asked. "Is that you?"

"Yes, Mr. Joe, it's me. Thank God, you're still alive."

"How ... how did you find me?"

"Never mind about that right now. You're hurt."

He stood and then squatted behind me. I felt a hand move under my right arm and another alongside my neck, then pressure as Jimmy audibly strained to lift me. "Try ... uhnn ... to sit up, Mr. Joe."

Somehow, the diminutive Jimmy Nolan was able to help me sit upright. As he knelt behind my back to prop me up, I wiped the mud from my face. It was then I saw Wears Loafers, sprawled awkwardly on the ground only ten feet away.

Jimmy noticed me staring. "He's dead, Mr. Joe, I checked."

"He tried to kill me, and I don't even know his name, Jimmy."

"Paul Ceborro. He runs this place. I ran into him years ago when I began investigating your godfather's story. He's a liar and a ruthless tyrant, but I never thought he would try to murder anyone, least of all you.

"And he left Dr. Chartier in pretty bad shape."

I stiffened and my eyes widened. "What did he do to her? Is she alive?"

"I think they'll both be fine. The hospital staff was in the room minutes after I found them. He must have threatened the lady with the painted hair to get Dr. Chartier to say where you were. I found her lying in her bed, nearly unconscious with a bloody face. She must have refused before he eventually beat it out of her. The lady with the painted hair woke up while I was there. She was the one who told me how to find you."

I could relax now, Anna would be OK. I tried to wrap myself around everything that had happened, straining to find the harmony, but it was futile. "As much as I've learned about my godfather's death, I think there's a lot more I don't know," I sighed.

I felt movement against my back, and a survival knife came suddenly across my face. I tensed and my right arm twitched instinctively, as if preparing to fend it off. But the knife continued around and began to cut gently at the left shoulder seam of my jacket, and I relaxed.

Jimmy slid the sleeve down my arm and over my wrist, then attempted to do the same to my shirt. It was blood soaked and it didn't cooperate, but he eventually freed it from the rest of the shirt and slid it off, too. Now I could see the hole where the bullet had entered just below my shoulder. It was caked with blood, but the bullet had entered cleanly from the front and had missed the bone. Jimmy grimaced out loud, and I realized he was looking at the back of my arm, at the torn meat of the exit wound.

"You're hurt pretty bad, Mr. Joe. The bleeding has slowed, but you need a doctor real soon."

But I was suddenly puzzled. "Jimmy, I remember turning around before he fired, but the bullet entered my shoulder from the front."

Jimmy hesitated. "Yeah, sorry, Mr. Joe."

"What? *You* shot me?"

I had only just finished the question when a handgun wagged in front of my face. "I guess I'm not very good with this thing," he said apologetically.

"Jimmy ..."

"Yeah, sorry," he said again, and he put the gun away.

He picked up the severed shirtsleeve and slit it lengthwise from one end to the other. He wrapped it twice around my wound as a bandage and tied it off. Then he slit my jacket sleeve into three lengths.

He whittled the twigs and leaves off the bowed branch. "Bend your arm, Mr. Joe, it's a brace." He held it beside my arm and I matched it with a cautious bend at my elbow, then he bound them together with the lengths of my jacket sleeve.

He removed his mac and worked at one of its sleeves the same way, but this time he tied all three pieces together end-to-end, making one long piece. He looped it under my wrist and over my shoulder, then tied it off as a sling. Then he cut off his own shirtsleeve, slit it into three pieces, and tied them end-to-end, too. This he used to lash my arm against my chest.

"That should help. Best to steady that arm, it's a long walk out of here," he said. Then he stood up and put his mac back on. "Can you stand, Mr. Joe?"

I grabbed his arm with my free hand, worked my legs under me, and pulled. I was suddenly queasy with pain in my arm and ribs and lightheaded with the abrupt change of position. I teetered into him, but I was standing.

"Huh. Nothing to it, Jimmy," I said uncertainly.

With my hand on his arm, we began to backtrack the same route I had been forced along by Wears Loafers earlier. The bridge was easy going, but the barren earth beside the canal had become a momentous challenge with the second rain, a mucky quagmire that sucked at our shoes and pulled us back.

The trussed up arm with a hole in it was a distinct disadvantage. Several times I stumbled or slipped and had to drop to my free hand and my knees to regain myself, then sit on a stump to let the pain subside. Things became easier again when we reached the trail beside the Conifer's natural channel.

At Pie'lik, Jimmy was half way across on the rock piles left by Young Footprint Woman when I called him back. "Jimmy, wait. There's something along this brook I have to find before we leave."

He hesitated and looked concerned. "Ohhh, I don't think that's a good idea, Mr. Joe. You're hurt bad. You should get to a doctor right away."

"I could use your help, Jimmy," I said, but I told him I would do this alone if I had to.

He shook his head in a scolding way, and he stepped toward me. "You shouldn't be anywhere except in a hospital right now. We both know that. This is a really, really bad idea, Mr. Joe."

I ignored his resistance, turned upstream, and for the first time in 21 years, I walked alongside Pie'lik, the brook named for me, on my way to find ... to find what? I still had no idea what to look for.

Pie'lik was the name my godfather had invented. I knew that wasn't its real name, but, at the age of seven, it hadn't mattered. My boyhood imagination had swelled with the idea that a whole river could have my name.

It had become our favorite place in this country. Only a few hundred yards from here, it had exposed its granite bottom and polished it as smooth as glass. Then, as if satisfied with the job it had done, it forsook the granite bench and plunged over the edge into a deep, crystal pool. It was in that glassy-bottomed trough that my godfather and I had often cheated the summer heat, two skinny-dippers pushed along on a free ride into the pool below, as if we ourselves were naturally a part of the waterfall.

But when I reached the age of ten, it had become apparent that something bothered my godfather deeply. His face had become drawn and his eyes had lost what had always been a youthful enthusiasm for the world around him, especially here in these woods. It was then I learned the secret he had harbored for over a year. With a heavy sigh, he told me Mkekkunit Malklit – my godmother Margaret, his wife – was ill with a terrible cancer. That was the last day Pie'lik swept us into its pool, and two years later, almost to the day, she died. Long after, he was still devastated by her passing.

"So, Mr. Joe, what are you looking for?" Jimmy's question brought me back to the present.

"I wish I knew, Jimmy, I ..."

He was quick to interject. "Then why are we here? I told you this was a bad idea! We should turn around right now!"

I stopped and turned to face him. "Jimmy, there's something important here. Somehow, the mercury that killed my godfather is coming from this brook, not the mine. I have to find it and stop it before it kills off the rest of my people, too. This could be my last chance to come back here for a long time. I have to do this now. I'll be alright."

"The mercury's coming from this brook? No, Mr. Joe, it has to be coming from the mine. How could it be coming from anywhere else?"

I suddenly realized I had learned a lot since our first meeting at the quay, a lot he didn't know. I began by telling him about my meeting with Anna, describing how she had doubted his theory mercury could be coming from the mine so soon. I told him she offered to test the Conifer, thinking she could disprove his theory before the falsehood gained a life of its own. I described the samples Anna took from the Conifer, and that she actually did find mercury in the some of the samples.

"I knew it!" he interrupted. "From the mine. Don't you see?"

"But there's more," I said, stopping him. "The mercury was in the samples farthest from the mine but not in the closest ones, and she found no cyanide in any of them. According to her, that meant the mercury could not be coming from the mine, that it had to be coming from somewhere else, and this brook is the only other place."

I told him a toxicologist in Ottawa confirmed that methyl mercury poisoning had been the reason my godfather died. Then I told him about the plate of wax and pins and the pots with my godfather's name on them, and how Mac had later confirmed they were the remains of Santeria curses. I finished with what Wears Loafers told me just an hour ago – that he had cursed my godfather to his death and he had tried to do the same to me.

Jimmy's jaw sunk with amazement. "Gosh, Mr. Joe, I had no idea. But curses? Do you really believe that?"

"I don't know Jimmy, I only know they can be powerful influences, especially to those who believe."

"Well, I don't, Mr. Joe. It was the mercury, you said yourself the toxicologist proved that. But it can't be in this brook. It's not possible, Mr. Joe, it has to be coming from the mine. There's no other way."

## The Sweet Bounty

"That's why I need to do this, Jimmy."

He stared blankly, as if not knowing what to say next. His stare became a look of worry as I turned to continue along Pie'lik, but once again he fell in behind me. "What about the bribery?" he asked a few steps later. "Did you find out about that?"

Bribery was the farthest thing from my mind right now, but I answered anyway. "Nothing, Jimmy, but I'm sure it's there. If it's all as you said it was, it has to be. Winslow prickled when I asked about the Sweet Bounty — he was certainly trying to hide something. Keep digging."

"But, …" he began, and then he just sighed.

At a bend in the trail, I motioned for Jimmy to stop and be quiet, but I was too late. Our noise had warned a browsing moose of our approach. It stared at us for a moment, then snorted and trotted away to better privacy. I stood quietly, watching the magnificent animal disappear into the trees.

That's when I heard it.

"Jimmy, did you hear that?"

"Hear what, Mr. Joe?"

"A click," I said, not certain I had really heard anything at all.

"A click? No, I didn't hear …"

"Shhh." I interrupted. "There it is again," I said. I was sure of it now. It was a faint, metallic sound that didn't belong here.

I waited and heard it again. And again. It was regular, but not frequent. Had I not stopped, it might easily have been disguised by the snap of a twig under my foot. I began to hunt for it.

"Where are you going, Mr. Joe?"

"It's close, Jimmy."

"What's close? I don't hear anything. I probably stepped on a branch, or the moose did. Let's go back — you're hurt, Mr. Joe."

I walked five slow steps and the sound came closer, almost beside me. I turned to my left and scanned my surroundings. A pile of birch branches lay partially hidden from view beside a tree. I might have missed it had some of the leaves not bared their branches. *Could it be there?* I walked closer to investigate. The sound became louder as I approached.

I cleared away the brush and found myself staring at the top of a black, rectangular case that looked like a steamer trunk. It was buried up to its lid, which overlapped the sides. I squatted to one knee and scooped away the dirt. I raised the lid, and nearly gasped at what I saw.

Inside were two clear plastic bottles, each containing a watery liquid. A length of clear, plastic tubing led from each of their lids to a small brass fixture in the shape of a Y. From the tail of the Y, a single tube led to the source of the click — a small electric pump powered by a car battery. More tubing led from the pump to a hole in the side of the trunk and to a narrow line of disturbed grass leading from the trunk toward the trail. I rose and followed it.

The disturbance crossed the trail, then disappeared under the brush at the edge of the bank. I stepped into the creek upstream of the brush and peered under it. The tubing emerged, and disappeared again under a pair of rocks in the creek bed. I moved closer, squatted down, and pushed one of the rocks aside with a stick. The tube floated to the surface, and a clear, watery liquid spurted from it in time with the clicks of the pump.

# The Sweet Bounty

I was stunned. *What was it? Could this be the what I was looking for? But mercury was silver, a heavy liquid, wasn't it?* Then, suddenly, my stupefaction ended.

"I told you this was a bad idea, Mr. Joe. You should have listened."

I looked up. The gun he had dangled in my face earlier today was now in his hand, pointed directly at me.

"Jimmy, what ... ?"

"Come out of the water," he ordered.

I stepped onto the bank. "What is this, Jimmy?"

"It's nothing, Mr. Joe, just forget you saw it and let's walk out of here. Now."

I resisted. "No, Jimmy, I won't. Not until you tell me what's going on here."

He hesitated. The gun began to quiver in his hand and he reached up with his other hand to steady it. "I wish you'd listen to me, Mr. Joe," he pleaded.

"Tell me, Jimmy," I demanded.

His voice began to stammer. "Can't you just leave it alone?"

"Leave what alone, Jimmy?"

"I only wanted to show them, Mr. Joe. Show them I could do it. I knew I could, I *always* knew I could. It was my chance to make it big."

I thought I detected a whimper in his voice. "What do you mean, Jimmy?" I asked.

"I couldn't believe it, Mr. Joe. Everything just fell into my lap. The payoffs, the deception. The corruption of power. An ignorant, victimized people, forced to bear an injustice heaped upon them by the unfeeling prowess of a cold international business. It had everything it needed to be a big story. Just like

Minimata. Everything except the mercury. It was going to happen anyway, Mr. Joe. It was just a matter of time. All I did was speed up the inevitable."

I pointed to the case. "Jimmy, is that what's poisoning the water? Is this your doing?"

He didn't answer.

"Why, Jimmy? Why would you do this? My godfather! My People! They've done nothing to you!"

His eyes began to water and he wiped them with his sleeve. "It wasn't supposed to happen like that," he stammered again. "No one was supposed to get hurt. Maybe a few salmon, but nothing more. They were just supposed to find it in the water."

Then he became visibly angry. "But no one cared! No one listened to me, no matter what I wrote! I didn't know he would die, but that's when things began to happen! Besides, it wasn't even my fault! Your godfather started it – *he* was the one who said the mine would cause it!" His anger turned suddenly to remorse. "And then ... it was too late. I couldn't stop it."

Stunned, I stopped questioning, trying to come to grips with what I had just heard. Jimmy Nolan – the reporter who had chronicled my godfather's struggle, the man who sought my help to bring the corrupt to justice, the man who had saved me from certain death at the hands of Wears Loafers – had poisoned the river with methyl mercury to bolster his flagging career. Young Footprint Woman wasn't a woman at all, she was Jimmy. He killed my godfather, and he was killing my people. And for what? A millisecond of fame?

Then, as quickly as he had lost it, Jimmy regained his composure. He cocked the hammer and pointed the gun straight at me. His hands ceased their quiver, and I suddenly had another worry. I realized he couldn't just let me walk away, not now, not with what I knew. Two shots left, I remembered. Unless I could talk him out of it, I'd be staring down the last moments of my life for the second time today. I desperately hoped his aim would be as poor as it had been earlier.

"Put the gun down, Jimmy. You don't want another death on your hands," I insisted.

"I didn't want *any* on my hands, Mr. Joe, but what choice do I have now? I'm sorry, Mr. Joe, but no one can know what I've done. Surely you must know that. I ..."

Out of nowhere, a voice boomed. "Do like the man said, son!" it commanded.

Instinctively, Jimmy and I turned. Two men in gray coveralls, bearing the Provincial Coat of Arms on their shoulders, stepped from the trees onto the trail and walked toward us. Both men had drawn their guns and both men aimed them at Jimmy. He glanced at me, then at them, then back at me. He froze, uncertain what to do next, and before he could decide they rushed him. The first man disarmed him and the other cuffed him from behind.

With the immediate tension over, First Man turned to me. "You all right?" he asked.

"About as good as someone about to be shot for the second time today could expect to be. Who are you and where did you come from?"

"Special agents, Ministry of Environment, investigating Ceborro and the Sweet Bounty. Orders changed and we were told to bring him in. We were searching the grounds for him when gunshots drew us to the canal where we found him already dead. Your tracks led us here."

He tipped his head in Jimmy's direction where Other Man had already begun to wrestle him up the trail. "Seems like we arrived just in time to keep you from being his second victim."

"Third," I corrected, "but I'm thankful to you both."

He nodded. "Come on," he said with a reassuring smile, "let's get you to a doctor."

"Gladly," I said. "But there is something I have to do first."

"Very well," he responded. "Just let me know when you're ready."

I walked to the buried case, intending to destroy it. But, for long minutes, I just stood there and stared at it. And the longer I did, the more incensed I became. An infuriating irony was at work here. My godfather's life had been a model of unselfishness, yet it was that very unselfishness that took him from me. I knew men had always placed themselves above others, had always been capable of evil. Yet, some part of me will never accept that it must be so. Men could be better.

Suddenly, an incendiary rage burst from within me. I yanked out the wires with my free hand and screamed my anger. I heaved them into the trees. My chest pounded and breaths bellowed from my lungs. I regaled in my vengeance.

Then, gradually, I calmed, as if some deep, instinctive urge had at last been satisfied, never to be felt again. And although it was only a small, insignificant sound I had stopped, a long, painful, and deafening roar within me was silenced. A harmony had been restored, and in my heart I felt the beginnings of a new peace. My People would be safe now. I released a sigh of relief,

turned, and began the long walk back.
    But as I walked, the question suddenly rose up again. It snagged at my step and I faltered to a stop. *Had the power of belief been so strong in my godfather?* I reflected yet again. I walked on, but I wondered if I would ever know ... ever know why he died and the others of my Tribe still live.

## Chapter 27

Two days later.

    I moved the wheelchair out of my way, sat on a chair beside Anna's bed, and gazed at her sleeping face. She lay on her back, her hospital gown covered to her waist by a blanket, and her hands rested by her sides. Her head tilted slightly away from me and she breathed quietly.

    I reached over and clenched her hand lightly. She stirred and turned her head toward me. With eyes only half open, she smiled drowsily. "Peter," she began softly. I felt her hand turn over, and the soft warmth of her palm enveloped mine. "How nice it is to see you," she said.

    My eyes moved to the faint row of stitches running from eye to ear against the backdrop of blue and black, and I remembered the cast on her leg. I winced. It wasn't fair she should bear even a single scar – she hadn't asked to come this far. She turned the side of her head into the pillow to hide it. "Don't look, Peter, it's hideous," she said, but she smiled anyway.

## The Sweet Bounty

I placed a finger on my own stitches. "We are like rag dolls, you and I – hand sewn," I said, and we laughed together at our own disfigurements.

Her eyes suddenly caught the sling on my arm, and her grip tightened. "Peter, your arm. What happened?"

I looked down at it, then back up at her. "Jimmy," I answered.

"Jimmy?"

I nodded and explained all that had happened since I left the hospital.

"My word, Peter. It is all so strange. I would not have believed any of it."

Just then came a knock at the door, and we turned to see Mary Benoit enter the room. The peaked cap and woolen skirt of several days ago had become blue jeans and a red sweatshirt. In her left hand she carried a folded newspaper.

"Kwe', Pi'el! Hello, Anna!" she greeted us. "My, the stories I have heard! I had to see you both for myself."

Anna broke into a broad grin as she said hello. I rose to welcome her embrace. "Kwe', Ma'lij," I said. "It's wonderful to see you again."

She released the embrace, took my hands in hers, and stood back, eyeing our wounds. "You two are quite a pair, I must say." As she lowered herself into the empty wheelchair across from me, she pushed the newspaper my way. "Here, you must read what is said of you."

I took the paper and unfolded it into my lap. A prominent banner above the headline story directed me to the editorial page. I opened it as instructed and began to read aloud:

## EW Finke

AN OPEN APOLOGY TO OUR READERS

To most of you, it will come as no surprise that these last few days at the Telegraph have been a period of heady and unprecedented activity. In a profession as passionate about truth, fairness, and objectivity as ours, we are led to ask ourselves how these events could ever have come to be.

We refer, of course, to the recent confession by one of our own journalists to a hideous crime which led to the death of two men and to the life-threatening illness of many others. We patiently await the results of a related investigation into an alleged 'fees for favors' conspiracy to deceive the Provincial government and people of Newfoundland. And we trust the Province will see to the appropriate disposition of the mine itself.

As much as we abhor the crimes themselves, we abhor even more the erosion of trust in us as couriers of news that the journalist's crime will inevitably leave in its wake. We assure you the Telegraph has no complicity in any of these crimes, and we have pledged the Telegraph's full cooperation to the Department of Justice and the Royal Newfoundland Constabulary. We will continue to report on these investigations as we may be permitted, and we promise to you, our readers, to maintain the highest standards of journalism in these and in every story we publish.

We are grateful to all those who helped bring these crimes to light, but we are particularly indebted to Mr. Peter Joe and Dr. Annamarie Chartier, who incurred serious injury and great personal hardship in doing so. We applaud their selfless and courageous

The Sweet Bounty

humanitarianism, and we wish them speedy recoveries.

    I lifted my eyes to Anna and Mary and learned that all three of us beamed smiles. I continued:

Lastly, we turn our hearts to the Mi'kmaq People of Conifer. With the death of Chief Abraham Jeddore they have suffered a great loss, and many more have become ill themselves. With compassion and great respect, the Telegraph has endowed a fund to help the Mi'kmaq as they undergo lengthy and costly medical treatment. We have seeded that fund with an initial donation of $300,000, and we pledge twenty percent of subscription profits for the next two years. We invite contributions from anyone who feels the desire to help.

We at the Telegraph thank you, our readers, for the many generations of loyalty and support you have shown us. May your god bless you.

    Mary nodded her approval as I folded the newspaper and laid it on the bed beside me. "It is a great kindness they do for our People, Peter. Chelation therapy will be long and difficult."
    I acknowledged her with a nod and scratched absentmindedly at the bandage on my healing shoulder. Briefly, we each sat quietly, saying nothing, looking at nothing, recounting in our own individual ways the events of the past eight days. Mary seemed to know something still lingered for me, and it was she who broke the silence.
    "Peter," she began quietly, "what do you know of your father?"

I was stunned at the very question. I hadn't thought about him since I was old enough to realize what his abandoning my mother and me meant. I knew nothing about him, and, until now, I had preferred to keep it that way. But, with Mary's question, something changed within me. What did she know of him, and why did I suddenly want to know? I hesitated for a long time before I gave an answer. Then, it just came out, pulled by a suppressed longing to fill the emptiness he left in that part of my life, and pushed by anger and contempt for the man.

"What can I possibly know about him? He never saw fit to be part of my life!" I said as if to scold her for asking. I was shaken by my tone and I looked away.

Mary only nodded. She had the patience and wisdom of the Old Ones, and that is how she began. "It is long past time you knew, Peter.

"Since boyhood, your godfather and your father were best of friends. They did all things together — played, fished, hunted, swam, danced, canoed. Whenever mischief demanded two people, they were the first to rise. Their imaginations were limitless. When they were together, no dare was too daring.

They even fell in love at the same time. Your godfather Abram and your godmother Malklit wed first, but it was not long before your father and mother would do the same. There were great celebrations among the families at both of those weddings.

"But only your mother bore a child. No one knew the illness that aborted your godmother's child would become the cancer which later would take her life."

"I remember that time," I said thinking back. "Her cancer weighed heavy on Nkekkunit Abram."

"Yes, it did. As did something else."

"What do you mean?"

"On the night of your mother's and father's wedding celebration, there was an argument among them and your godfather, an argument so terrible the man who was to be your father left the Reserve forever that very night. Only they knew why, and it remained so even as it became unbearable for your mother many years later. It was only in her last hours on the Reserve that she confided her truth in me. She could hold it inside no longer."

Mary had captured my complete attention, but I still didn't understand. *What could be so terrible it must be kept from everyone, and for so long?* My expression urged her to finish.

"Your mother was a caring and loving woman, Peter, and your godfather a noble man. But even the best among us are human, and we must forgive them this weakness. It happened long ago in a moment of irresponsibility, but they willingly fulfilled the responsibility they brought upon themselves."

Now I was anxious. "I'm confused, Mary. What weakness? What irresponsibility?"

She hesitated for a moment, as if to gauge my reaction to news I hadn't yet heard. Then, at last, she spoke.

"Peter ... the man who was to be your father did not become so. You are the son of your godfather. Abram is your father."

She stopped and waited patiently for the full meaning of her words to settle within me. But I could only stare at her wide-eyed, as if my ears, being no part of me, were not to be trusted. *My godfather was my father?* Emotions I could find no words for seared at my gut and ripped at my heart. *How can this be!*

I could hold back no longer. "No, Mary, that cannot be! He would have told me this if it were true, I'm certain of that!"

No sooner did I speak than his voice came back to me with the same words I heard a little more than a week ago, the last words I would ever hear from him. It was suddenly clear why I never knew the man who was to be my father, why it became so important to my mother that she leave the Reserve, and that my godfather, or rather my father, must have resisted her taking me away. The emotional burden on both of them could only have been very great for a very long time.

"They told no one ..." she began, but I interrupted her.

"Mary," I said, abruptly calm now, "he was going to tell me, I see that now. I was in Montreal when he reached me. 'It's something you must know. You must come right away,' he said. He wanted to tell me before he died, but he never got the chance.

"But why then, Mary? Why not years before, when we still had time? And why did my own mother not tell me?" I asked incredulously.

"They could not forgive themselves, Peter. They could not see beyond this frailty."

Then she narrowed her eyes and leaned forward. I knew her well enough to know she would not let me wallow in my daze. A teaching was in the making, and she was about to deliver it.

"Now you know you are the son of a Chief, Peter. Thus, great opportunities are provided to you, and so are great things expected of you. You have the Power to confront the truth no matter what it may portend. We may never overcome our weaknesses, but we must learn to see beyond them. Can you do this?"

I asked myself that question. Had I judged the man who was to be my father and the man who was my father, and even my mother, without seeking the whole truth? The answer that came was a resounding 'yes.' I had learned much about myself in recent days, but would I do the same again under other circumstances? Or worse? How could I say? One cannot know what his future will bring.

"I am no better man than any other, Mary," I began. "I can only say I am wiser for having learned from my actions and the actions of others."

She leaned back into her chair, folded her arms, and scrutinized my face with a furrowed brow. I felt like a schoolboy about to be scolded for bad playground manners. Then, without giving a clue to her thoughts, her face relaxed, as if some deeply personal need had at last been satisfied.

"You have answered truthfully, Peter, and that is good," she said, "because there is one thing more you must know."

My brow rose involuntarily. *Another long-hidden secret? Another teaching?* "And what is that?" I asked with trepidation.

"I have heard the Elders," she said. "There is talk of a new Chief."

My eyes drifted down as I considered the weighty task they had before them. "I wish them well, Mary. It will not be easy to find so great a Saqamaw as Godfather."

"Yes, you are correct. He was one of our best," she acknowledged with a sigh. "But it may not be so difficult as you suggest."

As if under their own power, my eyes lifted to probe hers. "You speak in riddles, Mary. What do you mean?"

She tilted her head slightly as she studied my questioning eyes. "The Elders say you are more Mi'kmaq, Peter."

She paused. Then she added, "They say *you* will be Saqamaw."

## ABOUT THE AUTHOR

"It would be no exaggeration to say that I eagerly read every one of Tony Hillerman's mysteries while they were still warm. I can't explain what it was about them. I can only say that where I might be distracted away only a few pages into any other novel, I would regularly finish a Hillerman in a single evening, trying to solve it before Joe Leaphorn, Jim Chee, or Bernadette Manuelito did. They were enthralling stories.

So it was that Tony Hillerman was the inspiration for writing my own mystery, and *The Sweet Bounty* is the first result of that inspiration."

- EW

EW Finke writes from knowledge acquired during over 30 years of experience in environment and natural resource management. He has been enthralled by Newfoundland – its history, its people, and its landscape – ever since his first visit in 2001 and he has returned many times. He lives in Bellingham, Washington.